Berkley Prime Crime titles by Rochelle Staab

WHO DO, VOODOO?
BRUJA BROUHAHA
HEX ON THE EX

HEX ON THE EX

ROCHELLE STAAB

BERKLEY PRIME CRIME, NEW YORK

THE BERKLEY PUBLISHING GROUP
Published by the Penguin Group
Penguin Group (USA) Inc.
375 Hudson Street, New York, New York 10014, USA

USA | Canada | UK | Ireland | Australia | New Zealand | India | South Africa | China

Penguin Books Ltd., Registered Offices: 80 Strand, London WC2R 0RL, England
For more information about the Penguin Group, visit penguin.com.

HEX ON THE EX

A Berkley Prime Crime Book / published by arrangement with the author

Berkley Prime Crime Books are published by The Berkley Publishing Group.
BERKLEY® PRIME CRIME and the PRIME CRIME logo are trademarks of
Penguin Group (USA) Inc.

For information, address: The Berkley Publishing Group,
a division of Penguin Group (USA) Inc.,
375 Hudson Street, New York, New York 10014.

ISBN: 978-0-425-25201-7

PUBLISHING HISTORY
Berkley Prime Crime mass-market edition / May 2013

PRINTED IN THE UNITED STATES OF AMERICA

10 9 8 7 6 5 4 3 2 1

Cover illustration by Blake Morrow.
Cover design by Diana Kolsky.
Interior text design by Laura K. Corless.

This is a work of fiction. Names, characters, places, and incidents either are the product
of the author's imagination or are used fictitiously, and any resemblance to actual persons,
living or dead, business establishments, events, or locales is entirely coincidental.
The publisher does not have any control over and does not assume any responsibility for
author or third-party websites or their content.

ALWAYS LEARNING   **PEARSON**

Acknowledgments

A warm thank-you to the generous folks who gave me their time and expertise in the writing of this story: Jeffrey Bloom, Jeanne Robson, Pat Sabatini, Charlie Springer, Sylvia Tchakerian, and Gerald Tinker; my baseball experts Mark Langill, Ken Levine, and Scott St. James, with an assist from David Schwartz and George Wilson; the always helpful members of the LAPD, particularly detective Joel Price, Officer Sebring, and Judi Breskin; and my first readers Carole Bloom and JoAn Brown.

I have the pleasure to work with an amazing team of people at Berkley Prime Crime. Thank you to all, especially my editor, Michelle Vega. Her warmth, wisdom, and wit encourage me through every stage of the process.

A hug and a tip of the hat to my critique partners V. R. Barkowski, Lynn Sheene, Donnell Bell, and Tammy Kaehler, whose feedback, intelligence, cheerleading, and good common sense keep me sane(-ish) and on track. You guys are the best.

And finally, my deep gratitude for the readers, librarians, and booksellers who embraced Liz and Nick from the very beginning. Your enthusiasm is my happy-ever-after.

Chapter One

Hitting the gym at dawn for a week sounded like such a good idea on day one. Wake up early, exercise and shower at the facility, and then attack unpacking the rest of the moving boxes at home with a fresh attitude—sure, I could do it. Right. Game On, the private Studio City gym co-owned by my ex-husband, Jarret, and his trainer, spanned three storefronts at Coldwater Curve, a small strip mall across the street from Jerry's Famous Deli on Ventura Boulevard, a few miles from my new house. On day two, I had to drag myself out of bed. By then I had no choice.

Half awake and incognito— no makeup, not even lipstick, hair twisted in a ragged ponytail, rumpled cotton sweats, and faded Nirvana T-shirt— I tossed my backpack into an empty cubbyhole on the member wall beside the front desk.

Only one trainer plus Jarret's partner, Kyle Stanger, knew me by name but I nodded hellos to my fellow daybreak warriors scattered over the three rows of equipment lined by type in the cardio room. An athletic jock ran full speed on one of the treadmills. Another man read the newspaper on a stationary bike facing the windowed wall to the mat room, and behind him, a woman paged through a magazine on an elliptical machine.

I stepped onto a treadmill in the last row and programmed the machine for a twenty-minute run. Course: Manual. Age: 38. Weight: 125 (-ish). Speed: 5.5. Incline: 0.

In the row ahead of me, a male exec type looking like money in designer track pants and a Cannes T-shirt, clicked the remote to switch channels on the mounted TV from news to a scripted "reality" program titled—according to the superimposed caption—*Atlanta Wife Life.*

Seriously? The guy wants to watch reality TV? Now? Waking up was enough reality for me. But like a gawker rubbernecking at a freeway pileup, I couldn't resist a peek at the show's unfolding theatrics.

Onscreen, a fortyish babe with lips plumped to a duck pout, false eyelashes heavy enough to require props, and earrings like road barrier reflectors dangling at her jawline, fumed at the camera. *"I hope she dies alone and I never see her again. She stole the man that my girlfriend loved since high school."*

Cut to—well, calling either woman onscreen an actress would be an insult to the profession—wannabe celeb number two: a fleshy, sobbing brunette with chasm-like cleavage. *"She stabbed me in the back."* Snurf.

Sympathy enlisted for the whiners in designer duds? Zero. I clicked my iPod on and ran at an easy pace with Journey's "Don't Stop Believing," drowning out the TV noise.

Blame my plumber, Stan, and an utter lack of showering

resources at home for necessitating the early morning gym visits. I had to wait two months after moving into my new house for Stan's schedule to clear so he could complete the overhaul of the upstairs bathrooms. Weeks of bathing in the squeaky-piped, worn-porcelain bathtub and mildewed showers left by the prior owner inspired me to sacrifice convenience for new fixtures, prompting my rise at dawn to shower two miles away. I opted for the gym as a bonus—the move had added a few pounds of stress-driven, comfort-food weight to my waistline.

As of yesterday, I couldn't shower or bathe in my bathrooms. Tile torn out, tub and shower unusable in the master bath. The guest bath upstairs was crammed with boxes of winter clothes waiting to be unpacked. My friends and family offered me access to their homes, but vanity—dropping those pounds—won out. I couldn't beat the price: my ex and his partner charged me half of Game On's monthly membership dues.

Stan promised the new fixtures in and ready for use in a few days or so. With my limited plumbing vocabulary, Stan's "or so" worried me. I notified my clients of my vacation, and closed my psychology practice down for the week to stay home, finish unpacking, and supervise. As if my presence would speed things up. I'm an optimist.

A middle-aged, corkscrewed blonde got on the treadmill to my right. She started to power-walk, loping the rubber track with stamina impressive for her short, bulky girth. I offered a smile. We jogged on the same treadmills yesterday at the same time, qualifying her as my foxhole buddy. She pointed to the pink-lipped reality star on the television, and then mouthed something to me.

I paused my music and slowed the treadmill to a fast walk for the last half mile. "I'm sorry, what did you say?"

"That woman up there on the TV is lying."

"She's definitely alienated," I said, following her gaze. "And closed off. Her arms and legs are crossed, creating a barrier."

The channel-changing exec turned around and said, "You're both right. In person, she's an angry shrew and a compulsive liar."

"You know her?" the blonde next to me said.

"I'm Billy Miles." He enunciated his name with exaggerated importance. "Our network produces that show."

She tilted her chin. "I bet you don't know your star hasn't let her husband touch her for three years."

"Wouldn't surprise me if he didn't care, hon." Billy turned back to the TV.

Smiling, my blonde buddy said to me, "I'm Tess, by the way."

"Nice to meet you. I'm Liz." I cocked my head toward the TV, curious. "How do you get three years out of her actions?"

"I'm a psychic. I read her aura."

And I can cook. I forced a polite smile, struggling to act interested.

"Uh-oh." Tess curled her lips in a mischievous grin. "You don't believe. Give me a chance—I'll change your mind. I'm very good. I do readings for people all the time. And I get visions in my dreams. You have a sharp eye for body language, what do you do?"

"I'm a psychologist. My PhD is in behavioral science—the physical response to emotion fascinates me. First our bodies react to a situation, and then our minds connect a

4

feeling to the reaction. Body language is often more truthful than the spoken word."

"Ooh, you're good at this stuff. We have a lot in common," Tess said. "The only difference is that I can see energy fields from the past and into the future, too. For example, I've been reading your aura. You have good energy, but what are you going to do about the two men in your life?"

My boyfriend, Nick, and my ex-husband, Jarret? I checked myself—Tess made a generalized guess, of course. Doesn't every woman in her thirties have a man in her present and a man in her past? "The only two men I'm concerned with this week are my plumber and his assistant. They're bringing me a new bathtub."

"I sense there's a lot more than plumbers going on with you, Liz. I see a man lying to you. We should talk about this some more."

"I don't . . . We . . ." Faltering for a way to dodge the discussion, I glimpsed past her and saw my excuse come into the cardio room.

"Two mornings in a row, Liz. I'm impressed." Kyle Stanger, my ex-husband's crony, personal trainer, and partner in Game On patted the top of my treadmill then stopped at Billy's side.

A walking ad for Game On and the benefits of pumping weights, Kyle, mid-forties with the body of a middleweight boxer, wore his brown hair in a military crew cut with a sharp widow's peak above his small eyes and thin mouth. His thick neck melded into a mass of muscles rippling across his wide, bulked-up shoulders, past a slim waist, and down to well-developed calves. Popped veins accentuated his powerful forearms and biceps.

I wasn't a fan. We had met a decade ago in Atlanta when the Braves signed my husband. Kyle became Jarret's team pitching coach and new best friend. In addition to Kyle's coaching role in the bullpen, he was Jarret's enabler in partying, drinking, and drugs. Too many nights Kyle dropped my then-husband at home in sorry shape. But when Kyle concealed Jarret's involvement in a barroom brawl and took the fall—effectively saving Jarret's professional baseball career—Jarret never forgot. After Kyle was arrested for battery and fired from the Braves, Jarret hired him as his personal trainer and paid him until Jarret and I relocated to Los Angeles. Two years ago, Kyle moved here and opened Game On with Jarret as his silent partner.

As Kyle and Billy talked, a chunky, round-faced brunette in her late thirties sauntered into the cardio room. She picked up the TV remote and began to change the channel.

"Don't do that, Gretchen. We're watching Billy's program," Kyle said.

"You gotta be joking." Gretchen clicked her tongue, dropping the remote in disgust. She turned on her heel toward the adjoining weight room. Tess and I swapped eye rolls. I knew I only had so much politeness in me after one cup of coffee, but Gretchen's stomping exit seemed overly dramatic.

"What's Miss Snit's story?" Billy said.

"She joined the gym a few months ago," Kyle said. "New in town."

"The girl obviously has no taste in good television." Billy laughed.

Tess turned to me. "Gretchen found out about my psychic talents and asked me for a free reading. It took time to get a strong fix on her. Strange aura. Focused, yet muddy. But she's not bad once you get her talking."

"Do you read everyone?"

"Sure. I like to share my gift," Tess said.

Kyle called from the side of Billy's elliptical, "Hey, Liz. Big game tonight at Dodger Stadium. You going?"

I brushed a stray, sweaty lock off my forehead and nodded. "We're celebrating my dad's birthday there. He and my boyfriend, Nick, are Cubs fans."

"You're not rooting against the Dodgers, are you?" Kyle said.

"Never. I was born here. My first crush was on Steve Garvey. Believe me, the Illinois contingent in my group will be surrounded by plenty of loyalists."

"I'll be at the game, too," he said. "Billy is hosting a party in the ATTAGIRL luxury box. I'm taking an old sidekick of yours from Atlanta. Remember Laycee Huber?"

I almost tripped off the treadmill. Laycee Huber in Los Angeles? The last time I talked to my ex-friend and Atlanta neighbor was four years ago, the day I knocked on her front door to return the pink-and-black polka-dot bra she'd bought on a shopping trip with me. At the store, she claimed she wanted something sexy to seduce her husband. Two weeks before Jarret and I moved to L.A., I found the bra, reeking of Laycee's distinct burnt sugar scent, under my bed.

Chapter Two

Kittenish Laycee and I began our friendship in Atlanta the morning we moseyed out to our adjoining mailboxes in identical sweats and T-shirts. After swapping witty observations on our impeccable style, she invited me to go mall hopping with her on weekends. She introduced me to her hairdresser, facialist, and the best shoe store in Atlanta. Though we shared the same size, our clothing tastes beyond mailbox garb were vastly different. Laycee shopped for low-cut and tight; I wore trendy at home and tailored to work. We shared our hopes and secrets over wine in my kitchen on the nights Jarret traveled with the Braves and her lawyer husband, Forrest, worked late.

The couple came to our barbeques and helped celebrate our birthdays; Jarret and I went to their pool parties and Super Bowl bashes. Forrest, thirty years her senior at sixty-one, watched his young trophy wife flirt with every man in attendance. The four of us were chummy until the day I learned Laycee was swapping spit with my husband. I divorced Jarret soon after our move to Los Angeles, my hometown.

"Sure, I remember Laycee," I said to Kyle over the top of my treadmill while swallowing back bitterness I thought I jettisoned years ago. "She's in town?"

"Yeah. She's going to call you. She told me she wanted to get together with you." Before I could tell Kyle to discourage her, he said, "Hey—I talked to Jarret. A string of lefties load the Cubs lineup so he'll probably pitch relief for at least a few innings tonight. Should be a great game. You sitting in the team section?" He projected his voice loud enough for everyone in the cardio room and in the cars parked in the lot outside to hear.

"I don't know where our seats are. My parents got the tickets." I knew damn well Jarret gave my mom his player seats for the game, but I wasn't about to play celebrity can-you-top-this with Kyle. And I didn't want him to hunt us down at Dodger Stadium with Laycee in tow.

I hopped off my treadmill and crossed through the weight room to the mirrored studio at the rear of the gym. After the two-mile run/walk, I just wanted to lie down. I rolled out a mat on the floor by the mirror and began a series of knee-to-elbow sit-ups.

Across the room, a trainer counted reps for a client on an aerobics step. Another trainer joked with a zaftig redhead squatting on a balance disc. Gretchen did crunches on an exercise ball. Earl, the sociable, ebony-skinned trainer I met my first morning, supervised a girl transferring a medicine ball from over her head down to her toes.

"How's your renovation going, Liz?" Earl said.

"Getting there," I said, crossing my left elbow to my right knee. "The plumber showed up yesterday. I consider that progress. At the rate he's working, I'm estimating a few months. If I'm lucky, my new bathtub might be in by the time the World Series starts in October."

"Sounds like a party to me." Tess strolled in and rolled out a mat next to me on the floor. "All this crowd needs is food, music, and ice in the tub for the beer. I love baseball. What time is the game tonight?"

"First pitch is at 7:10 P.M.," Gretchen said from across the room. "The players are out on the field by 6:30."

I paused mid-crunch and caught Gretchen's eye. "Are you a Dodger fan?"

"I've been a *baseball* fan since high school. My boyfriend gets me tickets," Gretchen said with a superior smile.

At seven-fifteen, I finished my sit-ups and stretched, picked up a towel, then removed my backpack from the shelf of cubbyholes where the club members left their wallets and keys in open slots on the honor system. I took my gear and headed to the ladies' room for a fast shower. Rush-hour traffic willing, I had just enough time to collect the boxes of my old books from Jarret's garage before he took his morning run, and then drive home to Studio City to let in Stan with, hopefully, my new tub.

I scrubbed and toweled in record time, jumped into my jeans and a Red Hot Chili Peppers T-shirt, and decided to let the stifling August heat wave blanketing Los Angeles take care of drying my hair. Makeup? To meet Jarret or the plumber? Not even lipstick. I opened the ladies' room door and stopped short.

A giddy laugh I knew too well pierced through the music and crowd noise. Laycee Huber stood near the desk with Kyle, Billy, Gretchen, Earl, and Tess. She called to me as I turned to escape through the back.

"Liz, Liz, oh Liz! Kyle told me you were here." Laycee ran over, fluttering her hands like a baby bird. She wore her dark brown hair parted into matching pigtails, a trick to cover her pointed, Spocklike ears. Stunning in a turquoise tank top, black tights, and pristine white cross-trainers, Laycee greeted me like the Atlanta bra-under-the-bed incident was forgotten or had never happened, then stopped short, showing as much concern as her Botoxed forehead allowed. I think one eyebrow actually twitched with pity as she studied my face. "Oh, Liz. Has it really been that long?"

Good ol' Laycee—the Southern belle who loved a good dig to make herself feel better. *Note: never again assume I don't need makeup.*

She threw her arms around me in a histrionic hug as I stiffened, backpack dangling from my hand. Air-kissing my cheek with pink-glossed lips, she batted her lashes and said, "I missed you."

I missed her like I missed a case of food poisoning. The people circling us took in our little reunion, grinning. Well, actually, I suspected the men admired Laycee's spilling cleavage. Their gazes were fixed below her neckline.

"What are you doing in town?" I kept my tone as light as my disdain for her allowed. The tips of my cars sizzled with annoyance—I wanted to get away from her with my temper in check.

She glanced over her shoulder at Kyle and Billy then said to me, "I'll tell you later. Can we get together? Do lunch?

Go shopping? I'll be here a few days, maybe longer if every-thing goes well."

"I'm having work done at my house. I don't have time."
Especially for you.

"Oh, come on. Just for an itsy drink? The workers don't sleep at your house—or do they?" She winked. "Do try to call me. My cell phone number is exactly the same. We must catch up, Liz. I want to hear all about your new life here. I need *all* the details. Let's do coffee early tomorrow morning after we work out. The café at my hotel opens early."

"We'll see," I lied, glancing at the clock. "I'm in a rush. I have to pick up some boxes then meet a contractor. Enjoy your trip."

Tess trailed me to the door. "I'll see *you* in the morning, Liz." She cocked her chin back toward Laycee. "That woman has one chaotic aura. I want to hear her story."

"She'd probably love to tell you herself, Tess."

Ventura Boulevard traffic jammed in a slow crawl through Sherman Oaks and became a worse mess after I turned left on Sepulveda, costing me precious time on the way to Jarret's. I passed the entrance to the 405, creeping behind traffic until my right turn into the exclusive Royal Oaks section of Encino. I checked the dashboard clock: twelve minutes until Jarret left for his five-mile run around the Harvard-Westlake track. He stuck to his ritualistic regimen with superstitious caution, especially on game days. Any break from the routine threw him off. He wouldn't hang around to wait for me if I arrived late.

Parked cars and vans lined both shoulders on Royal Oak

Road, however, I sped along the road alone until another car turned onto the street from two blocks behind me. No joggers or dog walkers visible in the neighborhood of green-shuttered, white-shingled, and redbrick houses up on hills or nestled in lush landscaping behind picket fences.

A mile in, I made a left at the stop sign. I remembered the first time I drove up the same street four years ago with Dilly Silva, Mom's good friend and Encino real estate agent extraordinaire. When Jarret's trade to the Dodgers brought us to my hometown, Dilly found the three-bedroom, white stucco, adobe-roofed dream of a house in the hills above the San Fernando Valley. As great as the house and neighborhood were, I knew then I wouldn't live there for long. My fifteen-year marriage was on life support before we moved in. Laycee was the last of Jarret's flings—I filed for divorce and moved out six months later.

I hooked a sharp left up the hill toward his house, then a quick right through his open gate. At the top of the sunflower-lined driveway, Jarret stood waiting for me. Six feet of tanned, sinewy muscles, a jackpot smile, and messy sandy brown hair, he jogged in place by three cardboard boxes on the asphalt near the garage. I shut off the ignition and popped open my trunk.

"You're late," Jarret said.

"I got sidetracked. Laycee Huber showed up at your gym this morning."

"Who?"

"Don't," I said, annoyed by his pretense of ignorance. "I'm surprised she didn't call you the minute she got to town."

"Why would she?"

"Why wouldn't she?" I turned away, concealing my irritation. *Why did I bring her up? To provoke him? Hurt myself?* I thought I had moved past the sting of their betrayal. Guess not.

"Forget her. Are these the right boxes?"

I checked the cartons on the stoop. "Liz psych textbooks 1 of 4," "Liz cookbooks 2 of 4," and "Liz book-books 4 of 4." I left four boxes behind in his garage when I moved out. "There's one missing."

"Those are the only ones I found." He looked at his watch then rolled his shoulders. "You can stay and go through the garage yourself. I have to leave in a few minutes. It's game day. I can't be late for my run."

"I don't have time either," I said. "The plumber will be at my house in a half hour."

"I'll search again later. If I see the other box, I'll call you. Mind coming back?"

"As long as I don't run into any of your female house-guests. You don't want the ex-wife showing up to spoil your love life."

He grinned. "Thanks, but you already do, Lizzie-Bear. When they get that look on their face like they want to move in and redecorate, I call them by your name or talk about how much I still love you."

"That's mean, Jarret. You'll be a lot happier if you'd let a woman get close to you again."

"Not the ones I've been dating lately. A model here, an old friend there. No one special. No one as special as you are."

We locked eyes for a moment. I shook my head. "I prefer

14

being your friend. You deserve a woman who will love you in return, Jarret."

And that was about as much affection as I could dish out and he could handle. He turned and loaded the boxes into my trunk then closed the lid. "I'm pretty sure I'll be pitching relief tonight. Are you coming to the game?"

"With the whole family. It's Dad's birthday."

"Are you getting Walter another autographed ball?"

My shoulders sunk. "I'm trying, but can't seem to find one Dad doesn't already have. I'm starting to panic."

Each year for his birthday, I gave Dad a small box wrapped in blue and tied with a red ribbon—the Chicago Cubs' team colors—holding a baseball autographed by one of the old Cub players. "Last year I gave him a ball signed by Ernie Banks, his favorite player when he was a kid. I need to find something before Mom's party for him Saturday night."

"What if I get the current Cubs players to sign a baseball for him? Would that work?"

"He'd love it. But I can't ask you to go into the Cubs' locker room to get autographs for me. It's insulting to you."

He waved me off. "It's no big deal. An old friend of mine from back in the minors is on their pitching staff. I'll call him for the autographs this afternoon. The ball will be in your hands by Saturday."

"That would be amazing. How can I thank you?"

"Spend the weekend with me," he said with a playful glint in his eyes. "We'll make like old times."

I laughed. "And that's not going to happen. Maybe I'll buy Dad a watch."

"Okay, okay. No thanks needed. I'll get the ball signed." Jarret smirked. "Tell Walter it's nothing personal when I pulverize his Cubs from the mound tonight. My old man will be watching the game in Illinois. Twists up his loyalties bad every time I pitch against his beloved Cubbies, and I have a strong hunch about this game. Ma still can't understand why I won't apply for a job with a Chicago team. She'll never get it."

"Your parents adore you and you know it. Are they resigned to living in the house the Braves paid for yet?"

When Jarret began to make major league money pitching for the Atlanta Braves, he paid off the mortgage on Bud and Marion Cooper's home in McHenry, Illinois. To show their gratitude, they hung a lone Braves' banner on Jarret's wall of fame in their den. Chicago team posters papered the rest of the room.

"You know my parents. They're too stubborn to accept me playing for a rival team. I still can't get them on a plane out here to visit Dodger Stadium. I'm happy you'll be at the game, Lizzie-Bear. Are you bringing the egghead? Or is he writing a book report tonight?"

I ignored the question and Jarret's refusal to call my boyfriend Nick by name. If "he" or "him" didn't fit, Jarret used nicknames degrading Nick's job teaching religious philosophy at NoHo, the progressive community college in North Hollywood. Somehow in Jarret's mind, my relationship with brilliant scholar, accomplished author, and oh-by-the-way adorably sexy Nick rated inferior to being married to a cheating, drinking, smoking, seven-figure Major League Baseball player in the twilight of his career. Jealous for my

16

attention, Jarret dug for excuses to get mad or feel bad—as if the real reasons for our divorce never happened.

"Mom, Robin, Dave, and I will be cheering for you, Jarret. Pitch a winner." I started my car.

"Lizzie, wait."

"What?"

"If you give me a lucky kiss good-bye, maybe I'll hit a homer for you tonight."

Our affectionate game-day ritual from the past warmed me into a smile. "Here." I blew him a kiss. "And when you hit your home run, blow the kiss back."

Bypassing the morning rush on the 101 Freeway, I took Ventura Boulevard east to Studio City. Twenty-five minutes later, I turned left on Tujunga Avenue and crossed the bridge toward my two-story bungalow tucked into Colfax Meadows on Farmdale Avenue.

I parked at the curb, leaving my driveway clear for Stan's truck. *My driveway.* I reveled in pride each time I walked the brick path to my porch. The bungalow had deteriorated into an eyesore before I bought it two months ago, left abandoned until lawyers and out-of-state relatives sorted out the estate of the deceased owner. Each new sign of improvement, like the row of purple-and-white pansies planted along the path, reflected a new beginning for both of us. House-proud.

A gardener had trimmed the overgrown trees and shrubs, reseeded the lawn, and cleared out the backyard so the neighbors would stop glaring at me as if the property was haunted. Dilly helped me organize a crew to renovate the worn and dated interior. Before my move, they painted a spare bedroom so my year-old kitten, Erzulie, and I had a room to sleep in and my clothes had a place to hang while my new home came to life.

Spending my day juggling painters, electricians, deliverymen, and my full-time psychology practice became a time-consuming trick. Instead of the romantic summer jaunt Nick planned for us last spring, he took the research trip to Mexico alone last month while I tended to house renovations. Within six weeks, the team had stripped old paint off the fireplaces in the living room and master bedroom, scraped the wallpaper in the living room, dining room, and downstairs half bath and painted the rest of the house. New appliances were purchased and delivered, and the original 1940s tiles in the kitchen got scrubbed and polished. Except for the bathrooms, my home was coming together.

Stan swore he'd have the renovations on both bathrooms upstairs and the half bath downstairs done in five to seven days, tops. Stan was an optimist, too.

Erzulie watched from the bay window in the living room while I carried the boxes from the car trunk into the house. Stan, a middle-aged gay Adonis in white painter's pants and beat-up construction boots, arrived at nine with his assistant, Angel, a rotund Mexican sporting a walrus mustache and a sweet demeanor. While they worked their noisy magic upstairs in my bathrooms, I settled on the living room floor to arrange books into the built-in bookcases bordering the fireplace. Behind me, Erzulie, a blur of taupe fur hiding in, under, and behind furniture, never tired of exploring the nooks of her personal amusement park we called home. She came out for food, her litter box, and to cuddle.

Soon my college textbooks, a collection of old high school yearbooks, and an accumulation of unread novels lined the bookcases framing the fireplace. I left one shelf empty for the research texts waiting at Jarret's. The rest of the books in the final box—a blushing collection of erotica my best friend, Robin Bloom, had sent as a joke on my thirtieth birthday—would hide upstairs in a closet or a bottom dresser drawer.

I sat back on my heels and stared at the shelves, unsatisfied by the visual imbalance. Nope. I wouldn't be happy until I achieved symmetry.

Jarret called at ten. "I found the other box. What do you want me to do with it?"

"I can't leave now," I said. "Can you—"

"I can't. Ira wants to meet about an endorsement deal before I go to the stadium. If it's as big as he claims, it means a lot of money. I'll leave your box on the kitchen counter. You can pick it up whenever. The back door inside the garage is always unlocked. You remember the garage door code, right?"

"Gee, let me think. Your birthday?" I said. Jarret had used his birth date for every password, code, and Internet login since we met in college. During our first years together, I was too trusting to argue about safety. The last few years we did nothing but argue and the passcode took a backseat to bigger problems. Even his parents used Jarret's birthday for their house codes because their only child needed to focus on baseball instead of cluttering his mind with strange technology baloney. "You should keep your doors locked, Jarret."

"What for? There's nothing valuable in the house anymore. You moved out."

At eleven, my mother, Vivian Gordon, waltzed into my house in a crisp gray linen dress and designer sandals. "Yoo-hoo. Ticket delivery." Mom tucked a loose strand of her white pageboy behind an ear and furrowed her brow. "I need to sage this house again. I thought I cleared out the old spirits, but the air feels troubled and confused. Where's the negative energy coming from? What are you doing?"

"Stacking books. Nothing chaotic or strange going on here unless you count the plumbers working on the bathrooms upstairs." I gave up debating the supernatural with Mom years ago. She believed. I didn't. Sage cleansing ceremonies made her feel like she contributed to decorating my house. I conceded to her mystical whimsies to distract her from rearranging the furniture. "Maybe you're nervous about Dad's birthday party at the stadium tonight."

Mom clicked her tongue. "Your father will be happy with a hot dog, a beer, and his family around him while his beloved Cubs lose to the Dodgers. Here. Tickets for you and Nick." She gave me the pair and a parking pass. "Your brother Dave has his. I just don't understand why you kids insist on taking three separate cars to the stadium instead of all of us driving together."

Thirty-eight years in, Mom still referred to my older sib as "your brother Dave," a quirk I attributed to family pride. Dave somehow had managed to sweet-talk my best friend into dating him. Robin, an executive assistant at an entertainment management company, was widowed almost three years ago; Dave, a detective with the elite Robbery-Homicide Division of LAPD, was divorced. When Dave jailed Robin on suspicion of murder in October—a mess Nick and I spent a week unraveling—the possibility of a romance forming between them went from unlikely to nil. And in April, after Dave left Robin stranded in a ballroom while he and Nick came to my rescue near MacArthur Park, I thought she'd never speak to my brother again. They proved me wrong after Dave wheedled Robin into having dinner with him to apologize, and the two found each other. Ain't love grand?

Since Dave and Nick had been best pals since college, and Robin and I had been inseparable since seventh grade, the four of us created a strong block vote if needed.

"Dave is on call and needs his car in case he has to go to work," I said to Mom. "Robin won't ride with Dave unless she has a backup to take her home. Nick and I are Robin's backup. You and Dad sometimes leave the game at the top of the ninth inning to beat traffic. Nick likes to stay until the game ends. Separate cars will keep everyone happy." Especially me.

Truth was, I didn't relish listening to Mom gush over her famous ex-son-in-law to and from Dodger Stadium with Nick in the car. Though Jarret failed to convince me his cheating was a harmless mistake, he somehow charmed my mother into forgiving him. I remembered her comment after I explained my reasons for divorcing Jarret: "But he's such a nice boy."

"I can't see why your brother can't get one night off to celebrate his father's birthday," Mom said, picking up then setting down the snow globe on my mantel. "There are thousands of police detectives on the street solving crimes. It's the same complaint I had about the force before your father retired—you'd think the Gordon men were the only two homicide detectives in the LAPD."

"When you're the best, everyone wants you."

"You're lucky Nick Garfield doesn't have that problem."

"Excuse me? Nick teaches the most popular classes at NoHo."

"I meant no one calls a professor out in the middle of the night," Mom said. "Where is Nick? Why isn't he here helping you? School is closed for the summer."

"He's been here every day, Mom. He's at the UCLA library doing research this morning," I said.

"Research for what?"

"He's prepping for a new class he's teaching next semester—Religious Influences in North American Folk Magic and Occultism."

Chapter Three

I unpacked and arranged the last boxes of curios in the dining room then began my attack on loose ends in the kitchen, rearranging drawers and stacking my cookbook collection in an out-of-the-way cupboard. The new stainless-steel appliances in my gray-and-white vintage forties kitchen hummed, waiting for me to break out the measuring spoons and learn to cook—an art Robin, Mom, and Nick executed with panache. I executed my cooking like capital punishment, yet I remained determined to master the skill. Probably not this week, but soon. Swear. I could almost taste the lemonade I planned to make with the lemons from my tree one day. Baby steps.

As I folded up emptied cartons, Stan and Angel stopped to say good-bye before they left for the day.

"Same time tomorrow?" I said.

"Nine. I have to stop at the hardware store first," Stan said.

"And when do you think you'll put in the tub and tiles?"

"Soon."

"What day is 'soon'?"

Stan scratched his chin. "Friday, maybe?"

Friday, maybe wasn't a day either. Which Friday? They hustled out the front door before I could ask.

I carried the empty boxes out to the garage, made another check with my office service for client messages, then went upstairs to freshen up for the game. The current heat wave kept temperatures in the high seventies late into the night, so I opted for a white T-shirt, my favorite jeans, and black Converse sneakers. I added makeup and lipstick, and then bent my head to brush through the waves in my brown hair. Erzulie stretched on my down comforter, watching me dab a finishing touch of rose oil behind my ears.

"Are you hungry?" I said to my fuzzy companion.

The magic words. She meowed, hopped off the bed toward the door, stopped to see if I followed, and then darted downstairs, tail up. I found her sitting on the kitchen counter top, waiting for me to open a can of smelly delights from the sea. Erzulie let me know early in our relationship that chicken or beef was not acceptable to her palate.

Once Erzulie tucked into the sardine mush in the bowl on the floor, even the *tap-tap* at the front door and Nick's greeting didn't disturb her. Pretty amazing since Nick was Erzulie's hero-man.

"Liz?" Nick's rich voice echoed from the entry hall.

"In the kitchen," I said, shaking my head for one last fluff of my hair.

Nick, tall, fit, and tanned from his recent trip to Mexico and weekends playing basketball with my brother, leaned on the doorjamb between the dining room and kitchen. Wisps of gray and sandy brown hair peeked out from under a weathered blue baseball cap with the red *C* in the center, his beloved Chicago Cubs' logo. He crossed his arms over his faded navy blue sweatshirt, his brown eyes twinkling with a slow warm smile that reached into my chest and pulled at my heart.

I wiped my hands and went to him, letting the comfort of his arms envelop me. He brushed his lips on the top of my head, and then lifted my chin. Quivers feathered up my spine from his mind-swimming kiss.

With his lips a whisper from mine he said, "When do we have to leave?"

"Five minutes."

"Not enough time." He pulled me closer.

"Then we better stop now," I said, catching my breath. "Or you get to explain to everyone why we were late."

"Struck out and the game hasn't even begun."

I stepped back and tugged at the brim of his cap. "You wore this to our first baseball game together in college."

"The Illini were on their way to the Big Ten Baseball Championship and Dave brought you along to see the phenom rookie pitch. What was that guy's name? Jarret something?"

"Cooper, I think."

"Right. The only time my lucky cap let me down. My mistake for taking you down to the field to meet the winning pitcher. I should have asked you out instead."

"You? A big important junior dating a lowly freshman? Scandalous."

"I had to wait years for my second chance," Nick said.

"Was I worth the wait?"

"Endlessly. Are you ready to dine on Dodger dogs and peanuts?"

"I'm ready for anything."

He raised his brows, grinning. "Anything? Maybe we should stay here. Your parents—"

"Would never forgive us if we didn't show up tonight. Dad can't wait to see you."

"Me?"

"A fellow Cubs fanatic? I only hope he lets the rest of us talk to you during the game."

Nick steered his red SUV onto the 101 Freeway entrance at Vineland and Riverside, driving east to I5 South with the Dodger pre-game show on the radio. The ride from Studio City to Dodger Stadium in Chavez Ravine took thirty minutes in normal traffic. We hit rush hour.

"Did you find what you were searching for at the library?" I said as we crept through traffic.

"Not everything. I'm going again tomorrow. Hohman's version of *The Long Lost Friend* sidetracked me. The folklore and mythology specialist in the research section is trying to track down an eighteen-eighty English translation of the *Sixth and Seventh Books of Moses*. All of their Scheible books are in German."

"And this has to do with . . ." I circled my hand.

"Folk religion and magic systems in nineteenth-century Pennsylvania. Good-luck charms, medicine men, and curses."

"A list of your favorite things. I'm glad you came up for air to come to a nice twenty-first-century baseball game. Did you take time to eat?"

"We stopped for a sandwich off campus. You know, baseball and its superstitions go all the way back to the nineteenth century. The New York Knickerbockers baseball team was formed before the Civil War."

"We?"

Nick glanced at me. "No, all of baseball."

"You said 'we' stopped for lunch."

"Oh. I ran into Isabella at the library, doing research for a paper on Mexican folklore. I told you about her."

"Your former fiancée from Costa Rica?"

"*Pretend* fiancée."

"I still don't comprehend the pretend part. Were you dating her?"

"No." Nick snickered. "I didn't hear about my engagement until Isabella and I got on the plane from Costa Rica to Los Angeles. Her village has a machismo culture—her grandfather wouldn't allow Isabella to leave home to attend UCLA without a husband. When I stayed with the family in Playa Del Alma, Isabella and her mother came up with a plan for Izzy to return to California with me. Then, behind my back, they told the grandfather we were getting married."

I wrinkled my nose. "How manipulative."

"The women battled cultural standards. Her mother wanted Izzy to go to college in the States. The ruse seemed innocent enough. I was happy to help—both of her parents opened their home to me during my stay. After our plane took off, Izzy told me about everything, then promised to write her grandfather saying she broke the engagement."

"Did she?"

"I assume so. Izzy's a good kid. You'll like her."

Then why hadn't I met her? A jealous lump rose in my throat. After Nick and I got together, we were happily exclusive. Or so I thought.

"Isabella *happened* to be at the library today?"

"She's a student at UCLA, Liz. Yes. She *happened* to be at their library writing a paper. What's the problem?"

"Nothing." Then added with a sarcastic bite, "Did you two have a good time at lunch?"

"We had a great time. I want you to meet her."

"I've heard that before." I turned to the window.

"Okay, what's with the attitude?"

Good question. Nick had female friends. He worked with women, he taught women, and he never gave me reason to feel threatened or suspicious. Why today?

I stared out the passenger window as traffic slowed near the Griffith Park Golf Course. Behind the fence bordering the freeway, a group of female golfers sashayed to the green in shorts. The casual sway of their hips made me think of Laycee Huber prancing through my Atlanta backyard flirting with every man at our summer barbeques. Realization clicked in—my foul attitude had nothing to do with Nick and Isabella. My encounter with Laycee brought up unresolved indignation over her tryst with my ex.

Flushing with shame, I faced Nick. "I'm sorry. This morning at the gym, I ran into a woman I hoped I'd never see again—an ex-neighbor from Atlanta who had an affair with Jarret. She pretended to be my friend, then and now."

"What did you say to her?"

"It's not what I said, it's what I should have done. Maybe

if I had bopped Laycee on the nose like I wanted to years ago, I wouldn't be in a snit about you running into Isabella today."

"Before you punch anyone in the nose with that little fist, I'll make sure you and Isabella meet. I don't want you to have any doubts about our relationship. I'm not Jarret, Liz."

"Can I kiss you?"

"I don't know. I'm trying to drive. You might distract me and cause a pileup."

I touched his right cheek. "There. I'm going to kiss you right there."

"If you have to." He angled his head to the side for my smooch.

We exited the freeway on Stadium Way. Clusters of people picnicked and tossed Frisbees beneath the lush green trees in Elysian Park, surrounding the stadium in Chavez Ravine.

Fond childhood memories stirred my excitement as we pulled up to the gate at the top of Academy Road. Dodger Stadium, the oldest ballpark on the West Coast, stood majestic in the early evening sunlight, encircled with parking lots and framed by the distant southern skyline of towering downtown Los Angeles skyscrapers.

I loved the game long before I met Jarret or became a baseball wife. Mom became a Dodger fan when the team moved to L.A. in 1958. Dad grew up a Cubs fan in Chicago. My parents took Dave and me to Dodger Stadium as soon as we were old enough to gum a hot dog. Dad taught us how to keep box scores and waited with us in the parking lot after games to meet the players. At home, Mom and Dad would hold hands on the couch as their teams played each other. When Dave and I were in grade school, Dad worked the LAPD night shift. Mom let us listen to Dodger night games on the radio and we shared the highlights with Dad at breakfast. Even after my divorce, I kept a casual watch on baseball standings for sports talk with Dad.

Nick parked in the season ticket lot behind the bleachers. We walked hand in hand to the right-field entrance to the Grandstand to meet Dave and Robin outside the souvenir shop.

Robin waved at us over the crowd, her shoulder-length blonde hair glistening under the stadium lights. She carried her rounded curves like an asset, and more than one set of male eyes turned to check out her worn jeans and V-neck tee as she pulled Dave toward us. His Dodger T-shirt fit snug over the belly of his 220-pound frame, with extra pounds courtesy of Robin's excellent home cooking, no doubt.

"Excuse me?" Robin pointed to Nick's cap. "A Cubs' hat? What is your area code, sir?"

"Eight-one-eight," Nick said, grinning down at her. "However, I was born in the three-one-two and raised at Wrigley Field."

"You know why Nick studies the occult, don't you?" Dave said. "He's on a mission to learn how to reverse the Curse of the Billy Goat."

"What's that?" Robin said with a giggle.

"A very sad story," Nick said. "In 1945, a tavern owner got thrown out of a World Series game at Wrigley Field because the stink of his pet goat bothered the fans. He got so upset over the insult to the goat that he put a curse on the Cubs and swore they would never win another World Series.

The Cubs didn't win that game and they haven't won a World Series since."

"Are you really searching for a reverse for the curse?" Robin said.

"Always," Nick said with a serious nod. "But don't worry, I'll be gracious when they win tonight."

"We're not worried about your sorry Midwest team, pal. We'll even dry your tears after the Dodgers win," Dave said. "First team to third base buys a round of beer."

"You're on," Nick said. "I hope you're thirsty, because Cubs take the first at bat."

"What's in the bag?" I said, pointing to the white plastic pouch in Robin's hand.

"While we were waiting for you, Dave bought souvenir shirts for your mom and us girls." She opened the bag and showed me three pink T-shirts, each with a silver-glittered Dodger logo on the chest.

I slowed down to let Nick and Dave pass through the security checkpoint first. "Pink? You let him buy us pink T-shirts?"

Robin put a finger to her lips. "Please don't say anything. Dave picked them out. If he thinks I love the shirt, he'll feel confident buying me gifts. He says making me happy makes him happy. Getting presents makes me happy."

"Pink doesn't make me happy," I said.

"Why?" Robin squeezed the bag tight to her waist. "The shirt is cute."

"To you, sure. You look good in pink. I'm not wearing that thing."

"A little cranky tonight, Liz? Are you edgy about being at the game with Nick when Jarret might pitch?"

"No. Jarret will be on the field. He's too far away to cause friction."

"Then why the mood?"

"Remember when I told you about Laycee Huber, my old neighbor in Atlanta? The one Jarret—" I stopped to show my ticket and open my purse for the security guards.

"Slept with?" Robin said, passing through the gate.

"Right. She's in town. I saw her at the gym this morning."

"Ugh. Way to start the day, Liz."

Robin and I caught up with Nick and Dave at the Field Box entrance and the four of us wove our way through the thick stream of fans searching for their seats and lining up for food at the concession stands. Fifteen minutes to game time, the stands were less than half full with the rest of the fans stuck outside in traffic or being L.A. fashionably late. We took two sets of escalators up to the MVP Loge Boxes to Section 103 and the seats reserved for Dodger players' friends and family. Jarret gave my parents tickets in the fifth row above and behind home plate with a sweeping view of the entire field.

"Finally," Mom said after we filed to our seats. "Nick, you sit next to Walter. Dave, you sit—"

"Vivian, stop telling everyone what to do." My dad, in a gray Chicago Cubs T-shirt matching his thinning salt-and-pepper hair, hugged Robin and me then shook Nick's hand.

"Good to see you, Walter," Nick said. "Happy birthday."

"Thank you." Dad beamed with excitement. "I can't think of a better way to celebrate than at a Cub's game—"

"Dodger game," Mom and Dave said in unison.

"With my family and close friends," Dad said. "Nick, I

32

hope you're ready for a battle tonight. I'm not sure about Robin, but Dave, Liz, and Viv don't take losing lightly."

"We'll see who leaves here happy. Game's not over until the last out," Dave said.

Robin and Mom left to change into the "lucky" pink T-shirts Dave bought. I begged off, claiming I wanted to stay to hear the lineup and the national anthem.

"Superstitious?" Nick said.

I smiled up at him, aware that Nick, Dave, and Dad all insisted on being in their seats for the first pitch. "I can't let you and Dad take the advantage for your team. I'm staying to even up the Dodger numbers for Dave."

Fans waved white rally towels at the end of the anthem as the Dodger players took their places on the field and the first Cub batter stepped to the plate.

At the top of the second inning with the score tied at zero, Nick stood. "First round of beer and dogs is on me. Who's in?"

Five hands waved. I volunteered to help, following Nick up the steps and across the crowded aisle to the concession stand. As we took our places at the end of the line, I heard my name called. I turned. Laycee Huber and Kyle Stanger pushed toward us through the crush of people. It was too late to duck. Thank God I hadn't donned the pink T-shirt. Laycee wore the identical pink Dodger shirt with the silver-glittered logo stretched across her breasts. Though we measured the same height barefoot, she towered over me in three-inch heels peeking from beneath the hem of her skin-tight white pants. Her shoulder-length wavy brown hair dipped over her forehead from a side part.

"Sugar, we haven't seen each other in a month of Sundays

and now twice in the same day. But then, neither one of us were much for church, were we?" Laycee flashed a dimpled smile my way then settled her eyes on Nick. "And who is this? Why Liz, I think you've outdone yourself."

I nodded up at Nick with a grin. He slid an affectionate arm around my waist as I made the introductions. Kyle grunted back a *hello*. Laycee took in Nick like a predator eyeing her prey.

She turned to Kyle. "Kyle honey, I'm absolutely parched. Will you get me something cold to drink while I talk to Liz for a minute?" She took me by the elbow, tugging me away from Nick and across the aisle behind the last row of seats.

I shook Laycee's hand off my arm. "I want to get back to Nick. What's so important?"

"You asked what brought me to town. Well, I have huge, huge, huge news to tell you. Kyle trains Billy Miles, a producer for the ATTAGIRL Network. You know, the network that runs *Atlanta Wife Life*?"

"And?" I glanced over her shoulder, trying to spot Nick in the concession line.

"When Kyle told me Billy knew the casting director for next season, I told Forrest I was going to visit you then hopped on a little ol' plane out here. Kyle introduced me to Billy this morning, and after I use my Southern charm on him up in the suite tonight, you can bet I'll be auditioning for the show tomorrow." She winked at me.

"Why are you telling me this?" I tensed, irritated she had concocted a visit to me as an excuse to carry out her scheme, a scheme I knew her husband wouldn't like at all. Her narcissistic lack of boundaries was limitless. "And why would you tell Forrest you came out here to see me? You and I haven't talked in years and it's still not long enough for me. I don't care what you do on your own, but I'll be damned if you use me as an excuse to your husband while you bed-hop your way onto a TV show." I turned to walk away.

She grabbed my arm. "Don't tell me you're still upset about—"

"My alleged *friend* having sex with my husband?"

"Oh, please. You think I was the only one? You'd have to move to the desert to escape all the women Jarret bedded while you were married."

"This conversation is over. You're dead to me." I spun around, straight into Kyle and the beer in his hand.

Chapter Four

Kyle's cup of beer hit me full frontal, soaking my white T-shirt, splattering him, and spraying the two men passing us in the aisle. Laycee stalked toward the escalator, unscathed.

"Whoa, I'm sorry. Here, let me help you." Kyle pulled out a napkin while his eyes tracked Laycee through the crowd.

Pinching the hem of my T-shirt, I pulled the sopping material away from my body before the beer soaked my bra. "I'm fine. Sorry, I didn't see you."

Nick appeared through the crowd, balancing a tray stacked with beer and hot dogs. "What the . . .?"

"We had a collision," Kyle said.

"Go find your date, Kyle. Nick and I can handle this," I said, fanning my shirt.

Kyle apologized again then shouldered into the streaming crowd and disappeared.

"Nick, will you ask Robin to meet me in the ladies' room with the other pink shirt?"

"What happened?"

"If I had known a full cup of beer was right behind me, I would have thrown it in Laycee's face. But the beer had other plans. Get Robin, will you? I'm drenched."

Good thing the night air was warm, because the beer and my wet T-shirt were ice-cold. As I wove through the crowd and entered the restroom, I heard a loud cheer come from the stands. I found an empty stall and pulled the soaked fabric over my head. Standing in my bra, a calm fell over me. At least I had the chance to tell Laycee what I thought of her. Cathartic.

"Liz? Are you in here?" Robin's voice echoed through the concrete walls and metal stalls.

"Over here," I said, opening the door a crack.

"You missed everything. The Dodgers just scored a run."

"Me, too. A deep fly onto my center field."

"Huh?"

"Baseball talk. I crashed into a beer. The shirt, please?"

Fortunately, my bra was dry enough to keep on. I wiped the residual beer off my skin with the dry side of my white shirt, dropped the wet tee into the plastic bag Robin handed me, and then slid into the new pink T-shirt. I recapped my run-in with Laycee for her on our way back to the seats.

"My only question is why you ever hung out with someone like her in the first place? She doesn't sound like the type of women you're close with," Robin said.

"Proximity. Loneliness. I spent a lot of time working, and didn't make a lot of female friends in Atlanta. Laycee lived right next door to us. I doubt if I'll ever see her again. At least, I hope not."

Nick had saved two hot dogs and beers for us. After enduring a mini-lecture from Mom about missing an inning then getting the play-by-play recap from Dad and Dave, I settled down to watch the game.

At the top of the seventh inning with the score tied at one, the Cubs loaded the bases with two outs. Their ace left-handed batter came to the plate. The Dodger manager took a time-out and brought Jarret, his ace left-handed specialist, out of the bullpen. After three warm-up pitches from the mound, Jarret easily struck out the batter and retired the side.

Jarret's skill as a left-handed reliever extended his career beyond the life of normal pitchers. He usually worked only one or two innings, leaving his arm always rested. At thirty-nine, even his chronic sore shoulder didn't hamper his performance.

"Jarret's in good form today," Dave said. "There are three lefties batting in the eighth. I bet they leave him in."

"If they do, he'll have to bat. The Dodgers are near the bottom of the batting order." Nick turned to Dad. "Gee, it would be just awful to see Jarret strike out, wouldn't it, Walter?"

Everyone except sports-clueless Robin turned at Nick's snide remark. Dave leered. Mom sneered. Dad chuckled. I enjoyed Nick's heresy. Jarret's shoddy behavior during our marriage got set aside whenever our family came to see him pitch. Dave, who usually ignored my ex, let his Dodger loyalty soften his feelings toward Jarret only if and when Jarret got in the game. Mom, taken by Jarret's Midwest boyish charm, liked having a celebrity in the family and still referred to him as her son-in-law. She watched him on the field, enchanted.

I had spent fifteen years rooting for Jarret. I knew how much pitching well meant to him. He made a lousy husband and a sometimes irritating ex, but his skill on the mound demanded respect.

Although the sun had set, the temperature registered seventy-four on the scoreboard as we sang two choruses of "Take Me Out to the Ball Game" for the seventh-inning stretch. As we sat down, the first Dodger batter walked to the plate. Jarret followed him out of the dugout with his bat, and took a few practice swings in the warm-up circle.

The lead batter got to first base on a walk. Jarret came to the plate, took another practice swing, then set his stance. He swung at the first pitch and missed. He let the second pitch pass him for a called strike. One more strike and he would be out.

Mom, Dave, Robin, and I stood. A heart-pounding rush of nervous energy coursed through me.

The next pitch crossed the plate dead center. Jarret swung, and the ball and his bat connected with a sweet *crack*. The ball flew high just inside the first-base foul line and over the head of the first baseman. And as the outfielder leaped to the wall to make the catch, the ball cleared the fence and bounced into the second row of the right-field bleachers for a two-run home run.

The stadium erupted into a massive, earsplitting cheer. Jarret circled the bases toward home. Two women stormed down our aisle, screaming and waving their arms, and as he crossed home plate, they hugged each other. Mom, Dave, Robin and I exchanged high fives, and fans throughout the stadium circled rally towels, baseball caps, and fists in the air.

Dad and Nick slumped in silence, arms crossed.

Jarret took off his batting helmet and disappeared into the dugout while the crowd continued to roar. Home runs by pitchers were a rarity. This was the second one I had seen Jarret hit in fifteen years.

The two women who rushed the aisle pumped their fists and jumped up and down, yelling with the rest of the stadium for Jarret to come out for a bow. As they turned, chanting Jarret's name at the Dodger dugout, I recognized both women from the gym. Gretchen, the brunette from this morning, and a nameless, streaked blonde I saw yesterday. Screaming for Jarret at high pitch, Gretchen wasn't kidding about being a baseball fan.

Relentless cheers brought Jarret out of the dugout before play resumed. He touched his cap in acknowledgement, then pointed up into the stands and blew a kiss in our general direction. I bent my head, chuckling. *He remembered.*

Mom leaned over to Robin and me. "Isn't it sweet how the fans love him?"

"Very sweet," Robin said.

The inning ended with the Dodgers leading by two runs. The Cubs' defense cleared the field and the Dodger defense came out of the dugout and took their places. Jarret, the last player out of the dugout, jogged toward the mound.

As he skipped over the chalk between third base and home plate, a white pigeon swooped off the home plate backstop fencing and dive-bombed straight at Jarret's head. Jarret flinched backward onto the chalk line.

Mom and I gasped together.

"Oh, no," Mom said.

"Damn," I said.

"What?" Nick said.

"Maybe he didn't notice," Mom said. "I hope he didn't notice."

"He noticed," I said. "See how he's stomping his foot? He's trying to shake off the chalk."

"What happened?" Robin hunched forward, staring down at the field. "Why is Jarret doing a rain dance on the mound?"

"He's superstitious about stepping on the baseline," I said. "He believes a myth about the chalk between third base and home plate carrying runs. If he wears chalk to the mound on his shoe, the chalk will make him pitch runs to the opposing team."

Nick leaned over to Dad. "Then this should be very interesting. Let's see how the phenom pitches with chalk dust clouding his focus."

I rubbed my knees, watching the field. When Jarret performed on the mound, he had a canny ability to shut out distractions around him. Jeering crowds couldn't shake him. All-star batters didn't intimidate him. Being behind on the count, hung-over, shivering from the cold, or sweltering in the heat didn't faze him. But the run-laden chalk on his shoe would shimmy up his leg and into his head.

And it did. Jarret walked the first two batters and hit the third on the shoulder with a wild pitch, loading the bases. The next batter, the Cubs' left-handed leader in runs batted in, came to the plate.

"They have to take him out of the game," Dave said.

"They won't. The Dodgers only have righties warming up in the bullpen. Jarret is their leftie specialist. They have a better chance leaving him in," Dad said, nudging Nick.

The Dodger catcher and first baseman went to the mound to calm Jarret down. He bobbed his head as he listened to them. The catcher handed him the ball with an encouraging tap on the shoulder. I knew their assurances wouldn't work. Jarret was freaked, and the worse he pitched, the more freaked he became.

On Jarret's second pitch, the Cubs batter cleared the bases with a grand slam home run. The manager took Jarret out of the game and he left the mound to lukewarm applause and a few jeers from the crowd.

The Cubs won the game five to three. Dad and Nick exchanged fist bumps and smug smiles.

"Season's not over. We'll get you next time," Dave said.

"I'm happy for you, Walter," Mom said, kissing Dad's cheek before they filed into the aisle. "You got your birthday wish—your team won."

Dave, Nick, and Robin followed them out. As I tagged behind, Gretchen and her blonde friend climbed the steps toward me in dejected silence.

"Gretchen," I said. She glanced up. "I saw you at the gym this morning. I didn't have a chance to introduce myself, I'm Liz Cooper."

"Cooper?" Gretchen tilted her head.

"Are you related to Jarret?" the blonde said.

"I used to be. He's my ex-husband. Tough loss tonight." I stepped into the aisle and climbed the stairs with them.

"Jarret pitched a great seventh inning. Bad break on the eighth."

"I hope he remembers his home run and forgets about the rest of the game," Gretchen said.

"He looked pretty happy rounding the bases, didn't he?" I said.

The blonde stopped and turned. "Pretty happy? Didn't you read the note on the scoreboard? He's the only Dodger pitcher to hit a home run this season. The fans adore him."

"But you saw the kiss he blew into the stands, right?" Gretchen said.

I smiled, amused by the delight on her face. "I did. And don't worry about his attitude. He'll make a comeback with his pitching game. He always does. It's a long season."

Mom and Robin met me at the top of the stairs. "Liz, are you meeting Jarret at the pub later?" Mom said.

I exchanged quick good-byes with Gretchen and her friend. As they disappeared into the exiting throng, I said to Mom, "Believe me, Jarret would rather hang out with his pals at Fifth Base than with any of us. Especially tonight."

Robin, Mom, and I followed the crowd to the escalators with Dad, Nick, and Dave leading the way. When we reached the field level, Mom pulled me to the side. "I feel bad for Jarret. Someone has to cheer him up. You should call him, Liz."

"Not my job anymore. If you're concerned about him, call him in the morning. I have a feeling he'll be busy tonight."

Jarret soothed his losses with rebellion. Back in the minor leagues, he broke training with a few beers and went to bed. When he entered the majors, the beers became scotch or pain pills. Age and wear on his arm only served to escalate his dejection over losing. During his worst slump, a disastrous road trip with the Braves, I called his hotel room to comfort him and a woman answered. The next day he swore I'd called the wrong number. Women, each with a different voice, began phoning our house. I refused to stoop to searching through his cell phone messages or texts. The day before I found Laycee's bra under our bed, he had pitched a horrible game to the Phillies. His losses and our marriage went down together.

Robin waited in the aisle for us to catch up then we followed our guys into the parking lot.

"Thank you for inviting me to the game, Viv. I had a great time," Robin said.

"Dear, I'm sorry we weren't able to chat more. I expect you and Dave at the house Saturday night for Walter's birthday barbeque. And don't let Dave try to back out with a work excuse. I know all the ploys homicide detectives use to get out of going to functions. I cured Walter of his habit by throwing parties at home. I can give you a few other good tricks to use."

"Oh, I'm sure Robin has plenty of tricks to keep Dave in line," I said, laughing.

Robin blushed. "I want to hear everything you know, Viv. We'll be there. Should I bring anything?"

"Whatever you want to, dear. What will you be bringing from your brand-new kitchen, Liz?" Mom said.

"Wine."

I stopped to give Dad another birthday hug and smooch,

and then Dave, Robin, Nick, and I left my folks in the lot with promises to regroup on Saturday.

As we walked to his car, Nick pointed at the waning crescent glowing over the hills around the stadium parking lot. "The moon will be full in a few nights. The spirits are getting restless."

"I think your spirits made enough trouble for tonight," I said.

"You mean Jarret? Live by superstition, die by superstition."

"I was thinking more about what spooked the pigeon to fly into him."

"Ah, the white pigeon. Remind me to make a donation to the home for orphaned pigeons. That bird helped the Cubs win the game. I wonder if Jarret has heard about the legend."

"What legend?"

"White pigeons are death omens."

"What's with omens and birds, Nick? Seriously, last year you and Robin had me dodging crows. Now you're warning me about pigeons?" I laughed. "Forget it. Have you looked around the city lately? We're surrounded by them."

Nick opened the door of his SUV for me, tossed his cap into the backseat, and started the engine. I relaxed in the passenger seat for the slow ride to the freeway and home. As we inched into the thick stream of traffic creeping out of Dodger Stadium a sour, yeasty odor permeated the car.

"What's that awful smell?" I said, wrinkling my nose.

Nick tossed me a glance. "I didn't want to say anything, but . . ."

I sniffed a strand of my hair. Oh no. Me. The stink was on me—my hair and skin reeked from the odor of dried beer. I put down my window. Nick put down his. The loud blast of hot air blowing into the car and the freeway noise outside kept our conversation to a minimum all the way to Studio City. He parked in front of my house and we walked inside.

"I have to get out of these clothes and clean up," I said.

"How? Did the plumber put in your showers and tub already?"

"Not even close. I can't go to bed smelling like this. I'll wash my hair in the sink and take another sponge bath after you leave."

"I have a better idea," he said, tugging at a strand of my sticky hair.

"What?" I moved close, wanting to kiss him. The stench stopped me. I knew Nick loved me but embracing my smelly body warranted combat pay.

"Where did you put the garden hose I bought you?"

"Are you serious?"

Nick curled his mouth into a sexy, evil grin. "As serious as a shower and nightcap in your backyard. Take off your clothes, get some towels, and meet me outside."

Chapter Five

"Nick?" Barefoot, with two towels and an open bottle of white wine, I peered over the candytuft blooms shimmering under the moonlight in my backyard. Crickets chirped. A dog barked in the distance. Erzulie watched from the kitchen window.

Nick's shirt and jeans were draped over the back of a chair on the porch. I scanned the empty yard with caution. Despite the heat in the still night air, I didn't want to be ambushed with a blast of cold water.

I heard a *squeak* of a faucet turning from the side of the house, and then the sound of water splashing the driveway.

Nick strolled into the yard in his boxer shorts, with the garden hose in his hand and his fingers on the nozzle. "Ready?"

"I'm not taking my clothes off." I dropped my voice to a

whisper so the neighbors wouldn't hear. "Let's have some wine and enjoy the night air."

"Put down the wine and towels, Liz." He aimed the nozzle at my feet.

He moved toward the steps, teasing me off the porch with tiny squirts of water. I let out a nervous, frightened giggle. He grabbed the towels from me and tossed them on a lounge chair. Another squirt sent me dancing over the grass with wet toes.

"Give me the wine," he said.

I backed away. "No."

Nick came toward me and snatched the bottle out of my hand. When he turned to put it on the porch step, I darted across the lawn to hide under the lemon tree by the back fence.

I made three good strides before he blasted me with cold water, soaking the back of my clothes and hair. I stopped and turned. "You are going to be so sorry you did that."

"I don't think so." He drenched the front of my shirt this time. "What are you going to do to me now?"

"Use my secret weapon." I tucked a strand of wet hair behind my ear.

"And what's that?" He aimed the nozzle at me.

I pulled the soaked pink T-shirt over my head and tossed it across the yard. With my eyes fixed on Nick, I flicked my bra straps off my shoulders, reached behind me, unhooked the clasp, and let my bra drop to the grass.

He relaxed his arm with the nozzle at his side.

Unzipping my jeans, I lowered them inch by inch over my hips, my knees, and then stepped out of them. I snapped the side of my panties with my thumb. Nick moved closer, watching me. As soon as he got within reach, I seized the hose from his distracted grip and backed away, opening the nozzle full force over his body. He wrestled the nozzle out of my hand with water spurting over both of us. Dancing under the moonlight, we laughed until we couldn't breathe.

And though I didn't win the backyard battle, the peace treaty we negotiated in my bedroom was worth the effort. He left at midnight.

My alarm went off at five-thirty. I reached across the nightstand and hit snooze. Ten minutes later, I hit snooze again, this time vaguely aware I should climb out of bed and get to the gym for a shower before Stan and his crew arrived at the house, hopefully with my new tub.

Erzulie nudged me before the second snooze went off.

"Okay, okay. We'll get up." I shut off the alarm and crawled out of bed. After I brushed my teeth in my wreck of a bathroom, I pulled on my gym gear, threw some clean clothes into my backpack, and trotted downstairs. The dim gray light of dawn crept through the living room windows, illuminating my half-empty bookcase. *I have to pick up that last box.* Even though the rooms upstairs were stacked with unloaded cartons of clothes, I wouldn't be happy until the rest of my books filled up the bookcase. Somehow that simple accomplishment represented progress.

I got to the gym, left my backpack in a cubbyhole, and looked around. Tess power walked on a treadmill. A few familiar faces from yesterday worked out on machines. I didn't see Kyle.

Earl the trainer strolled over to the cubbyholes in a red

muscle shirt sculpted tight to his skin. He nodded in greeting then pulled a smartphone from his cubbyhole, scrolling and typing with his thumbs.

"Hey, Earl. Where is everyone? Where's Kyle this morning?" I said.

He shrugged. "He called me at four-thirty and asked me to open the gym for him. I guess he partied hearty last night. He's coming in later. Was he supposed to meet you here?"

"No. Just curious. It seems empty in here today."

"Too hot to exercise," he said.

Tess waved hello as I climbed on the treadmill beside her. "Did you have a good time at the baseball game last night?" she said.

The baseball game. Right. My backyard and bedroom romp with Nick blanked my memory of Jarret's disastrous game, Kyle's beer shower, and Laycee's brazen attitude.

"The Dodgers lost but my family had fun." I programmed the treadmill and as I began my warm-up, glanced through the cardio room window to the studio in back. "No Gretchen this morning? I saw her at the game."

Tess scanned the room. "Huh, she's not here. I didn't even notice. That's a first. Was she with a guy last night? I'm curious who she's dating."

"No guy. She was with one of the female members from here—the streaked blonde who rode the elliptical in front of us Monday morning. I don't know her name."

Tess laughed. "You'll get to know everyone. Streaked blonde? Maybe you mean Gloria? Did she have an attitude? A little full of herself?"

"Let's say she exuded self-confidence. Works out with a trainer with a shaved head?"

"That's Gloria. Comes here about three or four times a week. She works in television doing something that requires her I'll-snub-you-before-you-snub-me defense."

"To be fair, I didn't talk to her much."

"Don't bother," Tess said. "Gloria wears a nasty vibe like a designer label."

I felt honored to be on Tess's good side. "Another psychic read?"

"You didn't pick up on her prickly aura? She doesn't warm up to women. I'm surprised she and Gretchen are friends."

"They seemed like they were having a good time together last night at the game," I said.

"Go figure. Did you run into Kyle there?"

"Literally. I backed into a full cup of beer he held while I talked with Laycee."

"So is he dating Miss Atlanta or what? What's her story?"

"Lonely housewife." I cranked up my treadmill speed to avoid answering in depth.

My late rise set me back a half hour. I finished my workout and shower with an impossible five minutes to make it to Jarret's before he left at eight for his morning run. But aside from rushing to meet Stan at my house on time, I was in no hurry to see Jarret. Knowing him, he would be hungover and cranky after drowning his loss on the mound.

Kyle still hadn't come to the gym by the time I left. I wondered if he spent the night with Laycee. Wouldn't surprise me. Both of them were users. Both had agendas. How fitting they found each other. How sad for her husband, who thought she came out to visit me.

Traffic moving west on Ventura Boulevard crawled along

at a stop and start pace again. I made the turn off Sepulveda Boulevard into Royal Oaks a little past eight-thirty, driving along the deserted streets through the tunnel of trees toward Jarret's. I turned into his driveway, drove up the hill, and parked at his garage door. Just in case he was home, I rang the front doorbell. No answer.

I went to the garage and tapped 0118, Jarret's birthday, on the security keypad. The door rolled up and back, exposing the carless garage. I crossed to the door in back and entered the kitchen.

His blender pitcher and a glass sat in the sink, both filled with cloudy water and remnants from Jarret's morning power shake. Two half-empty glass flutes along with two empty bottles of champagne stood at the end of the counter. So the party came home with him last night. I checked myself. *None of my business.* The quarter-folded cardboard box labeled "Liz books—3 of 4" waited for me on the cooking island. I lugged the heavy carton to my car, closed the garage door, and left.

At the bottom of his driveway, I made a fast left turn past the middle-aged woman walking a tottering black-and-white spaniel along the street. The neighborhood busybody whose name I never remembered. The day Jarret and I moved in, she knocked on our door holding up Neighborhood Watch pamphlets, and then attempted to wheedle her way into the house. The day I moved out alone, she rang the bell with a petition to ban parking on our street, casually asking if we were leaving. I viewed her as my personal hello, good-bye committee.

I stopped at the corner to turn, and saw her wave through my rearview mirror. I made a half-hearted return wave then sped off. I needed to get home to let Stan in. And the unpacked box on the passenger seat preoccupied me. Deep down, I knew filling my bookcase wasn't important—I wanted complete closure from my old life. No more leaving boxes behind. Jarret and I would be better friends after a clean break.

The traffic was still ugly when I reached Ventura Boulevard. I opted to go straight up Sepulveda and get on the 101 Freeway East, a risky decision in the no-win morning rush. Wrong move made too late. The jammed freeway crept bumper to bumper, too slow to hope for a break, and I was too trapped to worry. I tried Stan's cell without luck and left a message. My dashboard clock hit nine as I passed the Laurel Canyon ramp and took the 134 split south to exit at Tujunga Avenue.

Stan's new Ford F-150 white pickup sat in my driveway. He and Angel perched on the open tailgate under the blazing morning sun, both bare-chested and smoking. They stood, crushing their cigarette butts on the cement as I parked and got out of the car.

I spread my hands. "I'm so sorry. I got stuck in traffic. Did you get my message?"

"No worries, honey. Angel and I caught some rays while we were waiting for you. It's going to be another hot one today." Stan rolled a white T-shirt over his head. "Your tub should be ready for pick up tomorrow, princess. Soon you'll be soaking in a bubble bath."

"Hallelujah. You just made my day."

"I live to see you smile," Stan said.

I chuckled, doubtful. Stan might live to see guys on Santa Monica Boulevard smile, but I was pretty sure Stan lived to see *me* write him a check at the end of the week. I opened the passenger door of my car and reached for the box.

"Let me help you, Miss Liz." Angel took the carton off the passenger seat and followed me up the brick path to the porch.

"You can set the box on the floor by the fireplace. Thank you," I said, following them in.

Erzulie waited in the center of the living room floor to greet me. At the sight of a man with a box heading her way, she jerked back, did a fake to her right, then swerved to her left, doing a low belly scramble around the sofa and into the den beyond the living room.

Though I was eager to get to work on emptying the box, my rumbling stomach had another idea. My lone Dodger dog at the game was my last meal.

Stan dropped his toolbox at the foot of the stairway, and then started back outside.

I stopped him at the door. "I'm going to run over to Aroma for breakfast. Do you want me to pick up some food for you and Angel? Lattes? Croissants?"

"No, thanks, we caught breakfast on our way and had coffee while we were waiting for you. We're good. You go. I want to get to work," he said.

"Running over" in L.A. speak meant getting in my car and driving the four blocks to Aroma, the popular café nestled in Tujunga Village amid artsy shops, yoga studios, and restaurants. With luck, I'd find a parking space nearby. Given a miracle, the line outside wouldn't be too long.

After I circled the block twice, a space opened in front of Two Roads, a sixty-seat local theater down the block on Tujunga. Only four people waited in line outside Aroma.

Before long I sipped a creamy latte, people watching while I waited for an Aroma Panini to be delivered to my sidewalk table.

Just as the waiter set the plate of focaccia filled with scrambled eggs, cheddar, tomato, avocado, and smoked bacon on my table, my phone rang. I checked caller ID. Area code 404—Atlanta. Ugh. Laycee? She had the nerve to call me after last night? To tell me she aced her audition? Despite my dislike for the woman and a strong wish to forget I knew her, I could still recite her cell phone number from memory. And it wasn't the number on the screen.

Curious, I slid the unlock bar on the screen to answer.

"Liz? This is Forrest Huber. Laycee's husband."

I eased back in my chair. "Forrest, it's been a while. How are you?"

"I can't find Laycee. Do you know where she is?"

Damn her for using me as her excuse.

"I don't. I'm sorry. She doesn't answer her cell?" Laycee wore her cell phone like a lifeline. She may have been born holding one.

"No," he said, clearly irritated. "I haven't heard from her this morning. I tried her cell several times. She's not at the hotel. I thought she was spending the day with you. Are you meeting her later?"

I closed my eyes and sighed, reminded again of Forrest's possessive hold on Laycee. It would be so easy for me to blow her cover. Such great revenge to tell Forrest his wife lied to him, that she was probably running around somewhere with Kyle or auditioning for a reality show. I really wanted to tell Forrest his cheating tramp of a wife would be the last person I would spend my time with. Forrest didn't deserve being the target of my wrath, however. So why upset him more?

"I saw Laycee yesterday . . ." I hesitated. If I mentioned last night's ball game, he might ask for details. ". . . morning. She said she'd call me though I haven't heard from her today. If I do, I'll tell her to contact you right away."

"Please do." The distance between Atlanta and Los Angeles didn't temper the annoyance and suspicion in his voice. He hung up without saying good-bye.

I ate enough to satisfy my hunger then called my answering service. Three messages came in overnight—all hang ups. Rare but not unusual. My outgoing office message instructs clients to leave a message or, in emergencies, hang up and dial 911. Occasionally one or two hang ups preceded a call, a day or two later, from a nervous new client seeking an appointment.

My next stop was at Ralph's Market on Ventura and Vineland for supplies. Then, with my trunk loaded with milk, coffee, fresh fruit, and cat food in every fish-related flavor, I headed for home to face the task of emptying boxes.

Seeing my old tub in Stan's truck bed encouraged me. Progress. I carried the bags into the house and put away the groceries. As I finished stacking cat food by label color in the pantry cupboard, I heard my cell phone ringing in my purse in the foyer and went to answer.

"Hi, Mom."

"Oh, thank God you're all right." She sounded breathless.

"What's wrong?"

"Turn on your television. Hurry."

My stomach clenched, unnerved by the urgency in her

voice. I ran into the den and picked up the remote. "What happened, Mom? Are Daddy and Dave all right?"

"They're fine. You're alive. Beyond that, I don't know. Just turn on the television."

"What channel?" I fumbled with the buttons.

"Any channel."

The TV flickered on. A headline flashed across the bottom of the screen:

BREAKING NEWS: WOMAN FOUND DEAD AT HOME OF DODGER PITCHER.

Chapter Six

The brunette reporter spoke into a microphone from the middle of the upscale residential street. Behind her, I saw the iron fence bordering Jarret's house and driveway. I increased the TV volume and sat on the den couch, watching the screen in a stupefied daze as Mom fired off questions over the phone.

"Should we call Jarret? What if something happened to him? Should we call your brother Dave?"

Onscreen the reporter said, "We don't have a confirmed victim name or further details. The West Valley Division captain will make a statement at noon. This is Shazia Kapoor for Channel Seven Eyewitness News. Back to you in the studio, Jim."

"We have to call Jarret," Mom said. "Maybe we should go up there. Do you know who—"

"Slow down, Mom. What else did you hear on the news before you called me?"

"I was watching *The View*. I was about to turn off the set and start preparing your father's lunch when the news—"

My shoulders began to twitch. "Details, Mom. What did the news report say?"

"They led with the story about the dead woman in Jarret's house. Dear God, I panicked. I thought of you and ran for the phone. I thought maybe you were with him. Thank God you're all right."

"Sit down and breathe. I'm fine. You're fine. Keep the news on and see if you can learn anything else. I'll try to reach Jarret," I said.

"Call me back."

I fell back into the cushions, my mind spinning with worst-case scenarios. Did Jarret have it in him to kill someone? My instincts told me no. He had a temper but he never resorted to violence, especially toward women. Not possible. Was the woman an intruder? Did Jarret walk in on a robbery? I dialed Jarret's cell and got voice mail, and then tried his home phone number and got an answer on the sixth ring.

"Yeah." The raspy voice belonged to Ira Ryback, Jarret's sports agent.

"Ira, this is Liz. I just saw the news on TV. What's going on up there? Is Jarret all right?"

"He's a freaking nervous wreck, but he's alive," Ira said.

"What happened?"

"Someone broke into the house this morning and murdered a chick in the bedroom."

My breath hitched. I was at Jarret's house hours ago.

Alone. "What time? Was Jarret home? Who was the victim?"

"Some woman he brought home last night. He left her asleep in his bedroom and went out for his morning run. He got back home, found her dead, and called me to come over. We notified the cops when I got here."

"He called *you* and then waited for you to arrive before he dialed 911?"

"I *told* him to wait for me. He sounded too shaken to cope with the authorities alone." Ira added carelessly, "The woman was already dead from stab wounds."

Jarret had sat at home with a dead or dying woman, waiting for his agent to make the twenty-minute trip from Beverly Hills to Encino before he called for help? I shook my head in disbelief, though well aware of Jarret's tendency to panic in an emergency. His cocky attitude and self-assurance only applied to situations under his control. He left the remainder of his major decisions up to Ira, the slick business lawyer and promoter who protected Jarret's assets and career.

"Do you know the victim's name?"

"Laycee something."

My stomach flipped. "Laycee Huber?"

"Yeah. Don't tell anyone I told you that. The police have to notify her family before they release her name to the press. Listen, I need to get off the line. Jarret is with a detective, and I don't want him talking too much without me. I'll tell him you called."

As soon as he clicked off, my phone rang again.

Robin heaved a deep sigh. "I'm so glad you're there. I

just heard the news about Jarret. I got worried. I thought maybe—"

"No. It wasn't me," I said, curious why I topped everyone's victim list. "It was Laycee Huber."

"Are you serious?"

"Yes. Jarret's agent just told me on the phone. Jarret is with a detective now. Apparently he left Laycee asleep in his bed when he went out for his run this morning. She was dead when he got home."

"What was she doing at his house?"

"I don't want to guess. Do you want to hear something bizarre?"

"Worse than Laycee Huber dead in Jarret's bed?"

"I went to his house this morning to pick up a box. I must have missed the intruder by minutes."

"Liz, no. I had a strange feeling about you this morning. Did you see Laycee?"

"I only got as far as the kitchen. I didn't see or hear anyone." I flinched—Laycee must have been in the bedroom, dead or dying while I was there.

"Don't tell anyone you were there."

"Why not?"

"Ex-wife in the house and a dead woman in the ex-husband's bed? Keep your mouth shut. Trust me. Don't be helpful. Remember what happened to me? I volunteered to help the police last year and was rewarded with two nights in jail. Do not say anything," Robin said. "Maybe I should leave work and come over."

"Don't. I'm okay. I need some time to process this."

"Are you sure you're okay to be alone?"

"Yes, of course," I said, grateful for her concern. "This isn't about me. Poor Laycee. Her husband called me this morning, looking for her. What a mess."

"Why was she with Jarret? Didn't Laycee go to the game with another guy last night?"

"Kyle." I had forgotten about their date. "You're right. I don't know how she wound up with Jarret. I want to see if I can find another news report. I'll stay in touch."

"Just remember what I told you. No one needs to know you were there."

"Someone already does. One of the neighbors saw me pull out of his driveway."

"Then let the police come to you. Don't offer information. Call a lawyer. Protect yourself."

"This isn't about me," I said.

"I know. Let the investigation unfold on its own."

After we hung up, I scanned through all seven local TV stations for a story update but every station was in a commercial break. The floor above squeaked from the weight of Stan and Angel working.

I sat at the edge of the sofa, staring through the window while layers of complicated feelings reeled through me like ticker tape. I pictured Laycee at the game—once my friend, yesterday an irritation, and today the victim of violence. My heart ached over the shock and fear she must have felt in her last moments. Bitterness and disgust over her past betrayal. Then shame for dishonoring the dead. I didn't like Laycee, but she didn't deserve to die. And what about Jarret? A scandal might mar or even destroy his career. He was an idiot for leaving his house open to intrusion. Anger melded into horror—I may have missed the murderer by minutes.

Peace wouldn't come by sitting in a daze. I needed busy-work. As I rose to unpack the last box of books, my cell phone rang again. A familiar Illinois phone number flashed on the display.

"Liz? It's Marion Cooper." My ex-mother-in-law's voice wavered. "I couldn't think of anyone else to call. I'm trying to reach Jarret. He doesn't answer his telephone. There's a story on the cable news station about . . ." She hesitated. Usually talkative and amicable, Marion appreciated a good piece of gossip—but not if it targeted her family. Talking about a homicide at her son's home fell outside the province of her small-town comfort zone.

"I know. I saw the story on the news. Jarret is okay," I added quickly to ease her. "I spoke with his agent. I don't know exactly what happened yet. All I know is that Jarret found a woman dead in his house."

"What should we do?" Marion said. "Should I call the police station? Is Jarret in jail?"

"No. My best guess is that he's still at the house with the police. Let me make a call. My brother is a LAPD detective. Maybe he can get us more information."

"Yah. I told Bud you'd know what to do. Bud and I are worried. Everyone is calling here." She hacked out a smoker's cough. "I wish my son would get in touch with us."

"He will, Marion. Give him time. He'll be with the police for hours. Leave him a message. If I hear from him, I'll make sure he calls you."

"Thank you. It's hot and muggy here. How is the weather out there?"

"Hot and dry. The usual," I said, comforting her. Odd as her question was, I wasn't surprised Marion asked. She used weather as a neutral ground to escape unpleasant topics. *Bad news? How's the weather?* "Try not to worry. I'll call you as soon as I talk to my brother."

I hung up, and then left a message on Dave's voice mail.

Channel 7 broke into programming with a news bulletin. "This is Shazia Kapoor reporting from outside the home of Dodger pitcher Jarret Cooper, where a woman was found slain this morning. I'm here with Captain Eagleton from the West Valley Community Police Station."

She addressed the mustached man in LAPD blue on her left. "Captain Eagleton, can you update us on what happened here today?"

"911 dispatch received a call near 10 A.M. reporting a female victim of an intrusion at the Cooper home," Eagleton said.

"Have you identified the victim?" Shazia said.

"We're withholding ID pending notification of her family. We are, however, asking for citizens in the Royal Oaks neighborhood to report any unusual or suspicious activity on or near Royal Oak Road this morning."

"The West Valley Division phone number is onscreen for witnesses to contact," Shazia said. "Captain, can you tell us anything else? Who placed the original call to 911?"

"Mr. Cooper placed the call. The homicide unit in charge of the investigation is canvassing the neighborhood now. That's all the information I can give you." Eagleton glanced over his shoulder as if to signal the end to the conversation.

"Thank you, Captain." She turned to the camera and began a recap of her earlier report.

Eagleton crossed the street behind the reporter, and then

stopped to talk to a man at the base of Jarret's driveway. I held up the remote to mute the volume, then froze. I stepped toward the screen for a closer look. Unbelievable.

Though I only saw his hair and part of his face, I recognized the tilt of the head and the confident stance instantly. Nick—standing on the asphalt conversing with the captain. Eagleton turned and went back up the drive. Nick pulled out his phone. Within seconds, mine rang.

"You won't believe where I am," Nick said.

Still in shock, I said, "I don't—yet there you are, right on my TV screen."

He glanced back over his shoulder, saw the reporter, and then turned away fast. "Damn."

"Camera-shy?" I said as he sidled out of view.

"No one was supposed to know I'm here. Eagleton won't like this at all. Did you see my face?"

"Only your profile. But if you're going stealth, you better get out of there. Every major news and sports network is carrying the story. What are you doing there?" I said.

"Are you home?"

"Yes."

"I'll be right over to explain."

Chapter Seven

I made a pot of coffee while I waited for Nick. The high-pitched whir of Stan's drill upstairs distracted me from the tape of questions running through my mind about what could have happened at Jarret's house. As the rich brown liquid streamed into the coffeemaker on the counter, I wandered upstairs to check on Stan's progress.

I had to hand it to him. He worked slowly but with care. Tarps protected my bed and the furniture from the dust coming out of the master bathroom into my unpainted bedroom.

Inside the bathroom, stacks of soiled, broken tiles jutted out of a white plastic bucket on top of the toilet. The wall beneath the window where the old bathtub once stood was stripped down to drywall and exposed beams. White dust coated the mirror and countertops, paint chips and chunks

66

of plaster covered the floor. Stan and Angel kneeled at the far wall, an open sore of pipes.

I stopped at the threshold, facing the mess. "How's the work going?"

Stan sat back on his knees, wiping his forehead with a handkerchief. "Moving along. After we scrape away the old grout, finish clearing the walls, setting the floor, and checking the pipes, we can bring in and set the new tub and then begin retiling. The pipes are in better shape than I thought."

I nodded as if I understood. I heard at least another week of me showering at the gym. The guest bathroom upstairs wasn't an option—the previous owner hadn't used the shower in years and I had stacked the room with unopened boxes. My renovation plan looked more illogical by the hour.

Too late to change direction. I left them working, got a cup of coffee, and went to the den to flip through local channels for updates and wait for Nick. As soon as the bell rang, I ran to the door.

"You okay?" he said when he saw my face.

"Happy to see you." I led him into the den, where a newsbreak replayed Captain Eagleton's statement to the press.

Nick listened, arms folded, to the captain's comments. "Eagleton is so smart about community relations. I love his skill for placating the press without revealing too many details."

"How do you know him?" I said.

"Dave and I broke up a cult a few years ago in his jurisdiction. Eagleton is fair, honest, and tough. Before he took over West Valley, he ran the gang and vice units at Foothill. When he called me to the scene this morning, I had no idea whose house I entered. Imagine my surprise—I walked in and saw Jarret's photos in the hall."

"Imagine my surprise when I saw you on the news."

"Eagleton asked for my help to expedite the investigation. He wanted me to look at the body before the field investigation unit took over the scene."

"I don't understand. You're not a medical doctor."

He sat next to me on the sofa. "Before I explain, I have to tell you—for a minute I thought the small brunette face-down on the pillow might be you. I panicked until I got closer and saw the victim's face. You knew her, Liz."

"I heard. Laycee Huber. Jarret's agent told me over the phone." I held my hand to my chest. I had to know. "How bad was it?"

"Are you sure you want me to tell you?" he said. At my nod, he continued, "Someone repeatedly knifed her in the back, presumably while she slept. The slashes appeared angry, brutal. From her positioning on the bed, I assume she never woke to see her attacker."

"She would have fought if she did. I know Laycee. She would have fought with everything she had. What did he want you to see?"

"A symbol smeared into the blood on her back," he said.

I flinched, horrified. "What kind of maniac signs his victim?"

"The first responders assumed the mark was gang related. But Eagleton, who was a gang expert before he took over West Valley, disagreed. He recognized part of the marking and thought the killing may be cult related. That's why he called me to come over. He didn't want to risk e-mailing a photo. He wants the symbol kept out of the press, away from the public. I met him at the address he gave me, ignorant of what I was heading into."

"Was Jarret in the house when you got there?" I said.

"I didn't see him. Eagleton met me at the gate, guided me inside to the bedroom, and waited while I studied the symbol." Nick reached into his pocket and brought out a small sheet of paper with a sketch of a five-pointed star. The number 5, scrawled upside down in the center with three small crosses beneath.

"A star?" I said.

"A pentagram, defined by the connecting strokes. Wiccans use it to symbolize their beliefs. Christians, Mormons, and the Bahá'í Faith, among others, used the pentagram in artwork for centuries." He turned the paper to show the 5, upright. "The killer marked Laycee with an inverted pentagram."

I took the paper out of his hand and glanced down. "What's the difference?"

"The inverted pentagram is common to witchcraft and devil worship. It represents black magic to some groups. Others, including a satanic group organized in the sixties, use the three downward points to signify rejection of the Holy Trinity. In occultism, a reversed pentagram indicates evil. In black magic, the sign of fatality," he said.

"And the five?"

"In my opinion, the key to the killer's message. Laycee could be a fifth victim. When you take the components together, the five, the reversed pentagram, and the Petrine crosses—"

"Petrine?"

Nick pointed at the three crosses underscoring the five. "Inverted Latin crosses. The Petrine cross has conflicting meanings, from symbolizing St. Peter to denoting anti-Christian beliefs. In this context, I assume they're used to represent the devil. The inverted pentagram and crosses signal a killer tied to the occult, with the five completing the message."

"Saying what?"

"I can't tell yet. I have a vague sense I've seen this combination before, but I need to dig through some books and papers for the source," Nick said. "Eagleton is requesting a search of the FBI files for a match, too. My sketch is rough. The killer drew each part of this symbol on Laycee's body slowly and deliberately."

"He brutally attacks her then takes his time leaving a message?" I shuddered, wondering how close I came to confronting a madman. "Could the killer be someone Laycee and/or Jarret knew? Or do you think Laycee happened to be in the wrong place at the wrong time, like the Manson murder victims? A random killing by deranged zealots? Did you see any signs of a break-in?"

"All valid questions, and impossible for me to answer. I didn't stray beyond the hall and the bedroom. There were no broken windows that I saw. I'm no cop, but if it wasn't a break-in, I assume Jarret is the primary suspect."

I stood and began to pace in front of Nick. "Nothing fits. What would Jarret gain by killing Laycee? Their connection was casual as far as I know."

"As far as you know. But he left her asleep in his house, alone. Odd."

"She wasn't exactly a stranger, Nick. Jarret is addicted to his ritual morning run. If she was asleep, he probably left her alone to be considerate."

"He might have killed her before he left."

"In her sleep? Why?" I shook my head. "Jarret has his flaws, but he's not brutal or heartless. He wouldn't murder Laycee then go out for his morning run. He'd never leave a mark like that on her body."

"Then what type of killer leaves a message?"

"Manipulative. Someone craving attention and demanding to be engaged or caught. A clue challenging the police to find him or her. Or, in a twisted way, the message could have been meant for the victim."

"Laycee. An interesting thought," Nick said.

"It's more logical that the killer came after Jarret, found Laycee, and killed her instead."

"Then why not wait for Jarret to come home and kill him, too?"

"Right. Doesn't make sense. This symbol is the key." I handed the sketch back to him. "You think you've seen it before?"

"I do. I don't remember where yet." Nick folded the paper and slipped it back into his pocket. "I promised Eagleton I'd do some research and get back to him. You'll never believe who the homicide detective in charge of the murder investigation is."

"Not Dave." I cocked my head. "He can't be, because of his connection to Jarret. Who then?"

"Remember Carla Pratt?"

"The detective who jailed Robin?" I dropped my head back and sighed. "You have to be kidding. Carla works the Northeast Division, not the Valley. Did she transfer?"

"Pratt seemed less than thrilled to see me, so I didn't inquire about her career path. When Eagleton took me into the bedroom, she rolled her eyes and left without comment."

I sat at the edge of the sofa and tapped my heel on the rug. Wait until Carla learns I stopped by Jarret's house, too. Last year, Nick and I had worked to clear Robin of a murder charge, but Carla—ambitious, stubborn, and convinced of Robin's guilt—warned Nick and *I* to stay away from the case. "Carla probably took Jarret into custody already."

"Not unless she has probable cause to hold him," Nick said. "Why are you fidgeting? Are you keeping something from me?"

"Jarret phoned his agent before the police. In fact, he waited at least twenty minutes for Ira to arrive at the house before he dialed 911."

"Ouch. Why?"

"Jarret's not the greatest in emergencies?"

"And you're positive he didn't—"

"Kill Laycee? He's not violent, Nick. Yesterday when we talked, Jarret wasn't even aware that Laycee was in town. She went to the game with Kyle last night. I can't imagine how or why she ended up alone at Jarret's." I stopped myself. Sure I knew. Laycee liked a good time and Jarret needed a distraction from his colossal loss at the game.

"Maybe the three of them went to Jarret's and partied after the game," Nick said.

"Possible. Kyle didn't come to the gym this morning so maybe he *was* at the house late, but—"

"But what?"

"I only saw two glasses on the counter."

Nick drew back. "What do you mean, *you saw*?"

"I went to Jarret's this morning to—"

"This morning? What time?"

"While Jarret was out on his run. I stopped by to pick up that box." I pointed to the carton in the living room. "I didn't go beyond the kitchen. I saw the glasses by the sink."

"My God." Nick buried his forehead in his hands. "You may have been in the house with the killer. What if he saw you?"

The realization bolted through my body like lightning. I wrapped my arms around my waist and rocked. "I didn't see anyone. I was in and out of that house in less than five minutes."

"It's okay, Liz. I'm sure you're—"

"I had no idea Laycee was there."

"Take a breath." Nick pulled me in close, his chin resting on top of my head. "I'm getting the sense I should follow you around more."

"Thanks, but I don't need a babysitter."

"Not what I had in mind at all." He kissed the top of my head.

I leaned back and looked up at his face. "Bodyguard?"

"Something like that but with benefits—"

"Benefits? As in *ever after* benefits?"

"No . . . I mean . . . well . . ." Nick let me go and held out his wrist, making a grand show of checking the time. "I should get going. I want to stop at the UCLA library again and try to track down the symbol. Let's get together tonight and talk."

"About murder or . . . ?"

"I'll let you know if I find anything at the library." Nick

wasn't the type to squirm but when he did, he was kind of adorable at it. First, he reached to Erzulie purring at his side and scratched her between the ears before he stood to leave. On the way through the living room he mumbled something about library hours. At the door, carefully avoiding eye contact, he kissed me good-bye then hustled out. Fast.

I wasn't ready for ever after either.

The last box of books waited by the fireplace, ready to be unpacked. Great, something to do while I waited for Dave to return my call. I headed for the den and as I reached to turn up the TV volume, the phone rang again. Hopefully Dave. Probably Mom. Or Marion Cooper. I took my cell off the coffee table, glancing at the small screen. Area code 818—the Valley, and not a number I knew. I answered, hesitant.

"Liz Cooper?" The female voice on the phone sounded vaguely familiar. "This is Carla Pratt, LAPD. Do you remember me?"

I wandered to the window, nerves tightening my throat. "Of course I remember you, Carla. How are you?"

"Your name came up in a homicide investigation I'm working on. I'm hoping you can help me with some information. Can we meet this evening?"

"What kind of information?" *As if I didn't know.*

"A few background points. Where can we meet?"

Instinct warned me to pick neutral territory. I didn't want Carla nosing around my house for any reason. "There's a café called Aroma on Tujunga Avenue south of Moorpark. I can meet you there at seven."

She agreed and we hung up. As soon as I clicked off the call, I dialed Dave again.

When he answered I said, "Don't you return your calls? Do you know what's going on?"

"I return my calls in order of priority and, by the way, calls for the job come first. You're third on my social list after Robin and the folks."

"Good to hear I slipped in rank to number three. Doesn't blood mean anything in this family?"

"Between my job and your friends, blood seems to be the family business. I assume you're calling about the vic at Jarret's house? Don't you know anyone not connected to murder?"

"Funny. I'm amused. Did you talk to Nick today?"

"No, why?"

"Captain Eagleton called Nick in to examine a symbol the killer left on the body. He was at the scene this morning." I perched at the edge of my desk, eyeing the muted TV for news updates.

"Why Nick? Are they thinking ritual killing?" Dave said. "Voodoo? A religious sacrifice?"

"Nick mentioned witchcraft or devil worship. He's trying to track down more information this afternoon. I called *you* for details about the rest of the investigation. Jarret's parents called me, worried."

"Nick can tell you more than I can, if he was at the scene. I'm working my own cases down here."

"Will you just tell me what might be happening at Jarret's house? He doesn't answer his phone. His parents are in distress. They think he's locked up. I promised to call them back with information."

"I only know what I heard on the news, Liz. Jarret would be interrogated on the scene and, depending on what the detectives have, what Jarret told them, and—if he lawyered up—they either let him go or arrested him. The only thing I can do for you is phone the West Valley homicide desk to find out who took the call. Maybe I know the detective."

"Carla Pratt."

"And you continue to know more than I do. Do you just miss me? Is that why you called? I heard Pratt transferred from Northeast. She's good. I can't bug her. She'll be too busy securing evidence and talking to witnesses. Keep calling Jarret until he answers. You're good at that."

"Thank you. Dave, about talking to witnesses—Carla called me."

"She did? That was fast. An ex-wife from years ago would be far down on my list of people to talk to. Maybe Pratt already has a case and she's establishing the character angle. Hope Jarret has a good defense attor—"

"I'm not a character witness. I was at Jarret's house this morning. I need to fill you in on a few details."

He listened with his version of silence—grunts peppered with sighs and curses.

"Should I bring a lawyer to the meeting tonight?" I said.

"Damn it, Liz. Whose kid are you? A lawyer will tell you to keep your mouth shut. If you want to help the investigation, tell Pratt the truth. You're a witness, not a suspect. Just remember, whether or not she chooses to tell you, she'll tape your conversation. Remember what Dad used to say when we asked him what a homicide detective's job was?"

"To catch people in lies."

"Exactly. The first interview establishes your story. If

Carla finds no reason to doubt you, there won't be another. Do your interview and let it go. Let Jarret tell his parents what happened." Before Dave ended the call he said, "Try to stay out of it as much as possible."

I would. Right after I talked to Jarret.

Chapter Eight

I tried Jarret's cell again. No answer. His voice mail prevented me from leaving word so I left Ira Ryback a message for him or Jarret to call Marion and Bud to let them know what was happening. Then I phoned Marion and apologized for having nothing to report. Marion did. She updated me on Bud's latest bowling score, the upcoming county fair, and the birthday present Jarret bought her this year. Perceiving helpless anxiety behind her chatter, I listened until she ran out of topics. Marion and I were close before the divorce. I missed her, too.

The pounding, drilling, and banging upstairs ended at four-fifteen. Stan and Angel filed down the steps with their gear.

"Tomorrow at nine again?" Stan said as we walked out to the porch.

I nodded. "Are you any closer to finishing?"

"I think so. Any day now, you'll be soaking in a lavender-scented bubble bath."

"I'll be satisfied with a shower in my own home," I said.

"Soon."

Right. I stood outside in the blazing late afternoon heat and watched Stan back his truck out of my driveway. Though I had spent the day on the phone in my air-conditioned home, I felt sticky, grimy, and tired of T-shirts and jeans. I had an urge to dress up.

A shower and a sundress. There was an idea. Freshen up for my meeting with Carla and an evening with Nick. If I went to the gym for a quick shower, I might run into Kyle. Not a bad idea at all. I went inside, dashed upstairs, and came down carrying my backpack with a black-and-red-flowered sundress, lacy lingerie, and a pair of sandals inside. Erzulie gave me her abandoned kitty look.

"I'll be gone for less than an hour," I said. "You won't miss dinner. In fact, if you take a quick nap, you won't even know I'm gone. Or watch the birds in the backyard. You love watching the birds."

Yes, I reasoned with a kitten. Yes, she listened. Erzulie could be very understanding.

When I got to the gym, I eyed the scattering of people in the cardio room and working out on machines, looking for but not seeing Kyle though his Jeep was parked outside. I found Earl alone with a client in the weight room.

"Is Kyle here?"

"Somewhere," Earl said. "Did you look in the office?"

"I will, thanks."

I backtracked through the weight room past a TV with a cable sports station broadcasting the replay of Eagleton's press conference, and Jarret's picture posted in the lower corner of the screen. I passed the door to the ladies' locker room and rounded a corner to the west end of the gym along the wall of power racks and heavy weights facing the windows to the lot.

Muffled voices came from behind the closed door to Kyle's office at the far end of the building. I knocked lightly, turned the knob, and peeked inside the small room. Kyle sat behind the desk against the wall, talking to a twentyish, short and stocky kid with stringy hair and an acne-riddled face.

Kyle spun around, startled, and quickly dropped a brown bag into the bottom drawer. He shut the drawer with his knee, locked it, and dropped the key into the top drawer. The kid hid something behind his back and backed into a corner of the office, staring at the floor.

"Liz, you're a morning person. What are you doing here so late?" Kyle folded his hands on the blotter, clenching his fingers.

"My bathroom is still a war zone. I wanted to cool off with a shower before I go out tonight," I said, watching his knuckles turn white. "I apologize for interrupting your meeting. I heard about Laycee and wanted to see how you're doing. Will you be here for a while?"

"Yeah, we should talk," Kyle said. "I'm here until seven. Stop by and see me up front before you leave."

I retreated to the weight room, shutting the door behind me. What could be so private to make Kyle take a meeting inside a closed office in an almost empty gym?

With two clean towels from a stack near the desk, I took my gear into the ladies' locker room for a hot shower. I finished with a cooling rinse, then toweled off and smoothed moisturizer from my face to my toes. After I ran a comb through my wet hair, I got dressed.

When I came out to the weight room clean, scented, and feeling fresh in sandals and sundress, Earl wolf whistled from the side of the leg press machine. "You clean up good, Liz."

I grinned. Hell, I wasn't even wearing makeup.

Kyle sat behind the front desk, reading the paper. He glanced up at me then away, thumbing toward the office. "The kid wanted to talk to me about joining the gym. He's training to be a football player and—"

"You don't have to explain," I said though his unsolicited excuse, fast talk, and lack of eye contact suggested a lie. I was more interested in what had happened the night before than about whatever Kyle was trying to hide. "I'm sorry I barged in on you. Did you hear from Jarret?"

"Yeah." He lowered his voice and thumbed toward the front door. "Let's go outside. Jarret doesn't want me to talk about what happened in public. Nosey eyes and ears."

He opened the door for me and we walked out to the parking lot. Tall palm trees, motionless in the blistering late afternoon heat, bordered the sidewalk between the small parking lot and Ventura Boulevard. The asphalt cooked under the westward-bound sun. We got into my car and I turned on the ignition, letting the engine idle while the air conditioner cooled the interior.

Kyle fiddled with the vent blowing air in his face. "I talked to Jarret about an hour ago. He's staying at the

Sportsmen's Lodge until the cops let him back into his house. I'll tell you, Liz, he's freaked."

"I bet he is. What happened last night? How did Laycee end up at Jarret's house? I thought she was with you."

"Yeah, well, that's Laycee. She's with who she's with until she's with the next guy. She threw herself all over Billy Miles up in the suite at the game." Kyle snorted with disapproval. "I had to tell her to give Billy some space. That ticked her off. She was drinking heavy and kept on drinking after we met Jarret at Fifth Base."

"How was he?" I asked.

"After his pitching disaster? Can't you guess? Pathetic. Bitched and moaned about tripping on the foul line. Blamed the pigeon. Carped about being hexed. You know how damned superstitious he is."

I nodded. Jarret relied on his game day beliefs for a control mechanism to soothe his nerves and ease performance pressure on the mound.

"Laycee took Jarret's crappy mood as a challenge and started hitting on him right off. He knocked back the booze pretty hard. So did she. I guess when I went to the bar to order another round they made a plan to hook up. I knew by the way she cooed at him for the rest of the night. Didn't bother me." Kyle smirked. "I got up at four yesterday to open the gym. I just wanted to go home and get some sleep. She wanted to stay. She asked Jarret to drive her back to the hotel."

I held back from asking Kyle why, if he went home so early, he didn't open the gym this morning. His feigned nonchalance didn't mask the biting edge to his voice. Kyle took a backseat to Jarret's fame since the beginning of

82

their friendship. I often suspected that Kyle goaded Jarret into reckless behavior to knock him down a notch. Last night, Jarret wound up taking Kyle's "date" home.

"So you left them at the bar?" I said.

"Yeah. It probably was Jarret's idea to go up to his house after Fifth Base closed. He wouldn't go with her to her hotel. She was staying down the block at the Sportsmen's Lodge. He was too careful to be seen out with a married woman."

I flinched at Kyle's casual remark about Jarret's amorous cautions, a subject I didn't care to explore especially if those habits dated back to our marriage. "Did you see anyone you knew at Fifth Base?"

"Nah. The rest of the team went home after the loss. Why do you care about Jarret? You were too good for him, you know. You aren't like the rest of the women who hang around ballplayers." Kyle touched my bare knee, stroking his finger toward my thigh.

The jerk was making a move on me? Payback? Revenge? I moved his hand away, put my foot on the brake, and shifted the car into reverse. "I need to leave. I have an appointment to get to. Thanks for filling me in."

Kyle shrugged off my rejection and opened the car door. Before he got out he said, "Jarret is keeping his cell turned off. If you call the hotel, ask for Bruce Sutter."

I regretted engaging Kyle just to appease my curiosity. If I hadn't gone to Jarret's house this morning or Eagleton hadn't called in Nick, I wouldn't care what Kyle, Jarret, or Laycee did last night. Unless—was I still more connected to Jarret than I realized? I made a right turn out of the parking lot into the rush-hour traffic inching along Ventura Boulevard.

Tapping my fingers on the steering wheel, I replayed Kyle's narrative in my head, unable to shake off the bitterness I sensed in his tone. If Jarret got convicted of murder, Kyle would be left with full ownership of the gym. What if Kyle had stayed up all night drinking and stirring his resentment? Maybe he didn't like being used and decided to punish both Laycee and Jarret. Kyle knew Jarret's garage door combination. What if he saw Laycee asleep and murdered her to frame Jarret? Possible. What about the symbol? A diversion?

My phone rang as I passed the Starbucks at Vantage and Ventura. Mom.

"Did you hear from Jarret?" she said.

"Nope," I said, stopping for a red light at Laurel Canyon. "But I talked to his trainer."

"What did he say? Is Jarret all right?"

"He's fine. He's staying at the Sportsmen's Lodge and not answering his cell. Leave him alone, Mom. He'll contact someone when he wants to."

"Liz, he needs our support."

The light turned green. I passed through the intersection, biting down hard to keep from yelling. Then I took a deep breath and said, "You know what, Mom? *I* could use your support. Please don't draw me into Jarret's drama. If he's innocent, he has a team of lawyers and agents to help him."

"What do you mean by if? Of course he's innocent."

"Then don't worry about him. The truth will come out."

"You're upset."

"I'm hot. I'm tired of talking about this, and I want to get home. Let's talk tomorrow, okay?"

"I love you, dear."

"Love you too, Mom."

When I turned the corner onto my street, the phone rang again.

"Jarret's not registered at the Sportsmen's Lodge," Mom said, testing every strand of my nerves.

My rational side intervened. An outburst would be a poor prologue to my meeting with Carla. "He's registered as Bruce Sutter," I said, pulling into my driveway.

"Who is—?"

"Hall of Fame Cubs pitcher. Jarret's childhood hero."

"Isn't that charming."

Chapter Nine

I put on makeup and fed Erzulie, and then drove the four blocks to the Aroma Café. A rare parking space opened on Tujunga, giving me a short jaunt to the customers waiting in line outside. I didn't see Carla Pratt, so I cruised through the tables inside and on both patios. I spotted her at the rear of the courtyard, sipping an iced drink and reading her BlackBerry at a table tucked in the corner.

When I got to the table she removed her gold-rimmed glasses and smiled at me. Her sandy brown bangs were dark with sweat, her hair cropped even tighter around her ears and neck than the last time I saw her. In her mid-forties, she carried the guarded, pale-faced demeanor of a career city detective. Her gray two-button suit must have felt like a heating pad on her sturdy frame, but removing the jacket would mean exposing the gun I knew she carried on her belt.

"Dr. Cooper." She indicated the empty chair across the small table. "Did you order?"

"You can still call me Liz. I didn't order. I wanted to find you before I got in line. I'll be right back." When I returned to the table with an iced tea, Carla dabbed beads of sweat off her forehead. "Would you rather sit inside where it's cooler?" I suggested.

"Not unless you want to. I'm used to the heat." She pulled a small notebook from her jacket pocket. "It's private here, easier for us to talk. Nice place."

We eased in with small talk, and then she told me about her transfer from Northeast to the West Valley station. An opportunity, she explained as she handed me her new business card, for advancement to Detective II.

"Have you seen Dave recently?" she said.

"We were together last night at the Dodger game."

"Ah." Her brows shot up. "And are you still close to your friend the professor?"

"Nick? Yes. He told me he saw you today."

"He did." She opened her notebook. "As I mentioned on the phone, your name came up this morning in the homicide investigation I'm working on."

"At Jarret's house."

"Yes, Mr. Cooper's home. I understand he's your . . ." She tilted her head, waiting for me to finish.

"Ex-husband. We've been divorced for four years. What would you like to know? Ask away."

Carla clicked her pen. "Actually, I prefer for you to do the talking. Would you tell me in your own words where you were this morning?"

"Where do you want me to begin?"

"Wherever's comfortable. Take your time."

I stopped, considering how to verify my whereabouts, and decided to begin with the gym. "I went to work out this morning, early, around seven. After exercising I took a shower . . ." I rambled out details with nervous tension knotting my shoulders—hesitant to place myself at the scene of Laycee's murder. Carla jotted notes while she listened to my insignificant details with more patience than I would have had. I explained my decision to drive to Jarret's to pick up the last box of books waiting in his kitchen. "I left the gym and drove to the house—"

"What time was that?"

"I left Game On at seven fifty-five," I said. "I remember thinking I would miss Jarret when he left for his morning run at eight."

"Did anyone at the gym see you leave?"

I paused. "Earl Good, one of the trainers. A few members, but I don't have their last names. Earl saw me. He'll know me by name."

She made a note and gestured for me to continue.

"When I got to Royal Oaks, I pulled into Jarret's drive, opened the garage, entered the kitchen, got the box, and then went home."

"What time were you at the house?" Carla said.

"Traffic along Ventura Boulevard jammed on the way there. I'd say I arrived at his house a little past eight-thirty or so, picked up the box off the kitchen counter, turned around, and left. I didn't see or hear anything."

"Did anyone witness your arrival or your exit?"

"No one. It's a quiet—" I held up my finger. "Wait. I passed one of the neighbors walking her dog when I pulled out of the driveway. I didn't stop to talk to her. I was already late to meet the plumber at my place."

"How often do you visit your ex-husband's home?"

"Aside from yesterday and today? Never. And yesterday I didn't go inside at all. Jarret waited for me in the driveway, put some boxes in my trunk, then I left."

"Did you notice anything unusual about the house?"

"Unusual? No. No cars in the driveway. The garage door was closed when I arrived. Jarret leaves his kitchen door unlocked, so I opened the garage—"

She looked up, questioning. "How did you open it?"

"I have the combination. I used to live there."

"You knew the combination was the same or Mr. Cooper told you it was?"

"Both. He's been using the same combination for years." The sides of my dress stuck to my ribs and a bead of sweat trickled down my back. I excused myself and went to the condiment station for a pile of napkins to blot my face and neck.

Carla waited, composed. If she sweltered in her suit, she didn't show it. When I got back to the table she said, "Who else has the combination to Mr. Cooper's garage?"

"He never changes the code, so the list is likely long. You should ask him."

"I'm asking you."

"When we moved in, we gave the combination to the housekeeper, his trainer, and contractors. It's been years. I have no idea who else has it now."

"Let's go back to what you saw after you entered the house."

I shifted to unstick my sweaty thighs. Her repetitive

questions were annoying but I understood her goal: get me to tell my story, and then ask again to see if the facts change.

"I saw nothing," I said. "I picked up the box and left."

"Humor me. Describe the room."

Carla knew exactly what was in Jarret's kitchen. She probably had an inventoried list in her notebook.

"I saw appliances and dirty dishes," I said.

"What kind of dirty dishes?"

"A blender pitcher in the sink, some glasses on the counter. Empty bottles," I said. "I went in and out of there so fast it's difficult to remember. As I said, I picked up the box and left."

"Where did you go?"

"Home, to meet my plumber."

"I need his name and contact information." She wrote as I recited Stan's number then she said, "Where's the box now?"

"At my house."

"I'd like to see it." She flipped her notebook closed.

I had the right to demand she get a warrant, making an old carton of books appear far more meaningful than it was. Or I could grant her permission. I had nothing to hide. The sooner our interview ended, the better I would feel.

"Sure," I said. "I'm parked on Tujunga. Do you want to follow me home?"

"I'll meet you there. I have your new address."

The streetlights flickered on at twilight as I made the right turn into my driveway. Carla parked her steel blue, four-door Chevy Caprice across the street. She came up the brick path, waiting under the porch light while I used my key to open the front door.

Switching on the lamp on the small table by the living room sofa, I pointed at the brown carton on the floor in front of the fireplace. "There it is."

Carla snapped on a pair of latex gloves and crouched next to the quarter-folded box. "Did you open it?"

"Nope."

"Anyone aside from you touch it today?"

"Jarret, obviously. My plumber's assistant carried it in here from my car," I said. "Why the curiosity about the box? A bunch of old books are inside."

"If strangers entered Mr. Cooper's house, they may have touched it. Any foreign prints may be a clue. With your permission, I want to take the box in and have it checked for prints."

Made sense. The knot of tension at the back of my neck eased. Good. Carla sought suspects aside from Jarret. "You have my permission, as long as my literary taste won't be judged by the contents. The books have been in that box since our move from Atlanta."

With a half-grin on her face, she pulled a square of plastic from her purse and unfolded it into a large evidence bag. She covered the carton, sealed the edges, then took off her gloves and wrote out a receipt. "I'll need a set of prints from you for elimination since you touched it."

"I'm on file. The DOJ and FBI ran my prints when I applied for my license to practice psychology." I walked her to the vestibule.

As I opened the door, she stopped. "I'm curious about something, Liz."

"What's that?"

"You didn't ask for the identity of the victim."

I flinched. If I didn't know, or if the victim was a stranger to me, of course I would have inquired. Anyone would. Damn it.

"I already knew," I said lowering my eyes. "Ira Ryback told me when I called Jarret's house this morning after I saw the news reports. I didn't ask you because I assumed you couldn't say much."

Carla lifted her chin, squinting, and then she nodded slowly. I followed her outside to the porch. She stopped and turned. "One more thing. Did you know Mrs. Huber?"

What was she doing? Playing Columbo? Wasn't the damn box heavy? If Carla did her homework she already knew the answer.

"I used to," I said. "We were neighbors in Atlanta."

She started toward her car. "I'll be in touch."

I went inside, wondering if "in touch" meant a second interview. According to Dave, Carla wasn't likely to contact me again unless she doubted my story. I told her the truth, yet as she drove off my heart pounded in my throat.

Erzulie perched on the top of the sofa, watching me turn on lights from room to room. The cool air inside the house dried the sticky hair at the nape of my neck. My dress, wrinkled and wilted, was a lost cause. Too hungry to change, I pulled out my phone.

"Hey," Nick answered with the sound of computer keys clicking and soulful music playing in the background.

"Are you working?"

"If you can call going in circles working, yes. I—damn, it's already dark outside. What time is it?" When Nick focused on a mission, his preoccupation usurped even basic needs. Like food. Rest. Or me.

"Eight-thirty. Did you eat today?" I said.

"Eat?" He continued clicking on his keyboard. "I don't remember. I don't think so."

"Me either. I can fix that. I'll be over in a few."

I grabbed my keys and made a stop at Henry's, the taco stand on the corner of Moorpark and Tujunga serving the best homemade tacos in the Valley. Henry's wasn't the reason I moved to Studio City, although living near the walk-up stand under the yellow, green, and red "TACOS" canopy was a bonus. I bought five hard-shell tacos and hopped in my car to North Hollywood.

When I opened the front door of Nick's brown-shingled, one-story bungalow I saw him sitting shirtless on the paprika twill sofa in his living room. His legs stretched out with his feet resting on the coffee table and his laptop open on his knees. Books scattered over the Aztec rug on his hardwood floor. A mess of strewn papers covered the desk in front of the window.

As his fingers danced on the keyboard, Nick bobbed his head to Al Green's "Love and Happiness" playing through the corner speakers.

"Memphis soul tonight? What's the occasion?" I said, aware that Nick's taste leaned more toward Chicago blues and jazz standards.

He moved his laptop to the sofa cushion. "Felt right. Old Reverend Al's music got me through a lot of study nights in grad school. I can't say what made me think of him today, just an inclination. I'm having a hell of a time remembering where I saw that symbol. What's in the bag?"

"I made dinner."

"You? Made food?"

"Kind of. I made the drive to Henry's Tacos."

"You're unbelievable." Nick reached out his hand. "Come here. I need to ravage you right now."

So much for his usurped basic needs. I dropped the bag on the coffee table. He pulled me onto his lap with a kiss that shot goose bumps over my body. His hands stroked my bare arms and shoulders. Brushing his lips down to my collarbone, he slid the straps of my dress off my shoulders.

"I should forget perfume and wear hot sauce instead." I kissed the back of his neck, tasting the salt of his skin.

"You shouldn't be wearing anything at all." He began to unzip my dress. I walked my fingers down his chest to his belt. As his lips moved down from my throat, a ping sounded an incoming e-mail on his laptop. He turned his head slightly at the machine.

With his left hand still fumbling at my zipper, Nick moved his right hand to the computer beside him and touched the mouse to bring up the screen. He clicked the e-mail icon and opened his inbox.

I admired multitasking but not if I was one of the multiple tasks. I stopped unbuckling his belt to read the screen with him. The header on the lone e-mail read: *Con&grådülatons!* Spam.

"Where were we?" he said, fumbling at my zipper again.

"Distracted." I sat up and ruffled his hair. "Let's eat. You can tell me about the e-mail you're expecting over dinner."

Chapter Ten

"Well? E-mail?" I set two plates on the eating counter separating Nick's jade green kitchen from his living room and then opened the bag of tacos. My mouth watered at the first spicy scent billowing from the bag. I put out three for Nick and two for me.

Nick pulled on his T-shirt on his way to the stainless-steel refrigerator. "I'm hoping for news from Eagleton. I wasted the afternoon flipping through books on Wiccan symbols and hex signs. Useless. I didn't find anything replicating the specific position of the elements in the symbol left on Laycee's body. Yet I still have this hazy impression I've seen the combination before."

"What about the work you did at the library yesterday? Do you think you ran across the symbol in passing?"

He twisted the caps off two longneck bottles of beer and sat next to me on a stool. "I wish it were that simple. Of all the symbolism I've studied, the mark Laycee's killer left is too simplistic to be remarkable, yet the combination stuck in my memory. I just don't know why or from where."

"What about one of your research trips?"

"Not overseas or South America. It's not Southern voodoo or Native American spiritualism." He scratched his head. "The East Coast? The Midwest?"

"You're certain it's not a gang or cult sign? Or the rendering of a madman scribbling a nonsensical sign only he understands?"

He raised a brow. "A cult is a possibility, that's why I'm determined to shake my memory. Eagleton would have recognized a gang tag. Gangs mark their territory with symbolism their enemies would understand, nothing cryptic or complicated. For example, they slash letters to disrespect their rivals. If my Nick gang wanted to disrespect your Liz gang, I would slash through the letter *I* in my name because of the *I* in your name. Or if I tagged the word *Lincoln*, I would slash through the *L* and the *I* to disrespect you."

"Is the inverted pentagram common in cults?" I crunched into my taco. Heaps of shredded cheese burst from the sides and onto my plate.

"In devil worship cults, yes, but the devil cults are random, disorganized, and not geographically exclusive. The inverted Petrine crosses add a twisted religious tone. The five, however—"

"The five might be part of a series. Could Laycee have been the fifth victim of a serial killer?" I said.

"Eagleton will notify me if the FBI recognizes a pattern." Nick finished his first taco and bit into his second.

"So you're thinking religious fanatic?"

"I don't have an opinion yet. I'm preoccupied by this exasperating sense of familiarity." He took a long draw of beer, his face lost in thought. "Pennsylvania?"

"Pennsylvania?"

"A flash of intuition. I took a car trip east one summer to study the Amish and Mennonites, an unlikely group to practice devil worship. The trip crossed my mind earlier."

I popped the last bite of taco into my mouth and wiped my hands. "Your subconscious is working for you. Maybe talking about your trip to Pennsylvania will jar a specific memory. Try to relax. Talk free form. I'll listen."

His face lit up. "Like therapy? Let you delve into my psyche? I always wanted to observe you at work. Should I lie on the couch?"

"My clients don't . . . Oh, what the hell. Sure. Whatever helps you to remember."

"Should I turn off the lights?" Nick hopped off his stool and was flat on his back on the sofa in a minute. "Ready? How do we do this?"

I didn't want to get *that* far into his psyche. Laughing, I shut off the music then rolled the desk chair to the side of the sofa and sat down. "Begin wherever you like."

"Are you going to make me cry?"

"Only if you don't start talking."

He folded his hands on his stomach and closed his eyes. "I made the Pennsylvania trip during the summer between my first and second years at Oxford. I flew home to Chicago to visit my parents during an intense heat wave. My dad and I went to a couple of White Sex games, I mean White Sox—" He opened an eye and grinned.

"Nick—Pennsylvania?"

"Right. After a week at home with my parents, I went stir-crazy and decided to take a road trip."

As he talked, I glanced around the room at souvenirs he collected on his travels. The rug from South America, figurines and masks from Mexico and Africa, a cloisonné enamel incense burner from China. Intriguing. Even in his youth, after months spent away at school, Nick couldn't tolerate more than a week of being at home. *Maybe I should explore his psyche in depth.*

"This was the summer after I studied the Protestant Christian Radical Reformation of sixteenth-century Europe. I thought it might be interesting to view firsthand how Anabaptism evolved into the twentieth century through its Amish and Mennonite descendants."

Reformation evolution as a road trip? How did I fall in love with this guy?

"I drove twelve hours from Illinois to Pennsylvania and rented a room at an Amish dairy farm on the outskirts of Lancaster." He smiled. "I felt like Harrison Ford in *Witness*—the outsider in a closed society. I had the only room in the house with electricity. The Zooks. Nice family, a couple and their two kids. The daughter Ruth was in Rumspringa and she offered to be my guide."

"Rumspringa?" I said.

Nick opened an eye. "The years Amish adolescents explore the outside world before committing to the faith. Ruth turned eighteen that summer. Rumspringa gave her license to hang with me, a stranger, and ride in my car without being punished." Nick talked about the people Ruth introduced him to, places they visited in the hills of Pennsylvania Dutch country. "Simple, innocent, nonviolent people. Nothing related to the devil. Not a mention. I'm sure it wasn't—"

"Follow your intuition, not your mind. You're connecting to a memory. Don't force your thoughts. Relax. Let your feelings guide you. You came home this afternoon, and . . . ?"

"Remembered Ruth used to intern at the Lancaster Public Library. I took a chance and e-mailed the library, hoping to locate her. Hex signs are common in Pennsylvania. Then I put on an old Al Green album and began working," he said.

I tilted my head, reminded again of his preference for the blues. "Why Al Green?"

He bolted upright and cupped my face. "I love you, Liz Cooper."

"I love you, too," I said, delighted. "What did you remember?"

"I can do better. I can show you." He took my hand and led me through the house and out the back door. "On the drive to Chicago from Lancaster, I played an old Al Green cassette in the car a thousand times. My memory had nothing to do with being in Pennsylvania. If I'm right, I saw the symbol on the drive home."

We crossed through the yard. Nick opened his garage door to a chorus of crickets and we went from the balmy night breeze into the hot, stale air inside. He flipped a switch. A high-wattage lightbulb dangling on a wire from the ceiling illuminated the cement floored, open-paneled, two-car garage stacked with boxes. The chirping stopped. Something small and fast scrambled under the tool bench across the room. I edged closer to him with an eye on the floor.

He went straight to the floor-to-ceiling wall of cardboard

boxes in back, talking while he pulled cartons down. "I stopped for gas at a local rest stop in Indiana. The old coot behind the counter was listening to a preacher sermonizing on the radio. Before he would sell me gas, he asked if I was a religious man."

I glanced toward the noise rustling under the tool bench. "Nick, I don't think we're alone."

"It's probably a mouse. Shuffle your feet. They're more afraid of you than you are of them." He set another box on the floor. "When the old man heard I was studying religion, he told me he met the devil in person."

"The devil?" I said. "You must have loved that."

"I thought the old guy was a crackpot. Just to be a smartass, I asked him what the devil was doing in Indiana and he said, 'Fifty to life in the state pen for murder.' I bought a bottle of pop, sat down, and listened to his story about a family who lived outside a small town south of the interstate. The head of the family introduced himself around town as Rick, the son of Satan and an advocate of magic and self-indulgence. Rumors circulated about devil worship, moonlight rituals, and debauchery. Pets disappeared. His children were caught stealing candles from the church. A few months in, a town council member contacted Indiana Social Services to report Rick and his wife for child neglect." Nick slid another box off the stack and took off the lid. He looked inside and smiled. "Found it. Come on, let's go back to the house."

"What? Found what?"

"Go, go, go." He picked up the box. "I hope it's in here."

I led him through the yard and opened the patio door, taking a last look over my shoulder for tagalongs from the garage. The only creature behind me was one very animated professor.

He set the box on the living room floor, rifling through papers as he talked. "Rick printed pamphlets promoting devil worship and sex magick. The children sold copies door-to-door."

"He exploited his children?" I sat on the floor beside Nick. "You saw the pamphlets?"

"I think I have one. The man at the gas station felt sorry for the kids so he bought a few and kept the pamphlets as souvenirs after Rick got arrested. I convinced the old guy to sell me a copy. I wanted to show it to a professor at Oxford who studied devil worship."

"So you brought the pamphlet to Oxford?"

"No. Once I got to Chicago and read it, I thought the content was tripe. Rehashed satanic and devil worship tenets from the sixties. Here it is." Nick pulled out a five-by-seven booklet bound by staples. The cover, red print on a black background, showed an inverted pentagram with a goat's head drawn in the center. Across the top, the title: "Divine Rights."

Nick paged through, stopping intermittently. "I forgot how shoddy this was. He plagiarizes the hell out of every devil fad from the nineteenth century to the sixties, and rants like a hedonistic, occult flamethrower. How anyone deemed this—Liz, look, I found it." He held up the pamphlet, pointing to a yellowed page.

The page on the left showed the inverted pentagram with the number 5 in the center. Three blurred Petrine crosses underscored the 5. At the top of the right-hand page, the misspelled header read "Vengence." Beneath, "Thou shalt not turn the other cheak."

I read through the text, appalled by the theme of hatred and frustration within blustering statements from "nobody owes you nothing but respect" (sic), to "payback is you're right" (sic). The remainder of the pamphlet was filled with crass declarations of rules celebrating vices like indulgence, lust, and greed. Each rule was numbered inside the inverted pentagram image, some accompanied by crude drawings of figures enacting the benefits of self-indulgence and hubris.

"What do you think?" Nick said.

"Personally, his celebration of evil offends me. The author shows a lot of pain between the lines—a struggle to cope with disturbed, unresolved feelings. At a glance, I'd call him tortured. Someone taught to look at anger as wrong without defining or exploring the source. The text sounds like he moved to the dark side to justify his unresolved feelings and redefine himself to align with his pain."

"Any comment on devil worship?" Nick said.

"As a therapist, I view it as an ineffective and troubled attempt to resolve complex internal issues. His devil imagery projects sexuality and anger," I said. "How do you interpret this? Is his message meaningful enough to last thirty years? How would it relate to Laycee's murder?"

"Rick's message isn't unique. He plagiarized the core spiritual principles of Anton LaVey, a magician and occultist from San Francisco who started an atheistic sect glorifying the self in the sixties. I've seen the triple cross notation in spiritual and Wiccan practices, a shorthand instruction to repeat an incantation or prayer three times, but never in connection with the LaVey sect or any theistic devil worship groups," Nick said.

"Narrowing the field of possibilities for finding Laycee's killer. How many devil groups are there?"

"Countless. Devil worship is widespread, without a centralized leader, and the individual groups are intensely secretive. It's impossible to list or track down every sector. This is definitely the numbered inverted pentagram I remembered. I'll get the images to Eagleton, but this part of the trail might end here." Nick set the pamphlet on the table then repacked the rest of the box. "I wonder if the author is still alive."

"I want to hear the rest of the story," I said. "Who did Rick kill?"

Nick shrugged. "I don't remember. I'm amazed I recalled as much as I did. I don't even know his full name."

"I think I do."

Chapter Eleven

I opened the pamphlet and showed Nick the title page. "Divine Right" was centered at the top in large capital letters. In smaller letters below the byline: By Herrick Schelz.

"Rick—short for Herrick," I said.

"Can't argue with the obvious," Nick said, smiling.

"Now that we're this far, don't you have access to old newspaper articles? I'd like to read about his trial and see what happened to his family."

"I love it when you challenge me." He reached for his computer.

We curled up together on the sofa, my arm resting on Nick's shoulder as he clicked the keys on his laptop. Soon the archive section of the Fort Wayne *Journal Gazette* filled the screen.

He drummed the side of the keyboard. "Let's see. I was

twenty-three the year I took the trip. The guy said the family moved to town . . ."

As Nick studied the ceiling to work out the math, I opened the pamphlet to the second page. "The copyright is 1984. Start there?"

In a few quick keystrokes, a list of choices appeared on the screen. Nick clicked on the first article, and we read together.

DEVIL WORSHIPER SENTENCED TO LIFE
The Fort Wayne Journal Gazette
June 23, 1985

Herrick Schelz was sentenced to 50 years to life this afternoon for the 1984 murder of an Indiana social worker.

Early this month, Schelz, 38, was convicted of the brutal stabbing death of Adan Hunter at the Schelz home outside of Greenburg. Hunter, married and the father of three young children, was 34 at the time of his death.

In closing arguments in the penalty phase of the trial, Elkhart County prosecutor Carl Cates asked that Schelz be given the death penalty for the killing. Defense attorney Kenneth Rosenfeld urged the jury to be merciful, citing Schelz's extreme emotional disturbance as justification for a lesser sentence. He acknowledged his client's beliefs were "bizarre," then cited the right of religious freedom. He stated that Schelz could finish his life in prison without posing a threat to society.

Prosecutor Cates called Schelz a demon who corrupted his own children, abused his wife, and murdered

Hunter in cold blood after accusing the social worker of having an affair with his wife. During the trial Hunter's wife testified that she reported her husband missing when he didn't return home from a scheduled appointment with the Schelz family. In a warranted search, law enforcement dogs located Hunter's body buried in a shallow grave on the Schelz property. The victim was murdered with a knife found in the Schelz kitchen. Experts confirmed that blood found on Hunter's body provided a DNA match to Schelz.

Schelz's wife, witness for the prosecution, testified that her husband, an alcoholic and self-proclaimed devil worshiper, physically and psychologically abused her and their two children repeatedly after his failed attempts to organize a congregation of devil worshipers. Hunter, a social worker sent to the Schelz home to investigate reports of child abuse, encouraged Mrs. Schelz to leave with her children. On the day of the murder, Schelz learned his wife was pregnant, shoved her against a wall and beat her. Hunter interrupted the beating and Schelz accused him of fathering the child. Schelz attacked Hunter and stabbed him repeatedly with a knife. Schelz threatened to kill his wife and take the children if she reported the crime.

The prosecution produced a pamphlet Schelz had written, promoting devil worship, self-gratification, punishment for infidelity, and justified vengeance.

The defense countered with a claim that when Schelz learned his wife was pregnant with a third child, he was subject to extreme emotional pressure and guilt.

At the close of the sentencing, Hunter's wife said, "Justice has been served for Adan but our pain continues. We will never forget him."

"Disturbing. Sad," I said, sitting back. "At least we know Schelz's brand of devil worship didn't spread."

"Do we?" said Nick. "How did his version of the symbol end up on Laycee's body? Coincidence? I'd like to hear what Eagleton has to say."

"Do you think the police would try to interview Schelz?"

"If he's still alive. Or attempt to locate the publisher to see how many copies were printed and where."

"A vanity pamphlet from over twenty years ago?" I said. "Good luck."

"If the pamphlet can be tracked to Encino, you get the detective of the year award for triggering my memory," Nick said.

"I gracefully decline. Please don't mention my name to Eagleton. I didn't tell you about my conversation with Carla tonight." I gave Nick the highlights then said, "I prefer avoiding her if I can."

"What was in the box you picked up at Jarret's house?"

"Nothing important. Research texts. A small collection of erotica." My words flew out too fast to edit. Nick turned with a silly grin on his face. I put up my hands to bar the inevitable tease and said, "Robin sent me the erotica for my thirtieth birthday. As a joke. She said every old woman needs an erotica collection."

"Remind me to thank Robin next time I see her."

"Oh, sure," I said. "She'll be thrilled you approve of her taste in literature."

My cell phone rang and as I got up to dig it out of my purse, I glanced at the time. A call at eleven P.M. couldn't be good news but on seeing the caller ID, I knew I had to answer.

"It's Jarret. I should take this."

Nick closed his computer. He lifted the box off the floor and said, "I'll take this back to the garage while you're talking."

I slid the bar to answer and heard breathing. "Hello? Hello?"

"Lizzie-Bear? Baby? I'm s . . . so . . . sorry, honey. I didn't mean it."

I knew and despised that slur. Jarret was drunk out of his mind. I felt an urge to hold the phone away from my face or hang up.

"Where are you?" I said.

"I'm at . . . where am I?" He laughed. "I'm at the Sportsmen's Lodge. Will you come over? I have to tell you . . . explain what . . . I'm sorry, Lizzie-Bear. Please come. I'm in, wait, what room . . . ?"

"I'm not coming over. Jarret, are you okay?"

"I'm okay now that I'm talking to my Lizzie-Bear. I'm so sorry—will you forgive me?"

"Forgive you for what? What did you do, Jarret?" *Please don't let him confess to murder over the phone. Please don't erase the good I thought I knew about the man.*

"I'm not supposed to . . . come over? Lizzie? Please?"

"You're drunk, Jarret. Go to bed. We can talk in the morning."

"Promise, baby? You'll really come and have breakfast with me?"

"Promise. I'll meet you in the hotel coffee shop at

nine-thirty." I ended the call, curious why he chose me as his confessor.

Nick came through the patio door, talking on his cell. "Great. I'll meet you there at one." He hung up and said to me, "How's wonder boy?"

"Drunk," I said. "I agreed to have breakfast with him in the morning. He wants to apologize to me for something."

"Murdering Laycee?"

"I hope not. He was upset, too out of it to make any sense. Who was that? Eagleton?"

"Izzy. We're meeting at the library tomorrow afternoon. She needs advice, probably on a paper she's writing."

I tensed up. "What's the paper on? Seducing older men?"

"Yes. And I'm her lab rat." Nick pulled me into his arms and planted a knee-wobbling kiss on me. "You're cute when you're jealous, but you're wasting your energy. I'm attracted to older, brown-eyed brunettes with long legs and complicated pasts."

"Older?"

The next morning, I lolled in my bed half awake, realizing I should have planned better before I told Jarret I'd meet him at nine-thirty. Senseless to work out and shower at the gym and then drive home to let Stan in at nine, then drive back to meet Jarret at the hotel less than a block from Game On. Maybe if I buried my head under my pillow and slept for a few days, I'd wake up to a working shower in my own bathroom. Let Jarret work out his own issues, I'd sleep through Nick's date with Izzy, and Carla Pratt would forget about me.

Erzulie stood over me and nudged her nose on my bare shoulder. Twice. In other words, get up and feed her. I rolled out of bed, threw on shorts, a T-shirt, and my running shoes, then fed Erzulie and addressed my need for caffeine. While I waited for the coffee to brew, I turned on the small TV in the kitchen—a housewarming gift from my parents—to check the weather. Below the "Encino Homicide Puzzles Police" headline beneath photos of Jarret and Laycee, the temperature in the lower right-hand corner of the screen read seventy-two degrees. Already. The predicted high for the day was one hundred. Degrees. I shut off the set and went outside for a run through my new neighborhood.

As the sun rose over Universal Studios a few miles east, birds chirped from trees in landscaped, white-picketed yards bursting with summer flowers in bright reds and yellows. I did my two-mile run up and down the center of the deserted, residential streets. Squirrels scrambled up trees, lights went on in kitchens, and a middle-aged man in shorts, a pajama top, and sandals with socks, waved hello to me while his golden retriever sniffed at a tree stump.

I returned home sweaty and winded with time to kill before Stan arrived. I laid out a mat on my bedroom floor for a long leisurely stretch. Packed my backpack. Read the mail. Put in a load of laundry. Paid some bills.

Bless Stan for showing up fifteen minutes early. Damn him for being vague on a finish date for my plumbing.

"I'll return around eleven," I said as I left. "Make sure to close the door if you go outside so Erzulie doesn't get out."

"No problem, princess. We'll be inside all day," Stan said.

My dashboard temperature gauge read seventy-nine

degrees by the time I found a space in the crowded lot outside Game On at nine.

Earl stopped me outside the ladies' locker room. "You're late today. You okay?" He touched my shoulder, a concerned—*I heard all about the dead body, what gossip can you tell me?*—frown on his face.

"I'm great." I beamed, thumping my chest. "Woke up this morning and decided to go for a run outside. The fresh air was invigorating. I stopped in here to take a shower. How are you? Where is everyone?"

"I'm same-ol', same-ol'. Getting over a toothache. It's been slow here this morning. You just missed Tess. Kyle's in the office." Earl flicked his eyes from side to side. "You know."

No, I didn't know. Know what? "With a new client?"

"Yeah." Earl chuckled. "I guess you could say that."

The office door opened down the hall. A tall, spray-tanned, fortyish jock emerged in camouflage pants and a T-shirt stretched tight over a bulging, overdeveloped frame with biceps as big as cantaloupes. He passed through the gym without looking up, and left.

Kyle came out of the office, locked the door, and pocketed the key. He saw me with Earl and came over. "Did you talk to Jarret last night, Liz?"

"I'm meeting him at the hotel for breakfast," I said.

"He's in a mess of trouble, huh?" Earl said to Kyle. "Think he did it?"

"If they arrest him, he can kiss his endorsement deals bye-bye. Liz knows him better than anyone—or did." Kyle scoffed at me. "Think Jarret's crazy enough to commit murder?"

Ignoring the question, I asked Earl to excuse us then edged Kyle behind an empty bench, out of earshot. "Do you doubt Jarret's character? Or did you ask my opinion because you had an audience?"

"Well listen to you, protecting your boy." He stuck out his chest, posturing. "Jarret will love to hear that. You gonna bake him a cake in prison?"

"I'm surprised you can be so flip." I hoisted my backpack to my shoulder. "If Jarret ends up in jail, you lose your meal ticket."

"Easy, girl. Can't you take a joke?" he said. "Why are you so touchy? Are the cops on you about your fight with Laycee?"

"Excuse me?"

"The scene you made with Laycee at the ball game," Kyle said.

"What scene? We had a conversation. And how would you *or* the police know what was said? You were in the concession line getting beer."

"Laycee told me you threatened her."

"She lied. And you repeated that story to the police?"

He looked down at me smugly. "Maybe. Maybe not. The cops have all kinds of ways of finding out."

"Don't play games with me, Kyle. Who did you tell?"

"Jarret."

"Do me a favor," I said, my face radiating heat. "Don't repeat secondhand stories about me anymore. You weren't there. You have no idea what you're talking about."

Chapter Twelve

Late and in a rush, I parked in the Sportmen's Lodge tree-lined lot and dashed beneath the bougainvillea arbor to the side entrance of the Patio Café. I roamed over the red-and-black plaid carpeting inside, scanning the small legendary coffee shop for Jarret. The old-fashioned counter stood laden with glass-domed trays of pastries and doughnuts. A scattering of diners sipped coffee in the white leather, red-piped booths under autographed photos of John Wayne, Roy Rogers and Dale Evans, and posters of old Republic westerns—throwbacks to the 1930s and '40s cowboy flicks and B-movies filmed down the road at Republic Studios, now CBS Studio Center.

No sign of Jarret in the dining room so I exited the café on the hotel side, toward the grass-green carpeted pool area. Tourists slathering suntan lotion, chatting, or reading, filled the deck chairs around the Olympic-sized swimming pool.

Laughing, screaming children performed cannonballs into the water.

I spotted Jarret in a row of chairs at the far end of the pool. Long and lean with flat abs and muscular shoulders, he was stretched out on a blue-and-white lounge chair in swim trunks and black sunglasses. His face lifted toward the sun, he held a quarter-folded newspaper in one hand and a bottle of water in the other.

He took off his glasses, dashed bottled water over his sandy brown hair and face with posed flair, and waved me over. "Hey, gorgeous, where's your bathing suit?"

"At home, at the bottom of a box. I thought we were having breakfast."

"Sit down," he said, patting the chair next to him. "We can eat at one of the umbrella tables. What do you want for breakfast?"

"Eggs. And an air-conditioned booth where we can talk in private." I danced away from the edge of the pool seconds before an army of kids splashed up the steps.

Jarret toweled his head, face, and body, and pulled on a T-shirt. As we strolled into the restaurant, the waitress behind the counter waved and the host greeted him like an old friend.

"Pleasant staff," I said as we waited for a table.

"Ira got me a room here because they're used to dealing with celebrities," he said. "I told him I wanted to stay in the Valley."

"Interesting choice, considering Laycee stayed here, too."

He raised an eyebrow. "Did she? I didn't know."

A goateed waiter in a black shirt seated us in a private booth in the corner and then took our order. Steak (rare) and eggs (up), biscuits with gravy, orange juice, and coffee for Jarret, and two eggs easy with a side of rye toast for me. After the waiter brought the juice and poured our coffee, he left us alone.

I stirred cream into my coffee. Nothing like another steaming cup of java to cool off on a hot day. "Did your parents reach you?"

"I talked to them late yesterday afternoon after I left my lawyer's office. Mom told me she called you. I'm sorry they bothered you."

"Marion and Bud aren't ever a bother. They were anxious when they were unable to reach you. The news reports worried all of us. My mom called me more than a few times."

"Viv phoned me at the hotel last night. You're lucky you have such great parents. Your mom didn't grill me about what happened. She asked me if I was taking care of myself."

"And are you? You were pretty drunk last night."

He ran his fingers through his hair. "The last two days have been a living nightmare, beginning with the freaking bird going kamikaze and hexing my game. Everything went south from there. I just wanted to disconnect last night."

His response didn't surprise me. I understood his urge to withdraw—a need to escape was a common reaction to trauma. But what trauma was Jarret erasing? A bad game, finding Laycee's body, or a guilty conscience? I sipped my coffee and waited for him to continue.

"Every rumormonger in the Midwest contacted my parents yesterday— the neighbors, my cousins, the church ladies, hell—even Coach Olson from the high school. Anyone who ever asked my folks for tickets to see me pitch now wants to know if I'm a murderer."

"I'm sorry. I know how hard you work to protect your folks from gossip." *And his vices.* Unlike my family—where trouble sat open to discussion—the Cooper family harbored secrets. A problem concealed meant a problem erased.

Jarret clenched his fist. "I don't know what was worse: finding Laycee like that, the police grilling me all day, or hearing my mother cry."

"Last night on the phone you apologized to me. What for?"

He stared at his coffee cup with his elbow on the table, rubbing his forehead with the heel of his palm. "You know I didn't kill her."

"I believe you," I said, curious why he avoided my gaze. "Then what are you sorry about?"

"Kyle and Laycee met me for drinks after the game at Fifth Base. Kyle bailed at midnight. Laycee wanted to stay out and party. I didn't feel like drinking alone so I brought her up to my house with me. We got smashed on a few bottles of champagne. She blabbed on about auditioning for some cable show, then started telling me about Forrest's problems in the sack." Jarret stopped and looked up. "It's not what you think. I didn't sleep with her."

"I'm not here to judge, Jarret."

"I passed out on the couch. A garbage truck outside woke me at seven. Hell, I forgot about her until I saw her asleep on the bed. I dressed for my run and left her there. When I got home, I—" His face twisted. "I found her covered with blood. She was dead, Liz. I went in the bathroom and vomited. That's when Ira called me."

"He called you?" Odd. "Ira told me you called him."

Jarret shook his head. "You heard wrong. I was too

freaked to move. Ira told me to wait for him before I called anyone."

"Weren't you worried the intruder might still be in the house?"

"The police asked the same question. The house was quiet when I walked in. I called Laycee's name and when she didn't answer, I assumed she was asleep. I stopped in the kitchen for a bottle of water, and then went in the bedroom to wake her up. That's when I saw her facedown on the bed, covered with blood. I went numb. The room began to spin. As soon as Ira got there, we called 911. All hell broke loose. I spent the rest of the day with my lawyer, Ira, and the cops."

"Did the police clear you?"

He glanced away. "They didn't hold me. They made me repeat the story over and over and asked if anything was taken from the house. I won't be able to get back into my house until the field investigation units finish with the property. My lawyer took me to the station to be fingerprinted. Ira got me the room here at the hotel. I'm sorry, Liz."

"Why? There's nothing to apologize to me for." I reached across the table to take his hand.

"There is." He pulled away. "If I had kept away from Laycee in the first place, you wouldn't have . . ."

Me? I drew back, blinking. "I wouldn't have what, Jarret?"

The waiter appeared with our food. He set the plates down on the table and asked if we wanted ketchup, honey, or more gravy.

"No, thanks, pal," Jarret said, waving him off.

Before we could return to our conversation, a young boy

stopped at the side of our booth with a baseball glove tucked under his arm. "Are you Jarret Cooper?"

"I am." Jarret shifted into his public persona of the composed ballplayer. I waited with an affable smile, giving the boy his moment while an apprehensive knife sliced through my shoulder blades.

"What can I do for you, son?" Jarret said.

The boy shuffled his feet. "I was at the game Tuesday night when you hit that home run against the Cubs. I never saw a pitcher hit a home run before. That was pretty cool."

"Thanks. Are you a Dodger fan?"

The kid shook his head. "Cubs. I'm from Illinois. My dad said you are, too. I pitch for the Aurora Scrappers."

"So you're a Little League man." Jarret put up his hand and they exchanged high fives. "My respect. I played for the McHenry Stallions. Did you have a good season?"

"Not good enough, sir. We didn't make the series."

"Hang in there, kid. Baseball is about getting home safe. Remember that, keep up with your practice, and listen to your coach," Jarret said. "Would you like me to sign your glove for you?"

After an excited scramble for a pen, the boy took his autographed glove, thanked Jarret, and hollered as he darted across the restaurant. "Dad, look what I got!"

I reached across the table and grabbed Jarret's hand. "What were you about to say to me? If you stayed away from Laycee, I wouldn't have what? Say it."

He glanced through the restaurant then lowered his voice. "I saw your box of books missing from the kitchen when I went through the house with the police. Finding Laycee rattled me so much that I forgot you were coming to pick it up. I ended up telling the police the intruder must have taken it. Detective Pratt wanted to know if you were at the house the night before or that morning. I said no, and she asked if I was lying to protect you."

"And you answered?"

"I told her I hadn't seen you since the morning of the game. Did you come to the house yesterday morning?"

"Yes. For three minutes." I repeated the story I gave Pratt. "Your neighbor saw me after I pulled out of the driveway. I had no idea Laycee was in the house, dead or alive."

"What time were you there?" he said.

"A few minutes after eight-thirty. What time did you leave?"

"Same time I always leave for my run—eight."

"That gave the intruder a thirty-minute window. Did the police consider a burglary gone wrong? Someone who knew that you left at the same time every morning?"

"How could it be a burglary? The only things missing were a knife from the kitchen block and your box of books. There's an envelope of cash still in my dresser drawer." He leaned back, crossing his arms. "Was *he* with you?"

"He? I was . . ." I hesitated, confused. *Was he asking about the intruder? Or . . .* "Do you mean Nick? I went alone. The neighbor *saw* me alone in my car. What made you think Nick would be with me?"

"I don't know what I think, I'm just worried about you." Jarret picked up his fork and played with his food. "The killer smeared a witchcraft symbol in blood on Laycee's back. That devil crap is your boy's thing, isn't it?"

"If you're asking if the occult is Nick's field of interest, yes. Was he at your house? No. And since when do you recognize mysterious symbols?"

"Ira e-mailed a photo of Laycee's body to his office. They messaged back confirming the mark was witchcraft."

I pushed my plate to the side, glaring. "There are so many disgusting things wrong with Ira taking a photo that I can't even comment. Who decided Nick and I were suspects? You, or Ira?"

"Maybe we should change the subject." Jarret beckoned the waiter for the check. "My lawyer warned me against talking too much."

"Excuse me, but you brought this up. Say it out loud, Jarret. Do you seriously believe I killed Laycee?"

"That's why I wanted to talk to you. I don't think you did. But when Ira and my lawyer found out you came there that morning . . ." He opened his hands and shrugged.

"They decided to accuse me of *murder*?" I bit down, struggling to keep my voice low. "That's insane. How would I possibly know Laycee was at your house? If I knew, I wouldn't have driven up there."

"You hated her."

"Your words, not mine. As far as I'm concerned, I left Laycee Huber behind in Atlanta years ago. You told your lawyer and the police I hated her?"

"The cops tried to blame me for her murder. I was desperate. I had to tell them something to take the attention off me. I remembered you asking if I knew she was in town the other day."

I rolled my eyes. "So? That means I hate her?"

"Kyle said you threatened her at the ball game."

"I didn't. What else?"

"You called Ira to ask if they identified her."

Slowly shaking my head in utter disbelief, I said, "You're twisting the truth. I saw a news report and called your house, worried about *you*."

"Listen, I'm sorry I brought you into this but—well, everyone is a suspect until the cops find the murderer. Just watch yourself, Lizzie-Bear. Be careful of who you talk to and what you say."

"Take your own advice." I threw my napkin on the table and began to slide out of the booth. On a whim, I turned back to him. "Have you ever heard of Herrick Schelz?"

"Schlitz?"

"Schelz, like shelf with a 'z' at the end."

"No," Jarret said. "Why? Should I know him?"

"Never mind. Not important."

Chapter Thirteen

A chorus of cicadas pierced the air on my march through the hot parking lot toward my car. The high-pitched rasping bit on my nerves—raw, thanks to Jarret's big mouth. Lovely. I rubbed the bridge of my nose to ease a growing headache.

If I dripped sweat in a skirt and sleeveless blouse, the hefty man in a suit and tie lumbering across the blazing hot parking lot had to be suffocating. He stopped at his car, glancing over at me. We recognized each other at the same time.

I wove through rows of cars until I reached his side, clasping his arm. "Forrest, I'm so sorry."

"Thank you." Forrest Huber pushed a thin hair off his liver-spotted forehead, looking at me through dull eyes draped with loose pouches of skin. Lean and distinguished the last time I saw him, now his protruding stomach jammed at the buttons of his white shirt like a coronary waiting to happen.

"Is there anything I can do?" I said.

His jaw clenched. "Tell me how and why this happened. Laycee came out here to visit you. I don't understand why she was at Jarret's house or in his bed."

"Were the police able to give you any information?"

"Not yet. They won't even tell me how she got to Jarret's house in the first place. What was she doing there?" He snatched my wrist with fury flashing in his eyes. "Was she sleeping with him?"

"I don't know." I eased his hand off with a gentle squeeze to calm him. I pitied his frustration—Forrest had doted over Laycee like a prize and watched her like a coveted possession. Laycee and Jarret's encounter, whatever it was, wasn't my story to tell.

"I only have Jarret's old number, give me his new one," Forrest said.

"I'd like to help you, but Jarret doesn't give out his number. I have to respect his wishes."

"Why?"

"Did you just get to town?" I said, avoiding his question.

"The police called me yesterday afternoon. I'm going to the morgue to see her now."

"The freeways through downtown can be confusing. Do you need directions?"

"I mapped the route on GPS. I want Laycee to know I'm here for her. She's not alone. And I need to make the arrangements to bring her home to Atlanta. To bury her." He turned away.

I touched his shoulder. "Are you okay to do this right now?"

"I have to be. I want to talk to the police again before we leave. Someone is going to explain to me how my Laycee ended up dead in Jarret's bed and why he's not under arrest."

"If you need anything—help with local arrangements or someone to talk to—you have my number. Feel free to call me."

Forrest thanked me then said, "You were a good friend, Liz, the best girlfriend Laycee ever had. It broke her heart when you moved away. If you had stayed in Atlanta, Laycee would still be alive."

His comment stung but I left him with an encouraging hug, and then went back to my car with my head down. Poor guy. Laycee had lied to Forrest about everything—her reasons for coming to Los Angeles, who she was with, and especially why she and I no longer spoke. So much for love or loyalty.

Dancing my fingers under the hot door latch, I slid into the cooking interior and cranked up the air conditioner to high. As soon as I got home I called my office answering service for messages (none), and then checked in with Stan upstairs. His "just a few more days" estimate on completing the master bath tested my thin patience. I changed into a pair of shorts and a T-shirt. Enough was enough on the shower situation.

"Time to reassess and take action," I said to Erzulie, waiting for me at the bottom of the stairs.

Even if the tub and shower in the spare bathroom were in rusted and nasty shape, with some effort, cleanser, and bleach, maybe I could clean them up enough to use until Stan finished the master. I unloaded the washer and put my laundry in the dryer, packed a bucket with cleaning solutions and rubber gloves, and then went upstairs for some manual labor to clear my mind.

The bathroom at the top of the stairs shared a common wall with the master bath. To the left of the landing was my bedroom door; to the right, doors to the two bedrooms over the kitchen and dining room. I had planned to use the spare bedroom in front for a guest room and make the back bedroom a combination walk-in closet and craft room. If I ever decided to take up a craft. When I arranged the downstairs and my bedroom, I shoved the extra boxes into the spare bedrooms without paying attention to what I was putting where.

I opened the guest bathroom door and set the bucket on the small sink to the right. I could do this. First I had to move out the boxes of clothes stacked against the walls and in the tub. If the back room was going to be my closet, then the boxes of clothes should go in the guest bedroom to be unpacked. I lifted a box from the top and carried it through the hall.

Fueled by nervous energy and the desire to accomplish my goal, I moved seven boxes out of the bathroom and into the guest bedroom while the earsplitting screech of Stan's drill rang from the master suite. Setting the last box near the window facing the street, I stopped for a break and glanced outside.

A blue Caprice pulled up in front of the house. Carla Pratt got out of the driver's side in slacks and a white blouse.

She lumbered up my brick path with her gun holster and handcuff pouch visible for the entire neighborhood to see. Perfect.

I made it halfway down the steps before the doorbell rang. Erzulie darted past me up the stairs, and then darted back at the sound of Stan's drill. The last I saw of her was a tail disappearing under the sofa.

When I opened the door, Carla stood on the porch smiling. "Did I come at a bad time?"

Yes. This is a bad time. Any time is a bad time. Go away. "No, not at all," I said. "I'm unpacking boxes upstairs. What can I do for you?"

"May I come in?"

Chilled air poured out of my house. Unless I wanted to cool down all of Studio City on my dime, lingering half in and half out wouldn't work. I wasn't about to sit on the front porch in the heat, talking to a gun-toting detective in full view of the neighbors.

"Sure. Come on in." I led her to the living room. She sat on the sofa. I crossed my legs Indian-style on my white Camden chair and faced her. "How is the investigation going? Did you zero in on the origin of the symbol yet?"

Carla's brows shot up.

"Everyone knows about the symbol, Carla. I wouldn't be surprised if the tabloids posted it online by now. I heard that Ira Ryback e-mailed a photo from the murder scene. His source called the design witchcraft."

"What would you call it?"

"I have no idea."

"Let's not play coy with each other," Carla said. "You

and Mr. Garfield shared a fascination with the occult during the Darcantel investigation."

"The occult is Nick's passion, not mine. I don't have any interest in the supernatural."

"But you're familiar with the symbol left on Mrs. Huber's body," Carla said.

"No. I didn't know what the pentagram meant until Nick explained the history to me last night. Did Nick's report to Captain Eagleton help you?"

"Ask Eagleton. I'm too busy with the investigation to read. The FBI will tell us if the dated pamphlet means anything. My theory is the killer left a symbol on the body to *mislead* the investigation. Until I have facts convincing me otherwise, I'm focusing on the leads I have."

"Such as?"

"Yesterday you told me you 'used to know' Laycee, however, her husband told me Laycee came to Los Angeles to visit you."

"She lied to him."

"Yet the day before she died, you were seen with her at Game On and then again at the Dodger game."

My throat went dry. "Chance meetings."

"You didn't mention either meeting to me last night," Carla said.

"You didn't ask."

"And if I asked you now what really happened yesterday morning after you found Laycee asleep in your ex-husband's bed?"

"I didn't find Laycee or anyone else in Jarret's house. I didn't go past the kitchen."

"The truth is you hated her. What were your words at the ballpark after you accused her of breaking up your marriage?" Carla flipped through pages of a small notebook. "Witnesses heard you tell Mrs. Huber she was dead to you."

My stomach knotted. So beer-toting Kyle heard at least one part of the conversation. Great. I had finally expressed my feelings to Laycee—in front of an audience.

Carla continued, "The next morning, you walked into your old house and found Laycee in the bed. You must have been so angry, incensed even, realizing she had sex with your ex-husband while she was in town to visit you. A repeat of their fling in Atlanta. All the old feelings of betrayal returned. You went to the kitchen. Got a knife. I can understand why you couldn't stop yourself from stabbing her while she slept. Then you realized someone might have seen you drive up to the house, so you drew a symbol on her in her blood—a witchcraft sign Mr. Garfield showed you—to make the crime appear to be a random cult killing. Where is the knife?"

The knot in my stomach tightened to a chokehold. "Your imagination is astounding. You can turn off your recorder. This conversation is over." I stood, knees shaking, and crossed to the foyer. I opened the front door. "Get out of my house."

"We're not finished, Liz. You can tell me the truth now or we can talk at the station."

Chapter Fourteen

I knew Carla couldn't force me to respond to her accusations, answer her questions, or take me to the station without cause. Thank God I always paid my parking tickets. There weren't any random traffic warrants on me floating around to use as an excuse to take me in.

We stared each other down. I waited, refusing to budge from my stance at the front door. She rose from the sofa and hiked the strap of her bag over her shoulder. Taking her time walking out, her eyes scanned my living room.

"Next time you want to talk to me, contact my lawyer for an appointment." I swept my hand toward the porch, gesturing for her to leave.

"Have him or her call me. Today."

I shut the door behind her and leaned against the panel, my heart banging inside my rib cage. Erzulie scuttled from beneath the sofa to my side, arching her back against my leg. I looked down at her and said, "We need a criminal lawyer. Fast."

Erzulie trailed me into the den. I sat down and dialed Kitty Kirkland, our family attorney and the only lawyer I knew well enough to ask for help.

"Liz, it's good to hear your voice, dear. Is Lucia feeling all right?" Kitty said, referring to the woman she helped Nick and I rescue from fraud and elder abuse last spring.

"Lucia is very well. I'll tell her you asked," I said. "Nick and I had dinner with her last week. But that's not why I'm calling. I need a criminal defense lawyer."

"For Jarret? I saw the news about the homicide at his home. I had a bad feeling—"

"For me."

"Hold on." Her phone clattered. I heard a door click shut.

Kitty listened in silence while I detailed the whole story from Laycee and Jarret's fling in Atlanta all the way to Carla's accusation.

"Why didn't you call me before Pratt questioned you the first time?" she said in her drill sergeant manner.

"I didn't think I had anything to hide."

"The first half of your statement is true. Does your father know about this?"

"Not yet. You're my first call."

"Sit tight. I'll call you right back."

I entertained a short nervous breakdown until the phone rang.

"Oliver Paul will meet you at his office at four o'clock," Kitty said. "For God's sake, don't talk to anyone about this between now and then. If the police show up at your house with a warrant, you call Ollie and wait for him to get there. Here's his phone number and address."

I scribbled the info on a scrap of paper. "Thank you. Who is Oliver Paul?"

"A genius. The sharpest criminal defense attorney in the Valley. He was my star student when I taught criminal motion practice at Loyola. Don't let his attitude throw you. Trust me, you'll love him."

"I trust you." I had to—I didn't have time to be picky. "Will you do me a favor? Don't say anything if you talk to my mom. I want to tell my parents in person tonight."

"I won't say a word. I do want you to keep me updated, though. And Liz? Good luck."

I pulled up a Google map on the address she gave me. I had an hour to change clothes and drive to Oliver Paul's office in Van Nuys. I ran upstairs and at the top of the landing I spotted Stan in the now empty spare bathroom, on his knees in the tub. He raised a drill toward the wall.

"Stan, don't. I was going to—" Too late. Exposed pipes peeked through a gaping hole in the wall beneath the showerhead.

"Hey, Liz. Thanks for clearing out this bathroom. It's easier for me to get a full view of the plumbing from both sides."

I sagged against the doorjamb. "Maybe this will speed things up?"

"Yeah. It should." Stan cleared his throat. "Listen, we have to run out to an emergency job tomorrow. We'll be back on Monday."

He decided to tear up my spare bathroom wall then leave

me stranded for the weekend? I clenched my teeth, conscious of rule number one: don't insult the plumber mid-job. Not if I liked running water. I decided on a new rule: don't let the plumber off the hook.

"Monday? What about Saturday?"

"On the weekend?" His mouth dropped open. You'd think I asked him to work on Christmas.

I creased my forehead and blinked as if ready to cry. It was low but I was desperate. I sighed and said, "I smell. I haven't showered at home or had a decent bubble bath in over a month. I feel like I'm living in a tent. I'm going back to work next week and I—" I covered my face and sniffed.

Stan waved his hands. "Don't. Don't do that. I'll come Saturday morning and see how far I can get alone."

"Would you?" I touched his arm, sincere as a con man.

"Sure."

"Thank you, Stan. You're amazing," I said. "By the way, I have a last-minute meeting this afternoon. I need to lock up the house before I leave. I'm so sorry. We have to call it a day."

Stan grunted agreement and carried his drill and equipment into the master bedroom. He and Angel began removing the tarps off the furniture and packing their tools. I took a black sundress and bronze sandals out of my closet and crossed the hall into the guest bedroom to make a quick change of clothes. They shouted their good-byes from downstairs while I dotted my lips with red lipstick in front of the dusty mirror over my vanity.

With nervous adrenaline pumping through me, I closed up the house and jumped into my car with thirty minutes to get to my new lawyer's office. The air-conditioning kicked in high once I turned on Riverside Drive for a four-mile drive west. The right turn to Van Nuys Boulevard took me past the dealerships on "Auto Row" and the Van Nuys Government Center. After a quick left at a pawnshop onto Victory Boulevard, I passed a tattoo parlor and pulled into the parking lot adjacent to the address Kitty gave me, a five-story bank building. I got out and shielded my eyes from the sun while I surveyed my surroundings. A derelict curled under a blanket beside a Dumpster in the alley. Across the street, a Goodwill Donation Center and two bail bonds storefronts advertised in English and Spanish.

Granted, the bank building stood walking distance from the courthouse and jail complex, but Oliver Paul's office location didn't smack of elite, high-powered attorney. I entered the building, skeptical. Kitty had told me to trust her.

The directory in the glass-and-chrome lobby listed Oliver Paul, Esq., in Rm. 404. I got off the elevator on the fourth floor and wandered down the beige corridor bookended by green plastic trees until I located "404" posted on a small plate next to the third door on the left. No name on the door, no sounds coming from inside.

I knocked. No answer, I checked my watch. On time. I tried the doorknob. Unlocked. The door bumped a row of file cabinets lining the wall of an outer office barely large enough to house an old metal desk covered with a disaster of paper stacks, a dusty computer, and a telephone. The weathered chair behind the desk was empty.

"Hello?" I hovered inside the doorway.

A gravelly male voice answered from an interior hallway, "Back here."

As I curved around the desk and down the hall, I smelled

tobacco smoke. The sickly-sweet odor drifted out of the open door to a green shag-carpeted office. A tall red Chinese cabinet took up the wall to my right. A massive mahogany desk spread in front of a window overlooking the west valley. Behind the desk, an olive-skinned mid-fortyish man with curly brown hair rocked in a leather chair, puffing on a cigar. A striped tie hung loose from the open collar of his white dress shirt, sleeves rolled to his elbows.

With the cigar between his teeth, he stood and straightened his shirt. He stuck out his hand and with a glint in his eye said, "Oliver Paul."

"Liz Cooper," I said, accepting his handshake.

Short and slight, Oliver Paul exuded confidence as big and comfortable as the furniture surrounding us. He pointed at a banker's chair facing the desk. "Sit down, Liz Cooper. Tell me your troubles."

I sat with my purse in my lap, relating an extended, detailed version of how I wound up a suspect instead of a witness at a murder scene—my history with Laycee, Jarret, and Kyle, along with my reason for being at the house. Oliver listened without comment or expression until I started to tell him about my meeting with Carla Pratt at Aroma.

He doused his cigar in an ashtray and sat forward. "You went alone?"

"I had nothing to hide," I said.

"Go on." He dragged his hand across his mouth then rested his cheek on his fist.

Twenty minutes later, he was up to date on every conversation I had and every movement I made over the past two days, ending with Carla's accusation at my house. "That's when I told her to contact my lawyer if she wanted to talk to me again." I felt proud of my smart move to shut her down. I knew he would approve. "What do you think?"

"I think you're doomed," he said.

I closed one eye, not sure I heard him right. "Excuse me?"

"What? You want me to tell you everything is okay? Everything's not okay. You got a homicide detective accusing you of murder. What's okay about that?"

"What should I do? Jarret's lawyer is fueling her suspicions about me."

"Well, what can you do? Ya know?" He shrugged. "Give the cops somebody else to look at. Another schmo to tag the murder on. That's what your ex-husband, Jerry, did."

"Jarret."

"Jerry, Jarret, whatever. I don't know. What do you want me to do? I can bring in my private detective to follow him. Well, ah, you know, we'll have a . . ." Oliver rubbed his mouth again and studied the wall behind me. "Who is Jason's lawyer?"

"Jarret." I sunk into the hard-backed chair, my faith in Oliver shriveling. "My ex-husband's name is Jarret."

"I know." Oliver cracked a smile. "I know everything about Jarret Cooper. He graduated from the University of Illinois. He's a Major League left-handed reliever with an ERA of four-point-four in his career with the Dodgers and an ERA of four-point-one-eight when he played for the Braves. Want me to recite his win-loss statistics? His history in the minors?"

"No, I get it. You know who he is."

"No, you don't get it. You see, every time you correct me, I ask myself, 'Why does this woman care so much about me, a total stranger, getting her ex-husband's name right when she's accused of murdering his girlfriend?' You're lucky I'm not a cop, because right away I think four years after your divorce you still give a crap about him. He has a lawyer busy creating a smoke screen to cover his ass and you're upset that I'm getting his name wrong?" Oliver relit his cigar and blew smoke in the air. "Let's start again. Who is Jarret's lawyer? That's the guy who's pointing the finger at you."

"I don't know his name," I said.

"Find out. Now tell me about you and Jasper. You were married a long time. What happened?"

I sighed. "Fifteen years sounds like a long time, but we lived separate lives. Jarret spent the six or seven months during baseball season on and off the road. I buried myself in studies for my PhD, then built my career. It's painful to admit, but I dealt with broken relationships in my practice while ignoring the destructive signs at home. Jarret's affair with Laycee forced me to face the truth about his infidelities. He and I made a haphazard attempt to stay together after I found out, but I had stopped trusting or caring. I was done."

"You hated this Huber woman?" Oliver said.

"Laycee personified all of the women he bedded. But hate? No. I wouldn't give her that much of my energy. I didn't respect her. I'm angry with myself for befriending her." I fidgeted with my purse strap. Revisiting my marriage and the mistakes I made? Not my favorite subject. "How do we handle Detective Pratt? She wants to talk to me again."

Oliver sat back, puffing his cigar. "Let her wait. The cops got nothin' to bring you in or hold you on. They got guesses. Everybody's got guesses. Here's my guess: they don't have confirmed time of death, they don't have the murder weapon, and they don't have the fingerprint reports back. So Pratt is shooting out accusations at people like cardboard ducks in a carnival booth, waiting for someone to quack out a confession. Ain't happening. Ain't happening, honey."

I felt a little more encouraged, although not completely convinced about Oliver. "In other words, you want me to wait for her to find another suspect?"

"You can bet that right now, she's not looking at anyone but you and Jarret. Gives her something to do. That box you let her take out of your house, you know, the one she removed with your permission? What's in it?"

"Books I haven't looked at in years, just some . . . I don't know exactly."

"What do you mean you don't know exactly? You didn't open it when you got home?"

"No." I braced for another lecture.

Oliver sat forward in the big leather chair, sweeping a hand through his mop of hair. "You . . . you're kidding. What?" He sighed. "What if the killer dropped the murder weapon in the box on his way out? Oh boy, they must be having a party at the police lab. Commendation plaques are being ordered."

"Stop." I held up my hands. "First of all, Carla Pratt isn't ignorant, neither am I, and according to Kitty, neither are you. Carla had to know the contents of the box before she came to see me today. If the knife were inside, you and I would be talking from opposite sides of a table at the jail down the street instead of here in your office. Second, I'm not amused by the name game we just played. You're the man I'm thinking about hiring to protect my freedom. My freedom is precious to me. I don't know anything about you."

He pointed to the wall behind me. A JD degree hung above four framed commendations from the California State Bar Association.

"I have a wife and two kids who eat too much," he said. "I work too hard, I don't sleep enough, and I'm impatient. What else can I tell you?"

"Why did you opt to practice criminal law?"

"Is this the character interview part? I love the interview part. You're curious why I chose to defend criminals."

"I wouldn't put it quite that way but—"

"I like practicing law. I like seeing the justice system work. I like *making* the system work. I would rather read sports statistics than contracts. Divorcing couples are nastier than petty criminals. Probate and trusts would make me feel like a funeral director. Okay? So do I like working with criminals? Let me ask you this—did you become a psychologist because you like working with crazy people?"

I smiled. Maybe I could appreciate Oliver Paul. "I like all kinds of people. Kitty told me—"

"Gotta love old Kitty Kirkland, right? The gal's got balls."

"I wasn't finished," I said.

"Maybe you're not, but I am. I like you. You're thorough. I'll take your case. We have work to do. We need information to move the spotlight off you. I want the lowdown on the other names on Pratt's witness and suspect lists. I want to know what she knows. You haven't been charged—I don't have discovery to dig through. As I said before, I'll have my private detective do some checking."

"He won't have much time to investigate. How long can we stall Detective Pratt?"

"She'll have a hell of a time reaching me tomorrow. I'll be in court. She knows she can't talk to you without me present. Maybe I'll take the family to Palm Springs tomorrow night for a weekend visit to my mother. Ma misses me. She called me twice this week for money." Oliver rocked back in his chair. "But the longer we put off Pratt, the more ticked off and suspicious she'll get."

"Who's your detective?"

"His name is Hank McCormick. Ex-LAPD. He's been on disability since a rifle shot blew out his knee."

"I wonder if he knows my father and brother," I said. "Dad is a retired homicide detective and Dave is RHD. They may be able to help him out."

"We're not doing a potluck where everybody brings a dish." Oliver pointed at me. "I want your word—no 'helpful outsiders' to muck up the investigation."

I had heard and ignored the same warning a few times before. My life, my potluck, and my decision. "Not outsiders—family."

Oliver squinted at me and then broke into a half grin. "It's your neck, kid."

He opened his bottom desk drawer and took out a disposable cell phone encased in a large plastic shell. He ripped apart the packaging and dropped the phone, a battery, and the power cord onto the desk blotter. After he popped the battery into the phone and closed the casing, he plugged the phone into a charger then turned to his computer, typing furiously. Then he reached into another drawer, pulled out a card, scraped the back like a lottery ticket, and punched some numbers on the phone screen. "What's your cell phone number?"

I gave him my digits, he dialed, and my phone rang in my purse. I answered, amused and curious. "Hi, Oliver."

"See the number on the screen?"

"Yes."

"That's the number you call me at. Don't give it to anybody, okay? Hear me? Don't give it to anybody. Not to the police, not to your lover, not to your priest, family, or friends. Only you can call me on this phone. Did Pratt give you her business card?" I nodded, dug in my purse, and then slid her card across his desk. Oliver read the card and said, "Okay, good. I'll e-mail her tonight. If she calls you, all you say is 'Contact my lawyer' and give her my regular office number. Got it?"

"Sure," I said. "But why the intrigue with the phone?"

"There are people I want to talk to and people I don't. You're my client. I will always take your calls, but no one else needs to know how or when. After the case is over, you fire me, or I quit, this phone and the number disappears. That's the deal. All right?"

I liked his style.

Chapter Fifteen

On my way out of Oliver Paul's office, I bumped into a mountain of a man in a turquoise warm-up suit. He backed up to open the hall door for me and I squeezed past with a polite grin, eyeing the outline of a gun stuck in the waistband under his jacket. Bet he had a secret phone number from Ollie, too.

I dialed my parents from the lobby.

"I'm glad you called," Mom said. "Did you hear from Jarret today? He's not answering my calls."

"His phone is probably off. Is Dad home?"

"Your father is at the store picking up a can of creamed corn for me. I'm making my cornbread for dinner with salad and turkey chili. There's enough food for an army. Would you like to come over?"

Army? Perfect. "Can I bring Nick, Dave, and Robin? I need to talk to everyone about something important."

"Of course, but—"

"What time do you want us there?"

"Seven." Mom hesitated. I could almost hear her brain whirring. "Elizabeth, what is going on? Did you and Nick get engaged? Is that what you're coming over to tell us?"

"No, Mom. We're not engaged. I—"

"You're pregnant. I knew it. I told your father you were putting on weight."

Weight? I touched my belly. That did it. I'll be hitting the gym every day for the rest of forever.

"I'm not pregnant," I said, crossing through the parking lot. "I'll explain everything at dinner. I can't talk now. I have to round up Dave and Nick."

Using the hem of my dress like a glove, I opened the scalding car door handle. I put the car windows down and cranked up the AC, then phoned Nick.

"I need you. Can you pick me up at my place at six-thirty for dinner with Robin and Dave at my parents' house?"

"Sure. I thought your dad's party was Saturday," Nick said.

"It is. I'm calling a summit tonight. Carla Pratt came up with a ridiculous theory of jealousy and revenge to accuse me of murdering Laycee. I have to prove she's wrong."

"I'm in," Nick said.

I turned out of the bank lot onto Victory then made a right to Van Nuys Boulevard. While I crept along Auto Row in rush-hour traffic, I made my second call.

"Sam Collins' office. This is Robin."

"I need your help."

"You got it. What do you want me to do?"

"Find Dave and be at my mom's house at seven for

dinner. Nick and I will meet you there." I let out a frustrated sigh. "I just left a meeting with a lawyer."

"Well, I'm glad you took my advice," Robin said.

"A little too late. I'll fill you in on the details tonight when we're all together."

Nick and I pulled into the driveway of my parents' Encino ranch home at exactly seven P.M. He turned off the ignition and said to me, "I wonder what Viv's reaction will be when she hears Jarret threw suspicion on you by telling the cops you hated Laycee."

"Me, too. I didn't want to tell Mom on the phone and give her time to consult her tarot cards. She'll find some way to rationalize his idiotic thinking. Possession, maybe?"

"I'm with her if I can do the exorcism. I'd like to spin Jarret's head around."

"I wouldn't go in too cocky if I were you. Right now, Mom's convinced we're here to announce you got me pregnant." As I got out of the car, Nick sat frozen behind the wheel, staring through the windshield. I leaned in and said, "Are you coming?"

"Are you pregnant?"

I shook my head. "Accused of murder. Disappointed?"

"I need a drink."

Dave and Robin drove up in his white Ford Explorer and parked behind us. Dave hustled out of the car in a rumpled sport coat to open the passenger door. Robin exited as fresh as a spring bouquet in a silk rainbow sherbet sundress and heels.

As Nick and Dave walked to the front door, she slowed

her pace and said, "Dave's suspicious. I wouldn't tell him the reason you wanted us here. Better get this over with fast."

Decades ago, after my parents sent Dave and I off to college, Mom celebrated her independence from dirty uniforms, empty pop cans, and greasy pizza boxes by redecorating. She transformed the Gordon ranch house into a beige extravaganza, from the carpet to the walls to the bricks on the fireplace. Beige chairs and sofa in the living room, beige tiles and appliances in the kitchen. Dad joked that they were living in a carton of vanilla ice cream.

Give Mom a reason to entertain and the beige becomes her canvas. Dave, Robin, Nick, and I were greeted by bright splashes of summer. Bright yellow daisies in red vases dotted every table in the living room. Dozens of sunflowers in a tin bucket adorned the center of a dining room table set with a festive rust-colored tablecloth, six green plates, brown napkins, and a tall pitcher of lemonade.

Dave and Nick hung a left and joined Dad to watch *SportsCenter* on the flat screen in the living room. Robin and I headed to the kitchen, where we found Mom in a white linen tunic and tangerine capris, stirring a large pot of turkey chili. She tucked a strand of her white hair behind her ear and glanced knowingly at my stomach. I made a face and silently vowed to avoid the cornbread at dinner.

"Everything is ready, girls. Liz, take the salad out of the refrigerator. Robin, bring the cornbread. Call the men in and let's eat."

We took our seats around the dining room table. Mom, Dad, and Dave stared at me, then at Nick, then back to me.

I spread a napkin across my lap and said, "I was at Jarret's house yesterday morning before he found Laycee Huber's body."

They listened in hushed silence, a Gordon family first, as I told my story over the salad. Robin huffed with sympathetic indignation while passing the cornbread. I glanced at Mom, waiting for her to interrupt in Jarret's defense. She ate slowly without saying a word. Dad and Dave exchanged glances over Carla's trumped-up allegation then each took second helpings of chili. When I finished my tale, Nick circled his hand on my back.

"What did your lawyer say?" Dad said.

"Oliver thinks Jarret and his lawyer are using me to create reasonable doubt."

"Damn lawyers pull that crap all the time," Dave said between bites. "Carla leaned hard on Jarret so they turned suspicion on Liz. Makes sense."

Mom slapped her palm on the table. "Makes sense? Makes sense to accuse my daughter—your sister—of murder? To save Jarret Cooper? Not on my life. How dare that lowlife, miserable excuse of a man let someone use my daughter as his scapegoat."

Dad blinked in astonishment. Nick suspended his fork midair. Robin sat still. Dave shot me a who-is-this-woman look. I wanted to jump up and hug Mom for taking my side.

"Who is this lawyer of yours?" she said. "How did you find him?"

"His name is Oliver Paul," I said. "Kitty recommended him. She thinks he's incredible."

"He better be incredible. What is he going to do? Walter, how can we stop this? What—"

"Viv, calm down," Dad said. "Easy, easy."

"No. I will not take it easy. Absolutely not. We have to fix this. I want to know what Oliver Paul's plan is and I want to know now," Mom said.

"He's hiring a private investigator named Hank McCormick," I said. "I—"

"Private investigator? Another stranger?" She shook her head. "No. There are two men, excuse me, *three* men at this table who can investigate a murder case better than all of the police, all of the private detectives, and all the lowlife, finger-pointing lawyers in this city. Walter? David? Nick? Find out who killed Laycee Huber. If the evidence points to Jarret Cooper—fine. He can sit and rot in jail for the rest of his miserable life for all I care. Imagine, letting my daughter be accused of murder."

I clapped, proud and impressed. Dad, Nick, and Robin joined me.

Dave leaned back, crossing his arms. "I can't be involved. Internal aff—"

"We're *all* going to help Liz." Dad turned to me. "When did Laycee get to town?"

"I'm not sure. She was staying at the Sportsmen's Lodge," I said. "I first saw her at the gym Tuesday morning with Kyle Stanger and Billy Miles, the producer of *Atlanta Wife Life*. She went to the game with them that night."

"Nozzle, the bartender at Sportsmen's Lodge, is an old buddy of mine," Dad said. "Noz can find out the day and time she checked in, and tell me if she spent time at the bar with anyone. I need a photo of her."

"I think I saw one in the paper this morning. Give me a sec." Robin reached for her purse and brought out her iPhone. She thumbed the keypad, scrolled, and then clicked some buttons until the phone clicked. "What's your e-mail address, Walter? I'll send you the screen shot."

Dad gave her the address then left the table, returning with his cell phone. He opened Robin's e-mail. "You kids with your technology. How did you do this?"

"It's simple." Robin demonstrated.

"Great trick," Dad said. "I'll show Laycee's photo to the bartender. Who else did she plan to see in L.A., Liz?"

"Billy Miles, Kyle Stanger, and Jarret are the only people I know for certain," I said.

"A coordinator in the *Atlanta Wife Life* production office is a friend of mine. I'll call her for the inside skinny on Billy Miles," Robin said.

"If Billy is at the gym in the morning, I'll get his version of what happened between Kyle and Laycee at the stadium party," I said. "Kyle is the only other person who knew Laycee was with Jarret."

Dad pointed across the table. "Dave, run a check on Kyle Stanger. Find out if he has a record."

"Kyle is up to something at the gym," I said. "He takes short, closed-door office meetings with a stream of people who don't belong to Game On and I'm fairly certain they aren't vendors. I interrupted a meeting yesterday. He muttered out an excuse about membership."

"Do you see who he met with?" Dave said.

"A kid, late teens, early twenties with overdeveloped muscles like a bodybuilder." I said.

Dave sat back, folding his arms. "Kyle may be buying or selling steroids. There's a motive there if Laycee knew and threatened to tell Jarret."

Banned by Major League Baseball since the early 1990s, steroids were a hot topic in sports. Jarret, a purist when it came to his body and athleticism, adamantly opposed the hormone replacement therapy some athletes and bodybuilders took to build muscle mass.

"A steroid scandal at Game On could cost Jarret his career and his endorsements," Nick said.

"Why would Kyle kill Laycee at Jarret's house? And leave a symbol on her body?" I said.

"I can't comment on the symbol," Dave said. "But let's say Jarret knew or conspired with Kyle in selling the drugs—a felony. They would end up in jail if Laycee exposed them. Her knowledge may have gotten her killed by one or both of them."

Dad and Nick nodded agreement.

"Speculation doesn't help clear Liz," Mom said. "What do we do about it?"

"Build a scenario for reasonable doubt, Viv," Dad said.

"I'll snoop around a little more at the gym," I said.

"Watch yourself," Dave said. "If Kyle is dealing, he might be pushing anything—steroids, coke, Ecstasy, or worse."

Mom got paper and a pen from the kitchen, and made notes. "Liz, wasn't Laycee married? What about the husband?"

"Forrest was home in Atlanta," I said. "He thought Laycee was visiting me in L.A."

"What makes you think he stayed in Atlanta?" Dad said. "What if he followed her to L.A. and caught Laycee at Jarret's house?"

"How would Forrest know where to find them? Jarret and

Laycee left a sports bar and went to the house. Yesterday morning, Forrest called me, looking for her. I'm sure he was in Atlanta. I saw the area code on my—damn." I buried my face.

"Exactly," Dave said. "His cell number would register Georgia if he called you from the moon. Stalking his wife from Dodger Stadium to a bar to a tryst at her lover's house is nothing to a jealous husband. I've seen worse. I'll check the airlines. Dad, ask the hotel bartender if he saw the husband and when."

I gave Dad a quick description of Forrest.

"I have a question," Robin said, raising her hand. "What are we looking for?"

Dave and I answered in unison, "Lies."

"Shouldn't we be discussing the devil worship symbol?" Mom said. "Isn't that the most logical clue?"

"Carla doesn't think so," I said. "There were no signs of a break-in at the scene. She has a crazy theory that, in order to mislead the investigation, I used a symbol I learned from Nick."

Robin laughed. "Witchcraft? She sure didn't do her homework on you."

"Or she did. I know more about voodoo and Santeria than I care to." I turned to Nick and grinned. "No offense, darling."

"None taken. Now I understand why Eagleton didn't call today after he got my report. Carla's theory puts me on a list of potential witnesses," Nick said. "Tomorrow I'm meeting with a devil worshiper in Silver Lake who can tell me if the Schelz symbol was adopted by a local sect. Dave, can you tap someone at the Indiana State Prison for a list of Herrick Schelz's visitors? As far back as you can get them."

"Sure," Dave said.

Since my brother appeared to be in a cooperative mood, I added, "Let's not assume anything. Can you find out if Carla has the time of death and/or found the murder weapon yet?"

Dave shook his head. "Carla hears I'm helping you and her next call is to Internal Affairs."

"I still know some people in the Field Investigation Unit and in the coroner's office," Dad said. "I'll ask around."

"One more thing, and I guess this one's on me," I said. "I promised Oliver I would get him the name of Jarret's lawyer."

"I'll get the lawyer's name." Mom narrowed her eyes. "Jarret can't avoid me forever. I want to see if that lying, cheating dog is man enough to talk to me."

I set my napkin on my plate, my heart swelling with parental love. "What do you say? Shall we adjourn to the Sportsmen's Lodge for a nightcap?"

Mom sprung out of her chair. "I need a minute to freshen up."

Dad blasted a two-finger whistle as Robin, Nick, Dave, and I stood. "Sit down. *We* are not going to the Sportsmen's Lodge together. When I'm ready, I'll go alone."

"There's no time, Dad. The longer we wait, the more details the bartender will forget. We'll act like we don't know you and watch from the side. I want to see his reaction." Before he argued, I gave him my sweetest grin. "I want to see you at work."

Robin snuggled under Dave's arm. "We'll stay here to help Viv with the dishes."

I did a double take at Dave's agreeable nod. Prior to dating Robin, my brother's idea of doing the dishes was throwing his empty pizza box into the trash. What next? Sushi? Foreign movies?

Chapter Sixteen

Nick parked under the palm trees near the small, stone waterfall in the lot outside the Sportsmen's Lodge. The bell captain opened the door. Nick and I filed down the tiled steps into the hotel, turning right toward the mahogany bar in the lounge at the west end of the lobby. A lone couple sipped cocktails at a table in the corner. Nick pulled out a stool near the end of the bar. I slid onto the seat beside him.

The barrel-shaped bartender, late sixties with a white handlebar mustache and a red bulbous nose, strolled toward us from the cash register. He winked at me then smiled. "What can I get for you folks tonight?"

"Two dry martinis, shaken to waltz time," Nick said.

I turned, confused. "Waltz time?"

"Nick Charles, *The Thin Man*, 1934. The bartender knows."

"Sure do, bud." He looked at me and said, "Switching poison, eh?"

The bartender turned around and pulled bottles of gin and vermouth off the shelf. He set two martini glasses and poured the alcohol into a shaker. He shook slowly, gently—*waltz time.*

"I can't remember the last time I had a martini." I took a sip from the stemmed glass he set in front of me, then winced. Maybe I couldn't remember when, but I remembered why I didn't drink martinis. *Blech.*

Nick glanced over his shoulder then whispered, "Walter just came in. Here we go."

Dad crossed the lobby and sauntered into the lounge. He stopped four stools away from us and leaned his elbows on the bar. "Hey, Nozzle, what does a guy have to do to get a drink in this dive?"

The bartender broke into a wide smile. "Walter Gordon, you old gumshoe. I thought you were dead. Where the hell have you been?"

"On the golf course, lowering my handicap. How've you been?"

"You know, keeping busy. Tending bar keeps me off the streets and out of jail. What can I get you tonight? Your regular?"

"Sure," Dad said, slapping a twenty on the bar. "With a bowl of those stale peanuts and some information."

Nozzle poured out a shot of whiskey and set it on the bar. "Information, eh? I thought you were retired."

"I am. I'm doing some work on the side, for a pal." Dad downed his drink and slid the shot glass across the bar. He reached into his sport coat, took out his phone, and showed Nozzle the screen. "Have you seen this woman?"

"Sure. She's sitting at the end of the bar."

Dad casually glanced at me, then said, "You're slipping, Noz. That's not her. Study the photo with your glasses on."

Nozzle pulled specs from his pocket, took another look at the photo, gawked brazenly at me and then at the photo again. "Huh. You're right. The one down the bar is missing the—" He curved his hands out in front of his chest.

I cupped my fingers over my face.

"They're perfect," Nick whispered in my ear. "Pay attention."

"The girl in the photo has a Southern drawl, sweet as honey," Nozzle said. "She checked in late Monday and came back down here dressed like a call girl. Skirt up to here." He sliced his fingers across the top of his thigh. "A guy showed up for her around ten. They left together."

"What did the man look like?" Dad said.

"Mid- to late thirties, good looking, athletic, about six feet tall, maybe one-eighty, light brown hair. He checked into the hotel yesterday."

Jarret. My gut twisted. He had lied when he claimed he didn't know Laycee was in town Monday night. Why be surprised? The lie wasn't his first, certainly not his last.

"Are you sure she checked in on Monday?" Dad said.

"The legs, Walter, I never forget a great set of legs. I watched her strut to the check-in desk with her suitcase at the start of my shift. On Tuesday while I set up the bar, a different guy—bodybuilder type—met her in the lobby and they took off together. Didn't see her for the rest of the night. An older gent came down to the bar around ten, asking if I seen a brunette with a Southern accent around."

"A big guy? Sixties? Similar Southern accent to the girl?" Dad said, repeating my description of Forrest.

"Yeah, that's him. A guest here, too. Popular broad. Is she a hooker?"

"She's dead," Dad said.

"Christ. I thought she checked out."

I whispered in Nick's ear, "I've heard enough. Let's get out of here." I made a wobbly slide off the barstool. Damn martini. Hate those things.

Nick steadied me then left a few bills on the bar. "Are you going to make it?"

"I think I'll splash some water on my face. I'll be right back." I zigzagged through the lobby, up the steps, and into the ladies' room in the hallway leading to the restaurant and pool.

I looked in the mirror. Good grief, everything about me had wilted in the heat—hair, dress, makeup. Not a pretty sight. I turned on the cold water and cupped my hands under the faucet. As I bent over the sink splashing water on my face, I heard the bathroom door open. I peeked up and saw Gloria, the blonde-with-an-attitude from the gym, come in

She posed at the mirror in three-inch platforms, tight white shorts, and a hot pink tube top then opened her clutch and began applying nude pink lipstick to her lips.

"It seems like you and I are running in the same social circle this week," I said, reaching for a paper towel.

She glanced over at me then added another layer of lipstick to her bottom lip. With that kind of makeup mileage, she qualified for frequent flyer privileges at Sephora. "I don't remember your name," she said.

"Liz. Come here often?" Bad joke. No response. "You're Gloria, right?"

"Mm-hmm." She snapped the lipstick tube shut and dropped it in her purse. "I'm meeting someone at the pool for drinks. What about you?"

"I'm on my way out. The martini I drank at the lobby bar did me in." I picked up my purse. "See you at the gym in the morning?"

"Hope so." Gloria studied herself in the mirror and wiggled her tube top up. "Depends on how many martinis I can hold."

I tossed my paper towel into the trash and left. Nick met me in the lobby and with his arm wrapped around my shoulder, we wandered out to the parking lot to wait for Dad.

At the car, Nick moved a strand of hair off my face then stroked my cheek. "Feel better? You've had a rough day."

"I'm tired. I need sleep and a hot shower, not necessarily in that order. Let's talk about something else. I forgot to ask how your lunch with Izzy went today. Did you solve all her little problems?" I bit the side of my lip. "I'm sorry. That came out wrong. Isabella is your friend. I want to get to know her."

He hesitated, thoughtful, then said, "Let's talk about her another time."

"Why not now?"

"There's too much going on. After you're out of the predicament Jarret put you in, I'll tell you all about Izzy. Right now, clearing you is the priority."

I squeezed his hand. "Thanks. I can't believe Jarret shifted suspicion onto me."

"I think Jarret would do anything to save his own skin.

He must be at the top of Carla's suspect list. But you know what?" Nick leaned his forehead to mine. "We're going to save your skin."

I laughed. "You like my skin."

"I like your skin a lot."

"Do you think we're doing the right thing, Nick? Oliver is bringing in his own private investigator."

"Let him. Doubling and tripling up can only help you. Dave and Walter are the best and they're motivated. They love you."

"What if we're on the wrong track? What if Laycee's killing was random?"

"Without forced entry or robbery? I don't buy it," Nick said. "We need to learn more about the symbol. I don't believe it was random or meant to mislead. I still consider the symbol our best clue. And I'm going to find out what it means."

"Then *we'll* find out. I'm going with you to talk to the devil worshiper."

Nick rubbed his neck. "I don't know. Horus is odd."

"Perfect. Odd people are my specialty. Does Horus have horns?"

"You can judge for yourself. I'll confirm with Horus in the morning and text you a time."

Dad came out of the hotel checking over his shoulder, and stopped beside Nick's car. "Christ, I almost ran into Jarret in the lobby."

"Did he see you?" Nick said.

"I doubt if Jarret noticed anything around him. If he did, he saw multiples. He was drunk. But I ducked back in the bar and pointed him out to Nozzle."

"And?" I said.

"He confirmed Jarret met Laycee on Monday night. Go home, kids. Tomorrow I'll reach out to my buddies downtown then check in with you after." Dad took out his keys and started to walk away.

"Dad?"

He stopped and turned. "What Lizzie?"

"Thanks. I love you."

"I love you too, baby girl. Don't you worry about a thing."

After a night of restless tossing under my light cotton sheet, my eyes opened to the dark sky outside my bedroom windows. I glanced at the clock: 4:55. Didn't matter. I was done battling for sleep. Erzulie snoozed at my side, curled into a ball. Feeling sticky and grimy again, I sniffed under an arm and winced.

I canceled the alarm before it went off, threw on some shorts, a T-shirt, and my gym shoes, and then wandered bleary-eyed into the kitchen. At the first gurgle of hot water through the coffee filter, I perked up and remembered Stan and Angel wouldn't be working on my bathroom today.

"We've got the house to ourselves, kiddo," I said to Erzulie at my feet. She twitched her whiskers. "Yep, no Stan. This calls for a celebration. How about a nice *yellow* can of cat food this morning?"

Erzulie blinked in total agreement. Yellow was her favorite. She hopped on the counter and watched me take the can out of the cupboard then scoop the glop into her dish. While she inhaled her meal, I went upstairs to pack clean clothes and my wallet into my backpack. For once, I didn't have to rush out and rush home. I even had time to stop to pick up cash for the weekend.

When I arrived at the gym, I spotted Kyle and Earl in the weight room with clients. I parked my bag on an empty shelf and climbed onto my favorite treadmill in the deserted cardio room. With Sir Mix-A-Lot rapping "Baby Got Back" in my headphones, I set the speed and cranked the elevation to three. Thirty minutes later, I dropped the elevation back to one, gulping in air. I hopped off the treadmill and stopped for a towel at the front desk. Billy Miles walked in.

"Feels good to work out early, doesn't it?" I said, wiping my face.

"I'll get back to you on that in an hour." Billy tossed his wallet and keys in an open cubbyhole. "You're kind of new around here. Did you just become a member?"

"Ages ago, but I just started coming in again this week. I usually run outside and stretch at home. I use my membership for rainy days and emergencies."

Billy took off his sweatshirt and tossed it in a slot. "It never rains here. What's a gym emergency?"

"Heat waves and broken plumbing. I saw you train with Kyle the other day. How long have you been his client?"

"Since the gym opened. I can't get in here as much as I'd like to. I spend half of my time in Atlanta, on the set for my show. Kyle's great. He's become a friend. In fact, I helped him get into acting class. The guy has natural talent *and* he's an excellent trainer."

"Sad news about Laycee Huber, isn't it?" I said.

Billy's face went blank.

"The woman Kyle brought to your suite at the game Tuesday night?"

"Do you mean the Southern chick with the *Star Trek* ears?" he said.

"She was murdered Wednesday morning."

"No kidding? I don't pay attention to the news. What happened?"

"Someone attacked her at a home in Encino."

He stepped back, mouth open. "No kidding. Wow. I mean, no disrespect but I thought she was obnoxious. Wow."

"Obnoxious?" I said as Tess joined us.

"Relentless, actually. Laycee pitched for an audition for my show *Atlanta Wife Life* and wouldn't take no for an answer. Relentless and annoying," Billy said.

"You weren't interested in hiring her?"

"Honey, *she* wasn't interesting," Billy said. "No disrespect again, but her dull face, big ears, and cliché body came with a boring backstory. Married to a lawyer? Yawn. Not ratings material. The other stars on the show would have demolished her, and no one would have cared. Not even if she got a divorce. But wow—murdered? Man, that sucks. I'm sorry to hear she died."

Tess tossed her keys on a shelf. She swept her tight blonde curls off her face with a headband and said, "Are you talking about the murder in Encino? I saw the woman's photo on the news yesterday. Kyle's friend, right?"

I nodded. "Laycee Huber."

"You won't believe this—you and she were in my dream

last night. You, Laycee, and a cheerleader got into a fistfight over Charlie Sheen on a lifeboat."

Billy threw her a cynical glare and bolted to the cardio room, leaving me trapped.

"My psychic visions are never wrong," Tess said.

"Gee, I hope I didn't win the fight."

Chapter Seventeen

Tess cornered me, preventing an escape to the weight room. "I'm serious," she said. "I think my dream was a prediction."

"Okay," I said with patience I reserved for paying clients. "Lay it out for me. Tell me what *you* think the dream meant. Why Charlie Sheen?"

"Not him. His initials. C.S.? Crime scene? I think you were in the dream because you knew Laycee. And she was murdered at your ex-husband's house. I didn't get the cheerleader part until I heard Billy say she wanted to audition for his show. Competition, get it? A lifeboat is on water. Escaping a leaking ship, right? I think a plumber killed her."

Gretchen walked up and stuffed her purse in a cubbyhole. Over her shoulder she said, "A plumber killed who?"

"Didn't you hear the news?" Tess said. "The woman here

with Kyle on Tuesday was the one who got stabbed to death at Jarret Cooper's house."

"You knew her?" Gretchen said.

Tess gestured at me. "Liz did. I had a psychic vision about the killer's identity in my dream last night."

"What did you see?" Gretchen listened as Tess recapped her dream, then said, "I don't pay attention to dreams. It was probably something you ate."

"Trust me, I'm right."

I bit back sarcasm. I didn't doubt Tess's dream meant something— I've heard stranger stories from my clients— but a psychic vision from the beyond?

"There are many ways to interpret your dream," I said. "Freud might argue wish fulfillment. Carl Jung suggested every character in a dream represents you, the dreamer. The lifeboat may symbolize a facet of *your* personality. Water is sexual, the fighting is conflict, cheerleading is self-confidence. The subconscious layers multiple images in dreams, none of them literal. Instead of taking the dream at face value, see if you can relate the elements to your feelings."

"That's what I said. I have a feeling the dream provides a clue to Laycee's murder," Tess said.

Gretchen raised a brow. She turned to me. "You read dreams?"

"I can quote a few universal interpretations for fun, but I view dreams as personal messages from the psyche to the dreamer, especially if the theme recurs." I turned to Tess. "Do you write out your dreams after you wake up? The practice makes an enlightening trip into your subconscious."

"You bet I keep a journal. That's how I'm sure my visions are right. I go back and check."

Gloria bounced toward us in a T-shirt, sweats, and sneakers, looking like she had twelve hours of sleep and a facial though I knew she was out drinking the night before. She threw her keys onto a shelf. "Good morning. Nice day, isn't it? Guess who I met loaded out of his mind at the Sportsmen's Lodge pool bar last night."

"Who?" Tess and Gretchen asked in chorus.

"Jarret Cooper. You were right about those martinis, Liz."

"You were there, too?" Gretchen said to me.

"For a drink. I left right after I saw Gloria." I looked up at the clock, acting surprised. "Didn't realize how late it is. I've got to finish my sit-ups, shower, and get out of here. Excuse me."

Members performing a variety of sit-ups, push-ups, stretches, and balancing exercises filled the floor of the back studio. I spotted an open space beside Kyle and the middle-aged gent grunting out a round of push-ups at Kyle's feet. Nodding hello, I rolled out a mat then got on the floor and started my sit-ups.

"Liz, did you meet up with Jarret yesterday?" Kyle said.

"I saw him at the hotel. He was in a rush to meet Ira and—" I stopped mid-crunch and wound my hand in a circle. "What's his lawyer's name?"

"You mean Thaddeus Owen the Second?" he said with a bite of contempt. "The guy is more intimidating than my high school math teacher."

I nodded knowingly. "Right. Thaddeus Owen. I suppose Jarret spends a lot of time with Thad and Ira." *Scheming to shift more suspicion on me for Laycee's death.*

"Don't know. I worked all day." Kyle helped his client up, then led him to the weight room.

Tess threw a mat on the floor and plopped down at my side. "Did you notice?"

"Notice what?"

"Gloria and Gretchen have the hots for your ex," Tess said. "After you left, they kept talking about how sexy he is. Does that bother you?"

"Not at all," I said. "I'm with a man I adore. I wish the girls luck—Jarret can be a lot of fun. Exclusive? Not so much. But definitely fun."

After I finished stretching, I collected my things and a clean towel and went into the ladies' locker room to enjoy a long, hot shower in peace. I dropped my backpack and gym clothes on a bench, turned on the water full blast, and stepped into the stall.

As I shampooed and conditioned my hair, I pictured Jarret, sloppy drunk at the pool bar. The guy never could bear to be alone, especially in a crisis. Now, thanks to a rash comment, Jarret had made his latest problem mine. I toweled off, then slipped into black yoga pants and a light gray zip-up sweatshirt

Earl caught me at the door and we walked outside together. He scanned the parking lot then leaned in, con spiratorial. "I didn't want to tell you this in front of anyone inside. A woman detective called me yesterday afternoon. She asked me a lot of questions about what time you left here Wednesday."

"I apologize for involving you." I clenched the strap of my backpack. "You and Tess are the two people I know by name who saw me here Wednesday morning, and I don't know Tess's last name. Again, I'm sorry. What did you tell the detective?"

"The truth. That I saw you leave when my eight o'clock client came in." Earl squinted at me. "Are you mixed up in Laycee Huber's murder?"

"Mixed up?"

"You know, a suspect?"

I shook my head emphatically. "I'm not. Detective Pratt questioned me because they found Laycee's body in my ex-husband's house. I'd be the biggest serial killer in history if I attacked every woman who slept in his bed since I moved out. Did the detective ask you anything else?"

"Only how well I knew Laycee. I said I only saw her those two times she came here with Kyle."

"Two?"

"Yeah. First on Tuesday morning, and then she and Kyle came here that afternoon for a few minutes. I didn't talk to her either time. That's what I told the detective."

"Thanks for telling me in private, Earl. I'm trying to avoid the grapevine."

"I'll let you know if I hear from her again," he said, opening the door. "Good luck."

I strolled along the mall past a jewelry store and bakery toward the ATM kiosk at the end of the shops. At the ATM, I unzipped the side pocket of my backpack then gaped at the contents, puzzled. My wallet was opened upside down, my change, driver's license, and credit cards scattered at the bottom of the pocket. I rifled through and found nothing missing. Maybe the wallet jostled open when I tossed the backpack into the cubbyhole or onto the bench in the ladies' room? Fear of robbery wasn't an issue at Game On—members left purses, wallets, and smartphones in full view in the cubbyholes without concern. I shook off my bewilderment, slid my bank card into the slot, and withdrew some money.

On the way back to my car, I glanced inside the open bakery door. Behind the counter, a girl in oven mitts slid a tray of muffins onto a rack. Mitts plus a hot tray meant muffins fresh out of the oven to me. Not going in would be an insult to the baker. Five minutes later, I exited with a warm carrot-raisin oat-bran muffin and a cappuccino, and sat at a small sidewalk table.

With the sun beaming overhead and cars buzzing along the boulevard, I ate my muffin and sipped cappuccino, content to enjoy a moment of peace.

"Mind if I join you?"

I smiled up at Tess. "Please do."

"Be right back." She disappeared into the bakery, returned with an iced coffee, and sat across from me. "So, you don't believe my plumber theory, huh? Think it over. I told you, I'm pretty good at this stuff. I picked up on a shift in your aura. You've got a dark cloud around you."

"The last few days have been rough. Laycee and I were friends years ago in Atlanta. Her death was a shock."

"Do you know her family?"

"I ran into her husband yesterday. He's understandably a wreck. The police haven't been able to tell him what happened yet." I finished my muffin and downed the rest of my coffee.

"I know you think my dream is silly, but—"

"Not at all, Tess. Dreams are revealing but they're also very personal. You won't convince me a dream can solve a murder unless the dreamer had intimate knowledge about the crime." I sat back and teased, "Anything you want to tell me?"

She threw her hand to her chest. "Me? No way. I saw Laycee only once. You shouldn't resist communications from the beyond. They're all around us if you pay attention. I'm a messenger. My dream stayed with me because I was meant to tell you about it."

"Then thank you. I appreciate the thought. I'll keep the dream in mind." I stood and tossed my trash. Tess and I walked to our cars parked in front of the gym and wished each other a good weekend before she drove off.

Earl came out, scowling, and looked up and down the parking lot. "I'm sick of this, damn it. My client is late again. If he doesn't get here soon, I'm—"

The rest of his words were drowned out by the rattling tailpipes of a motorcycle blasting into the lot. A biker in fatigues parked the bike in front of the gym, climbed off, shot Earl a dirty look, then entered Game On.

"Member?" I said.

"Are you kidding? He's another one of Kyle's"—Earl fingered air quotes—"people."

Since Stan had taken the day off, I parked in my own driveway at home, a small luxury I would happily trade for completed renovations. I hurried inside to the den, plopping on the sofa eager to hear Oliver's opinion on Thad Owen.

Oliver answered on the first ring. "Give me some good news, Liz."

"Thaddeus Owen the Second is Jarret's lawyer. Do you know him?"

"He's an asshole," Oliver said. "You're sunk."

"Please quit saying that. You're not making me feel any better."

"You didn't hire me to cheer you up. What do you want me to say? Everything is peachy? Owen is a snake. Do you have any other news for me?"

"Jarret lied to me."

"Shocker," he said dryly. "When?"

"Tuesday morning, I asked him if he knew Laycee was in town. He said no. But the bartender at the Sportsmen's Lodge saw her with Jarret on Monday night. The bartender also saw Laycee's husband at the hotel the night *before* she died."

"Good. Lies are good. Jerome is hiding something," Oliver said.

"Jar—are you testing me again?"

Oliver chuckled. "You're wising up. I'll be in court all day. I'll get McCormick to check out the victim's husband. Remember—if Detective Pratt tries to contact you, have her call my office for an appointment on Monday."

"Pratt talked to a trainer at Game On yesterday afternoon. She asked him questions about me."

"Covering her bases, putting the pressure on us for a meeting, or both. Sit tight. We'll talk later."

Erzulie hopped on my desk for a scratch and some attention as I dialed Mom.

"I drew the Seven of Swords in my tarot reading this morning, dear," she said. "Sneaky. Lies. I can't wait to talk to that lowlife Jarret."

"You don't need to call him anymore. I found out his lawyer's name this morning."

She sighed. I shared her disappointment—Jarret deserved a dose of Mom's wrath.

"I left him another message an hour ago," she said. "I almost hope he doesn't call me back. I'm too angry to be civil."

"I wouldn't worry but if he does, don't let him rattle you."

"Your father and I are going downtown to talk to the people in the coroner's office then have lunch at the Pacific Dining Car."

I pictured Mom decked out in one of her pink suits and designer handbags, hanging out at the morgue. "Why is Dad taking you to the coroner's?"

"I didn't give him much of a choice," she said. "Either take me along or let me go to the hotel to confront Jarret. He decided on my company. But I'm worried about you, dear. What are you doing today?"

"Nick and I are meeting with the devil worshiper."

"You're going along?"

"Nick didn't have a choice either."

Bustling to the kitchen fueled by nervous energy, I took my backpack to the laundry room, put my dirty gym clothes on top of the washing machine, and cleaned out Erzulie's litter box. Then I puttered in the kitchen until I ran out of counters to wipe and dishes to wash. I was unpacking a box of winter sweaters upstairs in the guest bedroom when Nick texted he would pick me up at noon to meet Horus. Get ready in ninety minutes? Gee, I could try.

What would one wear to meet a devil worshiper? Red? Nick came with a colorful and unusual array of associates and I had to admit, the few I met fascinated me. The voodoo priest and Santeria *santera* I befriended through him turned out to be lovely people.

Robin called while I stood at the dusty mirror in my bathroom, adding a second layer of mascara to the slowest makeup job on record.

"You're going to love this," she said. "The gal I called at *Atlanta Wife Life* told me your Billy Miles is a fake."

I put the mascara down. "A fake what?"

"Producer. William H. Miles, the producer of *Atlanta Wife Life*, is fifty and lives in Bel-Air with his second wife and their daughter, a freshman at USC Film School."

Her description didn't fit the Billy Miles I talked to at the gym earlier. "Then who—?"

"*Billy* Miles is William's nephew and a professional slacker. Billy had one shot at a production and failed miserably. Uncle William demoted him to a useless job at the network to keep him out of trouble. Now Billy is little more than a gopher riding the nepotism train."

"I spoke to Billy. He acts and talks like he's connected."

"Oh, he's connected. Billy can speed-dial every maître d', car service, and florist in town."

"He told me he spends half of his time on the set in Atlanta," I said.

"Right. With William. Billy tags along to drive the uncle around, scout restaurants, get the laundry done. He's sort of like his uncle's road manager."

"What about the party Billy threw at Dodger Stadium? Kyle was there."

"The ATTAGIRL sales staff threw the party for advertisers. Billy has access to tickets to the ATTAGIRL suite at every sporting event," Robin said.

"I can buy a pretense of importance. Billy Miles isn't the first person in Hollywood claiming to be something he's not. Can he audition actors for the ATTAGIRL shows?"

"They won't let him near the cast," Robin said. "Everything you heard about Billy Miles is a lie."

Chapter Eighteen

Nick stopped his SUV at my curb at noon and I climbed in, neck damp from waiting in the sun, my jeans already sticking to my thighs. Cool and relaxed in a gray NoHo T-shirt, he leaned over and kissed me. "What happened to your eyes?"

I flipped down the visor mirror. Yikes. My over-mascaraed lashes framed my big browns like black centipedes. "Nothing. What time is our meeting?"

"Twelve-thirty."

Twirling my hair into a knot at the back of my neck, I grabbed Herrick Schelz's pamphlet off the console and fanned my face. "I thought you gave this to Eagleton."

"I included photos of the cover and the page with the symbol in an e-mail to him with my report. He still hasn't replied yet." Nick made a U-turn in the middle of my block and drove toward Moorpark Street. "I want Horus to check out the actual pamphlet. Either Pratt and Eagleton don't consider it relevant or they pulled me out of the loop because of you." He patted my thigh affectionately. "Pratt knows I'm in your gang."

"You're always *my* first choice as an accomplice," I said. As we traveled east on Moorpark to Vineland, then north to Riverside Drive and the entrance to the 134 East, I told him what I learned from and about Billy Miles.

"Billy Miles can describe his job any way he wants to. He's a fraud, but does that connect him to the crime?"

"I'm grasping for leads, Nick, so far we're getting a lot of information about nothing."

"We've been at this less than twenty-four hours. Maybe Dave came up with something." Nick autodialed the hands-free phone on the dashboard. On Dave's answer, Nick said, "Any luck getting Herrick Schelz's visitor list from the Indiana State Prison?"

"Waiting for a fax," Dave said over the speaker. "I'll let you know as soon as I get it. But I was about to call both of you. Seven years ago, Kyle Stanger was arrested and charged with misdemeanor assault in Georgia."

"Kyle and Jarret were in a bar brawl with a man in Atlanta," I said as we curved onto the Golden State turnoff heading south. "Jarret wasn't charged. Kyle took all of the blame."

"There's more," Dave said. "Three years ago, Stanger got arrested in Atlanta again, that time for possession and intent to sell Schedule II and III drugs—cocaine and steroids."

"Did he serve jail time?" I said.

"His lawyer convinced the judge to suppress the evidence

and the charges were dropped. Stanger moved to Los Angeles two years ago and applied for a business license."

"And opened Game On with Jarret," I said.

Nick glanced at me. "Do you think Jarret knew about the drug arrest?"

"I doubt it. Jarret is protective of his image. I doubt he'd risk going into business with a known drug dealer. Then again, he always felt guilty for letting Kyle take the assault rap for him."

"How about this—Forrest Huber was Stanger's lawyer in the drug case," Dave said.

I tapped my lip. "I knew Kyle got chummy with the Hubers at my parties in Atlanta. I was curious why he and Laycee stayed in touch. If she threatened to tell Jarret that Kyle was dealing drugs again in L.A.—"

"Kyle wouldn't have taken her to the bar to meet Jarret or let her leave with him," Nick said.

"True," I said, then added into the speaker before we hung up, "Good work, Dave."

"I know. You're welcome."

I stared at the passing roadside, puzzled by Kyle's relationship with the Hubers. Something didn't fit. "Nick, I'd bet anything Forrest had no idea that Laycee and Kyle were close. He wouldn't like it."

"Why?" He changed lanes and took the exit through a canopy of trees bordering the edge of Griffith Park toward Los Feliz Boulevard. "How jealous was he?"

"Edging toward morbid—the extreme version that can lead to stalking and violence. Although I've seen Laycee play on his jealousy and provoke him. I remember how she flaunted their age difference to make him crazy, making

175

jokes about their sex life and wearing revealing clothing. Forrest fumed over her flirtatious behavior at our parties. If Laycee and I went out together, he called every ten minutes asking when she'd be home. It wasn't much of a surprise when he phoned me Wednesday morning looking for her."

"Did he abuse her?"

"I can't say for certain. I didn't see visible bruises, but there were signs. After their arguments, she'd lock herself inside for days. Then a new car, new clothes, new vacation, or new pet would appear."

"Could be Forrest discovered her lie about the trip and used the call to you Wednesday morning as a cover." Nick turned south on Griffith Park Boulevard. "The question is, how would Forrest track his wife to Jarret's, and who let him in? Laycee?"

"Forrest and Laycee both knew our garage code in Atlanta, and Jarret still uses the same code. As Dave implied at dinner last night, tracking her movements would be tough, though not impossible. Laycee was a talker. Even if the bartender at the hotel didn't know where she went with Kyle Tuesday night, she might have told someone else she was going to the game—the bell captain, the desk clerk. Forrest would take extreme lengths to find her. Violence wouldn't shock me, especially if he caught her cheating. I can envision him parked on the street all night waiting for Laycee to come out."

"He sees Jarret leave in the morning, goes in the house, and finds Laycee in bed—his worst fears confirmed."

Nick turned right on Hyperion into the Silver Lake business district, cruising by a tattoo parlor, a dance studio, three auto repair centers, and a string of hipster restaurants. He parked in front of a one-story black building with a spectacular art deco starburst etched on the stainless-steel door in the center.

I picked up the pamphlet and got out of the car, approaching the building with curiosity. No windows. No address. "Horus works here?"

"This is her studio. She's an artist." Nick pressed the mother-of-pearl doorbell.

"She?" I stepped back. "Horus is a woman?"

"I didn't mention that?"

A whirring sound drew my attention above the door. A small camera mounted over the doorjamb rotated until the lens focused at our heads. Nick waved and the door lock clicked open. We entered a black vestibule four feet deep, as wide as the building, and as cold as an ice cave.

Nick grasped my hand before the outside door swung closed, leaving us in blackness. He rustled along the back wall, and then pushed open a swinging door into a large, dimly lit room.

A lone candle flickered inside a hurricane lamp on a black iron floor sconce in the far corner. Good thing I didn't wear a skirt—my jeans kept the lower half of me warm while every hair on my arms stood on end from the chill. We crossed the room and sat on two black folding chairs next to the candle.

As my vision adjusted to the dim light, I noted the bare walls around us. I crossed my legs and cradled my arms, leaning forward to protect my body heat and wondering if I could see my breath. Too dark to tell.

"You sure know how to show a girl a good time," I said in a whisper.

"Anything for you, baby," Nick said.

"Where's her art? The room is empty."

"*She's* the art."

Hinges squeaked. A door on the far wall swung open and Horus, slim as a boy and barefoot, entered the room wearing nothing but a string bikini bottom over her tattooed body. Rings pierced the nipples on her small breasts. Blue-and-black snake tattoos coiled up her calves to her thighs and hips, the snakeheads licking orange-and-red flame tattoos rising from her groin to her navel.

Nick stood and accepted her hug, gingerly patting his fingertips on her back. "Thanks for seeing us."

"It's about time I get to meet your lover." She stood, smiling, in the candlelight. Her sapphire blue eyes were framed with long black lashes and lightning-bolt tattoos instead of eyebrows. Holding out a slender blue hand to me, she said, "I'm Horus. I'll take him after you're done. He'll make pretty babies."

"I won't be done for a long, long time. It's nice to meet you. I'm Liz." I shook her hand, fighting not to stare at the horns implanted on her temples or her fringed black bangs, the only hair on her tattooed face and skull.

"Your hands are freezing. Is it cold in here? I can't tell," she said. "I'll get you a sweater."

"Please don't bother," I said between chattering teeth. "The cool air is a nice change from the heat outside."

"This is why I called you." Nick handed her Herrick Schelz's pamphlet.

Horus sat down and studied the booklet under the candle-light. She paged through, reading and rereading sections. Pointing at the title page she said, "I've seen a few of these old American pamphlets before. The devil made a big comeback—not that he was ever really missing—in the late sixties. Schelz's ramblings twist the hell out of LaVey's tenets, and not well. Why the interest in this guy?"

"A murderer used the inverted pentagram with a five and three crosses to mark his victim." He took the pamphlet and opened to a page. "Exactly like this."

"The fifth Satanic Statement. Vengeance," Horus said. "An eye for an eye."

"Or a twist of the fifth commandment," Nick said. "Thou shalt not kill."

"The fifth satanic sin—herd conformity."

"The fifth deadly sin," Nick said. "Lust."

"My favorite." Horus beamed with delight. "Perhaps the fifth satanic rule against unwanted sexual advances. Was the victim male?"

"Female," I said.

"Crowley's Libre five," she said. "The ritual of the mark of the beast."

Nick shook his head. "The killer used the pentagram, not a unicursal hexagram."

"Then perhaps wrath, the fifth heavenly vice," she said.

"Jealousy," Nick said. "The fifth poison in the Buddhist Mahayana tradition."

"Doubt," Horus countered. "The fifth defilement in Vasuhandhu."

"I'm sorry to interrupt," I said, "but it sounds like there are endless possibilities for the motive or message hidden in the five. Nothing for us to identify the killer. We don't even know if we're on the right track with Schelz's version."

"True," Nick said. "We can't rule out Schelz, however, until we've exhausted every effort to find out if his pamphlet went into circulation."

"Horus, you said you've seen other pamphlets like this. Locally?" I said.

"Like this, but not *this* pamphlet. I've seen similar," she said. "Fanatics with time and money have been printing religious propaganda since the fifteenth century. Before that, ink on scrolls, and before that, carved into stone. I've seen every variation. So have you, Nick."

"Not everything," he said. "I searched the library then online for numeric adaptations of the inverted pentagram, pre and post Schelz. Nothing."

"Go see Vic Walkowiak. If this pamphlet or a new version of the same is floating around, Vic will know. He collects religious propaganda. He owns the comic book store a few blocks north. Tell him I sent you." Horus reclined in her chair, stretching her legs. "Is that all?"

"Are there any new devil worship covens or cults in the area? Any rumors you care to share?" Nick said.

"As much as I lust over every inch of you, dear Nick, you know I can't break the code. You'll have to accept my word that none employ your symbol." She traced her fingers up the snake tattoos on her thighs with her eyes fixed on him. "Unless you're willing to barter your body for more information."

Nick glanced at me.

Seriously? He was thinking about it?

"Horus, I don't share," I said.

"Self-preservation and lust. You're a true lioness, Liz. I like you." She rose, walked over to Nick's chair, and straddled his legs. I watched, startled, as she wrapped her fingers around the back of his head and kissed him hard on the lips. She left the room without a word.

I stood outside on the sidewalk letting the sunlight thaw my body. Horus's horns, tattoos, and offensive, overt sexual innuendo created a massive shield, making it impossible to ignore her and a challenge to like her. Yet I sensed fragile vulnerability behind her toughness.

"Slut," I said when I got into the car.

"Don't buy into her sex-and-shock act, she's quite a genius," Nick said quickly. "She was a different person when we were in school together at Oxford. I'd always find her sitting at a table in the library, translating ancient Middle Eastern religious texts. She wrote one of the most compelling analyses of the Virgin birth I've ever—"

"Not her. You." I poked him. "You actually thought about having sex with her? Because if—"

"To keep you from getting arrested?" Nick made a half shrug with a *so-what?* look. "Damn right it crossed my mind—for a second. The tattoos don't bother me, but I draw the line at horns." He started the car and made a U-turn at the stoplight, driving north.

"So, if she didn't have horns, you—"

"Watch for a comic store. We didn't get the address."

I rubbed his knee. "You would have laid your body on the line for me? I think I'm getting teary."

"She didn't give us the shop name." Red-faced and ignoring me, Nick's eyes darted from the traffic ahead to the storefronts along the sidewalk. "What if there isn't a sign?"

"I think I see it. Pull over."

He parked at the curb then looked over his shoulder. "Where?"

"The white building three doors back."

We got out of the car and strode down the empty sidewalk past a manicure shop and a deserted dance studio. I stopped at a window filled with action figures from Star Wars to Harry Potter, Spider-Man, Superman, and Iron Man poised for combat on glass shelves. Nick nudged me when we entered, pointing to a small, red-neon sign on the rear wall. "THE COMIC STORE."

Packaged action figures hung on the walls above rows of white bins filled with alphabetically filed comic books encased in plastic. Featuring characters from comic book–action movies of the past three decades, the shop appeared to be nothing like the comic book store in the valley Dave and I frequented in grade school. Where were the dusty, dog-eared stacks of used *Donald Duck* comics? Where were Archie and Veronica?

"We're here to see Vic Walkowiak," Nick said to the clerk, a thick, freckled man with a combover and beard eating a burger behind the counter.

"That would be me." Vic popped a fry into his mouth and washed it down with a long draw from a Super Big Gulp, then wiped his hands on his Justice League T-shirt.

"Horus sent us," Nick said.

"What do you want?" Though Vic seemed to be a man of few words, at least he was fully clothed.

Nick gave him a business card. "We're researching the devil-worship renaissance in the sixties and seventies. I hear you collect religious propaganda."

"Some."

"Ever seen this before?" Nick laid Herrick Schelz's pamphlet on the glass countertop.

Vic glanced at it then scratched his chin. "What are the odds? Follow me."

Chapter Nineteen

Vic Walkowiak led us to a back room papered with comic convention flyers, autographed photos, and vintage Marvel Comics calendars. Around and above us, hundreds of pamphlets encased in plastic and separated in groups by yellowed paper tabs filled the floor-to-ceiling bookshelves.

Nick and I squeezed between stacks of open cartons of action figures and comic books and past a wastebasket overflowing with take-out cartons and crumpled bags. The air, thick with the odor of old paper and dust, tickled my nose. I sneezed.

"Excuse me," I said, reaching for the open tissue box on the scarred wooden desk tucked in the corner of the room.

"This is my collection." Vic swept his arms toward the shelves. "Twentieth-century handouts are my specialty."

I read the section titles closest to me. "Spiritism," "Kabbalah," "Voodoo," "Satanism," and "Necromancy."

Nick put on his glasses and sifted through booklets. "Amazing," he said as he slid out samples from the "Illuminati" section and studied them. He stood back, taking in the full array. "I've never seen a private collection this extensive. How did you find all these?"

Vic bared yellowed teeth in a proud smile. "Online, rare bookstores, religious rallies, yard sales—you know. Sometimes even at comic conventions. Two months ago, I would've paid you fifty bucks cash for your Schelz pamphlet. If you're looking to get rid of it now, I'll give you twenty."

"It's not for sale," Nick said. "What changed?"

Moving around us to a shelf tabbed "Devil Worship," Vic leafed through a row of plastic-covered booklets and slid out a copy of the Herrick Schelz pamphlet. "I found this baby."

I shuddered at his delight over the product of a madman. "Where did you get it?"

"There's a guy who collects spell-casting and witchcraft publications. You know, candle burning, scrying—the airy-fairy stuff. He knows I like the darker occult themes, like this." Vic pointed at the Schelz pamphlet. "Talk about twisted. Hell, I didn't know about Schelz's background until I bought this and did some research. What a find. A zealot turned murderer. This pamphlet is as rare as they come. The publisher went out of business in the nineties. How did you get your copy?"

Nick began to describe his Indiana gas station encounter. My phone rang in my purse. I pulled it out, saw Jarret's number on the screen, and silenced the ringer.

Vic tugged at his beard as Nick told his story. "No kidding. He knew Schelz?"

"And his family," Nick said.

"Do you mind if I take a closer look at your copy?" I said. At Vic's nod, I slid the pamphlet out of its plastic bag and paged through, searching for a handwritten name, date, or notes. The unmarked contents were in pristine condition. The stapled pages were stiff and wouldn't open flat, as if never read.

I handed the pamphlet back, ignoring the now vibrating phone in my purse. "How can we reach the man who brought this to you?"

"Why the interest in him?" Vic creased his brows, turning to Nick. "You said you were researching propaganda."

"Intellectual curiosity," Nick said. "We heard a few Schelz pamphlets were floating around. I'm curious who renewed the interest in his rantings. If you read the pamphlet, you have to agree Schelz lacks credibility."

"Yeah," Vic said. "Most propagandists do. I read through a few of Schelz's pages but I collect pamphlets for art, not rules to live by."

"I'm interested in the formation of belief systems and the origins of cults," Nick said. "I'd like to talk to the guy who sold you Schelz's pamphlet."

"I . . . don't remember his name." Vic slid the pamphlet back into place and then shut off the light. "He doesn't come in much either."

"If you hear from him in the next few days, tell him I'll trade him cash for information." Nick said at the door.

I traipsed back to the car with Nick, frustrated by what felt to me like a dead end. "I think Vic was lying. Did you notice how he shut down when we asked about his friend?"

"I told you the occult circles, and especially the devil-worship community, are closed to outsiders. Vic is either a member or he's protecting his source." Nick opened his passenger door for me. "Let's give him some time to approach his pal with my offer."

"I wish I had time to give. With Carla after me, I don't." I buckled my seat belt then took out my phone, turning the ringer back on. I opened voice mail and listened to Jarret's message.

"Lizzie-Bear, please call me. I want to explain."

Nick watched as I made a very unladylike gesture at the phone and hit "Delete." He cocked his head.

"Jarret, trying to apologize." I played the second message.

"This is Detective Pratt. I need to meet with you again, Dr. Cooper. Your attorney isn't returning my calls. Let's not make this difficult."

I erased her message then smoothed the heel of my palm against my throbbing forehead.

"What's wrong?" Nick said.

"That was Carla. I can't avoid her for long. Maybe we should have told Vic about the symbol on Laycee's body."

"Bad idea."

"You told Horus," I said.

"I trust Horus. Putting word on the street about the symbol won't score points with Carla and the LAPD." Nick steered onto Griffith Park Boulevard.

I picked up my phone again and dialed Dad. As he answered, I heard people talking and dishes clattering behind him.

"Where are you?" I said.

"Eating prime rib sandwiches at the Pacific Dining Car," he said. "We just left the morgue."

Ribs? After the morgue? Theme lunch?

"What did you find out?" I said.

"The coroner's office put a lockdown on the flow of information on the Huber case until after an arrest is made, though I did manage to dig up a few interesting bits of information," he said.

"Wait. I want Nick to hear." I hit the speaker button on my phone.

"Who's on the phone, Walter?" Mom said in the background. "Is that Liz? Give me the phone. I want to tell her what—"

"Easy, Vivian. You can talk to her in a minute. Where's the horseradish? I ordered extra horseradish," Dad said. "Liz? Are you there? Can Nick hear me?"

Nick turned the car onto the Golden State Freeway entrance. "I'm here, Walter."

"Good," Dad said. "They did an autopsy on Laycee's body yesterday afternoon."

"That happened fast," I said.

"Pratt requested the rush. They're looking for fingerprints on the symbol on Laycee's back, or a hair follicle dropped into her blood," Dad said. "Smart thinking on Pratt's part."

"Don't get so warm and fuzzy over Pratt's cleverness, Dad. She thinks I'm the killer, remember?" I said.

"And if they find hair or fingerprints, you're in the clear," he said.

"Walter, give me the phone." Another shuffle and Mom came on the line. "Your father is not telling you the best part.

I did my own detective work at the coffee machine with the coroner's intern, a nice college girl from Pasadena."

"And?" I said.

"Well, Forrest Huber made quite the scene when they told him he had to wait to view Laycce's body."

"He's grieving. I'm sure he wanted to—"

"Not a grieving scene, an I'll-have-you-fired-for-this scene," Mom said. "Forrest wanted to transport her body to Atlanta, and blew a gasket when he heard about the autopsy. He insisted on being present."

"Pratt, the field unit, and the medical examiner are the only people allowed at the autopsy," Dad said in the background.

"According to my little intern, Forrest is the only bereaved person who's ever asked to watch," Mom said.

"Morbid," Nick said.

"Or a strategy to cope with his disbelief," I said. "As a lawyer, Forrest should know the coroner owns possession of the body until the death certificate is issued."

"Well, listen to this." Mom took a dramatic pause. "After he signed for Laycee's things, he tore her purse apart on the counter, complaining about her missing phone. The police kept it, of course. Of all things, why be angry about her phone?"

"Maybe he needed a reason to lash out. Forrest loved Laycee but he didn't trust her. His jealousy is a familiar feeling, easier to manage than his anguish over her loss." I remembered the fury in Forrest's eyes as he clenched my arm in the parking lot. "He might be searching for Jarret's cell phone number so he can confront him."

"Aren't Forrest and Jarret staying at the same hotel?"

Mom said. "Should we warn Jar—never mind. Not our problem."

I loved the new version of Mom. "Did Dad talk to his guy in the Field Investigation Unit?"

"Walter?" Mom repeated my question to him.

I sunk in my seat, listening to mumbles and fumbles on the other end of the phone—my parents at their chaotic best. "Remind me to teach them how to put a phone on speaker," I said to Nick as we transitioned to the 134.

He threw me a doubtful look.

My father returned on the line. "No fingerprint results yet. No murder weapon. What happened at your meeting with the devil worshiper?"

"Oh," Mom said in the background. "Walter, come and sit next to me. I want to hear."

I nudged Nick. "You can field this one."

"Horus sent us to a collector in Silver Lake, where we found another copy of Schelz's pamphlet. The collector wouldn't give us the name of the guy who sold it to him."

"Nick thinks the seller will call. I have doubts," I said.

"Tell Pratt about the comic store," Dad said. "Let her convince him to reveal the source."

"Like she would take orders from me," I said. "I'm not talking to her without Oliver."

After my parents hung up Nick said, "I'm hungry. How about a burger at Carney's?"

"Love it."

He exited the 134 at Coldwater Canyon and made a left at Ventura. As we passed the Sportsmen's Lodge, he pointed through the window at the driveway. "Isn't that Jarret's car?"

Jarret gunned his red convertible sports car out of the

hotel parking lot. He sped in the opposite direction, too fast for me to catch more than a glimpse of the dark-haired passenger in the front seat.

"I wonder why he isn't at the stadium?" I said. Jarret often joked about not knowing what the world beyond a baseball diamond looked like on summer afternoons.

"You didn't hear? They took him out of the lineup. No official statement from the team. The press is calling his absence a forced leave," Nick said. "Who was the woman with him?"

"I didn't see a face. My guess would be a model, a lawyer, or a bartender."

"I know you're angry with him, but if Jarret is innocent the odds are he knows the killer. I don't trust the guy but he might be of some help."

"If we can believe him," I said. Hell was freezing over if Nick looked to Jarret for answers, but I knew Nick was right—I needed to talk to Jarret again whether I wanted to or not.

We parked in the lot next to Carney's, a bright yellow burger-and-hot-dog diner built inside a railroad car off the boulevard. Taking the metal steps to the platform, we went inside, dodging children running up and down the long, narrow aisle. The menu I knew by heart hung above the shoulder-height counter fronting the kitchen.

Behind the counter, aproned clerks took orders, poured drinks, and loaded hot dog and burger buns with tomatoes and onions, adding squirts of ketchup and mustard, and a ladle of chili. A cook flipped burgers and fried onions on the grill. Another cook manned the deep fryer.

Tables filled with customers sat along the long skinny

row of car windows behind us. Businessmen and women read BlackBerrys or chatted between bites of chiliburgers. Pastel-clad soccer moms broke hot dogs in half for the toddlers in high chairs.

I ordered a cheeseburger (no bun), and Nick ordered a chilidog and fries. While Nick waited for the food, I took our drinks outside to an empty picnic table on the empty redwood patio. I was hungry and curious. Jarret was tooling around town with some woman? Sounded to me like the perfect time to return his call.

He picked up on the second ring. "I didn't think I'd hear from you, Lizzie."

"And here I am. This better be good," I said.

"I can't really talk right now."

"I can. I'm listening."

He lowered his voice. "It's not a good time. I'm with . . . a business associate. Will you let me take you to dinner tonight? Alone? I can explain."

I reluctantly agreed, aware I might regret the decision. Nick came out of the diner with our food. He set the box on the table and sat beside me with a question on his face, nodding after I mouthed, "Jarret."

"What time should I pick you up?" Jarret said.

"Let's meet somewhere."

"Whatever makes you happy, Lizzie. How about the Daily Grill at seven?"

"I'll be there." I hung up and said to Nick, "I'm having dinner with Jarret."

"Great. Ask him who he really thinks killed Laycee. Want me to come along?"

"Wouldn't that be fun? No."

I ate part of my cheeseburger and a few of Nick's fries, too distracted to finish. I was foolish to call Jarret, stupid to agree to dinner. Jarret's apology wouldn't appease me. I had no idea what questions to ask him. The information we'd gathered so far felt like the mess in the spare drawer in my kitchen—a jumble of mismatched, half facts. What was the point of meeting with Jarret, aside from making him suffer? Well, actually, a little suffering would be good for the louse.

"Dave didn't call us back," Nick said.

"Another dead end."

"Research is a slow process. You have to follow each lead until you hit a wall or discover a turn." He tossed our garbage into the trash can at the corner of the patio. "Come on, we can call Dave from the car."

Nick started the engine and turned the air conditioner on full blast. "Now where to?"

I had no idea. Maybe we'd already hit the wall. "My house, I guess. Do you mind if we stop at my office on the way so I can go through my mail?"

He turned east on Ventura then parked in an empty space outside the small complex where I leased an office. Leaving Nick in the car, I entered the courtyard of suites bordered by a row of coral gladiolus and opened the door to my one-room office. A small stack of letters scattered on the floor beneath the mail slot. Junk. Junk. Junk. Phone bill. Bottled water service bill. I tossed the junk, left the bills on my desk to pay on Monday, checked the service for messages, and then locked the door behind me.

"Dr. Cooper." Building manager Yuri Ivanov lumbered out of his office in a geometric print shirt and held up a finger for me to stop.

"Hi, Yuri." I smiled, curious. The beefy Russian did an excellent job of maintaining the property but rarely chatted with the tenants. "Crazy hot out, isn't it? I came by to get my mail."

He grunted. "A woman detective come here about you today," he said in his thick accent. "You in trouble? I don't like trouble."

My ears burned. I didn't have to ask who or why, but I wanted to know *what* Carla thought she'd accomplish by annoying my landlord. If she sought my attention, she had it.

"I'm sorry she bothered you." I cringed with embarrassment. "I'm not in trouble. What did she want?"

"She show me picture of dark-hair woman and light-hair man. Ask me if they visit you. She want me to tell her if you pay rent on time. When you come to work. Sound like problem to me."

"Everything is fine, Yuri. I'll be back in my office on Monday. I assure you, nothing illegal is going on."

Yuri grunted, appearing wary but appeased. We crossed the patio together and he stopped outside his office door. "Rent is due on first."

"No problem. Have a nice weekend."

I had my phone out before I hit the sidewalk. I dialed Oliver's secret number and got an automated message. Great. He was probably still in court. "It's Liz Cooper," I said at the tone. "Please call me. Carla Pratt phoned, and then went snooping around my office building this afternoon, asking questions. I hope she isn't bothering my neighbors, too. We need to talk."

"She knows you're stalling her," Nick said, easing into

traffic after I got in and blurted out Yuri's account of Carla's visit. "Did you think she'd be polite and wait for you to call?"

My logical love. "I can't see her until I have concrete information to get her off my back. Is she trying to manipulate me into a meeting?"

"I think you already know the answer," Nick said.

We passed the Big Sugar Bakeshop near Vantage Street and I made a mental note to buy Yuri a box of doughnut muffins on Monday morning as a peace offering.

"Let's call Dave," I said.

We reached him at his office in the Police Administration Building downtown.

"I talk to you two more than I talk to Robin," Dave said over the speaker.

"Robin isn't avoiding the police," I said. "Give us some good news and we'll leave you alone."

"I don't know if you'd call it good, but I have news," he said. "Herrick Schelz is still incarcerated and he's not Indiana State Prison's model citizen. He's had eight disciplinary actions. There are two names on Schelz's approved visitor list. Kenneth Rosenfeld—"

"His trial attorney," Nick said. "Rosenfeld must be on the long side of seventy by now."

"And Margaret Smith, listed as his daughter. She's been visiting Schelz twice a year since the early nineties. Her last visit happened in January. No visits from a wife or other children."

"Schelz's wife testified against him, no love there," I said. "If I remember correctly from the article we found, both children were minors at the time of the trial."

"Right," Nick said. "The social worker Schelz murdered came to investigate complaints of child abuse."

"The abuse allegation would block the children from visiting Schelz in prison until they became adults," Dave said.

I did some quick math. "Which means if Margaret began visiting her father when she turned eighteen, she's close to our age or older. Did you get any contact info on her?"

"Curran Road in Bull Valley, Illinois—and I already checked," Dave said. "The house at that address was destroyed in a fire last December. No forwarding address on the owners or tenants."

Chapter Twenty

As soon as we entered my house, Nick put on his glasses and stood by the living room window, thumbing through e-mails on his phone. I plunked on the couch with Erzulie and opened the GPS app on my smartphone. I typed "Bull Valley, Illinois" at the prompt and hit the "Start" button.

A map flashed on the screen with a red pin marking the center of Bull Valley. I clicked the pin on the map to request directions. A gasp caught my throat.

Nick pocketed his phone. "What's wrong?"

"You have to see this." I pointed to the map. "Bull Valley, Illinois, is five miles west of McHenry—Jarret's hometown."

Nick sat beside me and studied the screen. "This means Jarret may have known Schelz's daughter Margaret. Hell, Jarret could have seen the pamphlet and remembered the symbol."

"Twenty years later? Jarret has no interest in the occult."

"He's superstitious."

"True," I said. "But his superstitions are meaningless baseball rituals and good-luck charms. It's not like he's some kind of fanatic with an altar to the devil in his stadium locker." I winced. Nick displayed occult symbols all over his house. "I'm sorry, I didn't mean you—"

"I understand what you meant. I just don't understand what you're doing. You seem determined to defend Jarret even though he didn't mind entangling you in Laycee's murder. Do you still have feelings for him?"

"Not in the slightest. But I know Jarret well—murder and devil worship are completely out of character."

"Like the man who walked into a beauty shop last year and gunned down his ex-wife and seven other people? His friends and neighbors thought murder was out of character for him, too."

"That case was a child custody dispute gone bad," I said. "Jarret didn't have a motive to murder Laycee."

"How can you be so sure? It's not up to you to understand his motive or solve the crime, Liz. Jarret put suspicion on you by telling the police you hated Laycee. Meanwhile, I see a viable case building against *him*. A connection to Schelz's daughter links him to the symbol." Nick went to the den and opened my laptop. "Let's see how many Schelzes and Smiths are listed in the Bull Valley phone book. If I have to, I'll call each one to find Margaret."

"And what will you say to her if you do?"

"I'll ask if she knows Jarret. If she does, I'll notify Eagleton."

"I asked Jarret about Herrick Schelz yesterday. He never heard of him."

"And of course, Jarret would never lie to you," Nick said with a sneer. "Think about it. What if Schelz's wife moved the children to Illinois after the trial? All three of them could live in the Bull Valley area."

"Four. The mother and three children," I said. "Mrs. Schelz was pregnant at the time of the murder."

"There's a chance Jarret and one of the two older kids are the same age. Five miles is a close enough area for the McHenry and Bull Valley school systems to overlap. Maybe he went to school with Margaret. What's your computer password?"

" 'P,' three pound signs, 'W,' two exclamation points, then 'D.' "

As Nick typed at my laptop, I stared at the small map on my phone screen, spinning through the possibilities of a connection two thousand miles away. Jarret would never remember a specific occult symbol after all these years. But Nick was right—the connection between the symbol and Jarret's hometown was difficult to ignore.

I stood behind Nick at the desk, watching him scroll through the Bull Valley White Pages. "Anything?"

"No Schelzes. Damn. I suppose that would have been too easy. Maybe Schelz's wife changed the family name to Smith after the trial to escape notoriety," he said, typing again.

"Smith" produced eight results in Bull Valley and over a hundred in the surrounding area. Nick printed out the list. "I'll begin making calls tomorrow."

"What if Margaret attended school and married in another city, and then relocated to Bull Valley long after Jarret left?" I said. "I realize Bull Valley and McHenry are small towns, but a lot of years have passed since Jarret lived in Illinois."

"We know Schelz's daughter lived near Jarret's hometown. We also know Schelz's symbol was left on a dead body inside Jarret's house. I say we follow the clues we have."

"I agree. Someone in Bull Valley must be able to help us locate Margaret."

"What about Jarret's parents?"

"Ask them to help incriminate him?"

"What if Margaret Smith helps to clear Jarret by telling us what happened to the rest of Schelz's pamphlets?"

Made sense. I folded my hands on the top of my head. Nick's cell rang and while he took his call, I dialed the Coopers in Illinois.

A recording came on after the fourth ring. "Yah, this is Marion and Bud. Leave us a message at the beep and we'll call you back. You have a good day."

"Marion, this is Liz. I talked to Jarret—he's fine. But would you please give me a call? I have a question for you." I hung up, hoping I did the right thing.

Nick finished his call with, "We'll be right there." He turned off his phone, smiling.

"Right where?"

"Vic Walkowiak came through. Some guy named Weisel will talk to us about the pamphlet for cash." Nick took his keys out of his pocket. "Let's go."

"Where? I have to meet Jarret at seven."

"We'd be able to walk there and still get you to dinner on time," Nick said. "Weisel works a mile from here."

HEX ON THE EX

* * *

Neon beer logos, discount offers, and "CAlottery" signs filled the windows of the liquor store on the southwest corner of Moorpark Street and Whitsett Avenue. We parked behind the store and crossed the small lot to the rear entrance.

Liquor bottles in every label, shape, and size lined the wall behind a long counter stacked with boxes of gum, jars of candy and jerky above, and cigars and cigarettes below. A lone customer paid for his twelve pack of beer at the register near the front door. Nick and I wandered along the refrigerated cases on the wall then through the wine aisles until the customer left.

"I'm Nick Garfield. Are you Weisel?" Nick said to the clerk at the register.

The long-necked, hook-nosed clerk furtively scanned both entrances and the security mirrors up in the corners. Apparently satisfied, he nodded at Nick. "Yeah." Then he ran his eyes over me. "Who's she?"

Be polite. We want information. I smiled. "I'm Liz. I'm sorry, I didn't catch your first name."

"Everyone calls me Weisel. Did you bring the money?" he said with a hushed tone.

"Let's talk about the pamphlet first," Nick said.

"Which pamphlet?"

"Can we cut the intrigue? I'm interested in where you got the pamphlet you sold Vic." Nick put a ten-dollar bill on the counter. "A nice, simple exchange."

Weisel reached for the bill and I spotted a tattoo on the

201

back of his hand, an inverted pentagram with a goat's head in the center. He pocketed the cash and said, "I got the pamphlet from a customer."

"You can do better than that," Nick said.

"A woman."

"Her name? A description?"

"Never got her name. She comes in to buy scotch." Weisel curled his lips in a wry grin. "If a customer looks old enough to buy liquor and pays with cash, I don't ask for ID—unless it's a girl I want to take out on a date. This lady is too old for me."

"How old?" I said.

"Like your age, maybe? Short brown hair. Flat-chested."

The combination narrowed our odds from one in a few million to one in a few hundred thousand. Locally.

Nick pulled out another ten-dollar bill. "How did you end up with her pamphlet?" The clerk reached for the money. Nick pulled back.

Weisel turned his palm down, showing his tattoo. "She saw my tat and asked if I worshiped Lucifer. I'm not into the left-handed scene anymore, but some people see my ink and want to save my soul. They come in Saturday night for booze and want me to meet them at church Sunday morning. This lady said her old man preached a different kind of religion and wrote something I should read. Then she gives me the pamphlet. Just gave it to me, like a gift. I took it, figuring Vic might be interested."

"Has she been back?" I said.

"I see her now and then, nothin' regular."

Nick gave him the second ten with his business card. "I'll pay you twenty more if you get me her name."

"Fifty," Weisel said.

"Twenty-five."

"Forty-five."

"Twenty-five. I'll make it fifty if she agrees to meet with me," Nick said.

"Deal," he said. "How come you want to meet her so bad? Are you cops?"

"The pamphlet is a classic. We've been trying forever to track down a tie to the author," I said. The past three days *felt* like forever. "You can't imagine how excited we are about talking to her."

A customer entered the liquor store, ending our conversation. Nick and I left through the back.

I buckled my seat belt. "Some detectives we are. We didn't even get the woman's name. I wonder if the weasel told us the truth."

"The weasel?" Nick laughed. "I thought Marty Feldman in *Young Frankenstein*, but you're right—Weisel's name suits him. If Weisel had something to hide, he wouldn't have called me. Jarret and Forrest still top my list of suspects. Jarret had means and opportunity."

"No motive," I said.

"No apparent motive. Forrest had a definite motive if he caught Laycee cheating on him," Nick said. "Forrest knew the combination to Jarret's garage, so he had means. The only piece missing is opportunity. How did he track Laycee to the house?"

My phone rang. I held up a finger. "It's Oliver."

Chapter Twenty-one

I clicked my phone on and said hello to Oliver as Nick turned out of the liquor store parking lot toward my house.

"Sorry, kid," Oliver said. "I was in court when you called. I just hung up from Pratt. She's been after me all day to bring you in for an interview—left me four damn messages. The woman can hound worse than my ma, and that ain't pretty. I told her you'd be at the station tomorrow at eleven."

"Tomorrow?" I panicked. "Aren't you leaving town tonight?"

"Change of plans after I got your message," Oliver said. "I get what Pratt is up to—she wants to embarrass you by hassling your neighbors, friends, and anyone else until you come in. I wish I had something to distract her. So far McCormick got zilch on Forrest Huber."

"Nick and I found an interesting piece of information off

Herrick Schelz's visitor list at the Indiana State Prison. His daughter lived five miles from Jarret's hometown."

"That *is* interesting," Oliver said. "And I guess you called the prison all by yourself and they gladly gave you the list? Man, those Midwest folks are cooperative."

"We may have had some outside help."

"What a surprise. The next time you have a family crime powwow on this case, invite me," Oliver said.

"How did you—?"

"Kitty Kirkland told me all about your bent for solving murders." Oliver's tone shifted to grave. "I'm warning you— be careful where you poke, kid. A twisted sicko murdered once, the second kill will be easier. What kind of trouble are you into tonight?"

"I'm having dinner with Jarret. I want him to explain why he put me in the middle of this mess."

"Don't go. Meet me at my office tomorrow at ten and we'll drive to the station together. You know how to reach me before then."

I turned off my phone and released a deep sigh.

"Start from the top," Nick said as he stopped the car in my driveway.

"Oliver and I are meeting Carla at the station at eleven." My throat knotted with apprehension. "The plumber is coming tomorrow as a favor. Now I have to cancel. What if Carla decides to hold me? What about my clients on Monday? What about Erzulie? My house? My . . ."

The lump in my throat escalated into a burn behind my eyes. Without warning, tension from the past three days poured out in tears streaming down my cheeks.

Nick got out of the car. He walked around to my door, coaxing me out with a gentle hand, then led me into the house. Leaving me sniffling with a box of tissues in the living room, he came back with a glass of water. "Drink this."

Puffy-eyed and spent, I took a sip.

"Pack a suitcase," he said. "You and Erzulie are spending the weekend with me. I have a working shower and bathtub. I'll meet the plumber here in the morning and stay while you're at the station."

"You don't have to take care of me," I said.

"I don't have to." He stroked my hair. "I know you're tough. I love that about you. But when you're vulnerable and you let go like this? Try to stop me."

Erzulie hopped on the couch between us and nudged my hand with her head.

"See?" Nick said. "Even she agrees with me."

I blew my nose, laughing. "I'm pretty sure she just wants her dinner."

Nick trailed me into the kitchen. As I pulled a green can of seafood stew from the cupboard, he said, "Before Oliver called, you were going to tell me how Forrest Huber could have tracked Laycee all over town Tuesday night."

Erzulie hopped on the countertop and watched me peel the lid off her can of food. "Laycee never went anywhere without her phone. Forrest knew her password. All he had to do was log into her mobile account and click on 'Find My Phone.' A GPS map opens to the phone's location, down to street level. He didn't have to leave his hotel room to locate her."

"And this works for any phone?"

"Pretty much. One of my patients calls it the Cheater-Beater. You know my password. Try it. Find me."

I set Erzulie's food on the floor and refreshed her water while Nick typed into his phone.

He held up the satellite map with a blue dot on the roof of my house. "There you are. Outstanding. Tell me—how can you be so certain Forrest knew her password?"

"Laycee was a technical klutz. Forrest bought and set up all of her equipment, including her passwords."

I went upstairs, packed for the weekend, and brought my bag to the door as Nick coaxed Erzulie into her carrier with ease. Sure. Whenever I brought out the carrier, she dove under the bed. Nick merely picked her up, scratched her head, and slid her into the cage. He carried her out to the car without so much as a whimper and then returned for my suitcase.

We shared an awkward moment at the door—nothing like sending off my boyfriend before I got ready to meet my ex.

"Do you have cat food?" I said, unwilling to let him go yet.

"I'll pick some up."

"Should I call you when I'm done?"

"Just come over."

"Want me to bring you dinner?"

"Don't bother." Nick pecked me lightly on the forehead and turned to leave.

I pulled him back and into my arms for a kiss he wouldn't forget. A lot of groping. A lot of promise.

He came up for air, chuckling. "What was that for?"

"To hold my place," I said.

"Right here." Nick tapped his heart. Then he paused before he left. "Be careful what you say to Jarret. I don't trust him."

I shut the door behind him and used the half bath downstairs to freshen up. Then I headed upstairs to solve the wardrobe dilemma. What to wear? Though I couldn't care less about impressing Jarret, dining at the Daily Grill required an upgrade from my grubby T-shirt and jeans. I twirled and pinned my hair off my neck in a knot. Lipstick, the porcelain-and-pearl earrings Nick gave me last Christmas, a red linen shift, and sandals. Good enough. Better than good enough.

The Daily Grill, located on the second-floor balcony of a small mall at the intersection of Laurel Canyon and Ventura Boulevard, was a five-minute drive west into the cool purple and golden red sky behind the evening sun. Cars jammed the mall's street-level parking lot. Apparently everyone in Studio City had come out to dodge the stifling heat or to kick off the weekend. At six fifty-six, I found a space in the underground lot and rode the outside escalators up to the second floor.

A small crowd waited outside the revolving glass door to the restaurant. Jarret, in a white shirt, khaki pants, and black sunglasses, waved me over to a table at the farthest end of the patio dining area. As I approached, he stood and pulled out a chair for me.

"I'd rather not sit out here in the heat," I said. "Let's get a booth inside. We'll have more privacy."

"This is private," Jarret said, sweeping his hands at the empty tables around him. "Look around. There's no one out here."

"Exactly. No one is sitting out here because it's too hot. I'd like to eat inside."

"It'll cool off as soon as the sun goes down."

In less than two minutes, our egos tangled in the dance familiar to both of us. Jarret refused to lose; I refused to give in. Compromise wasn't an option, never was. At the beginning of our marriage, our quarrels ended with makeup sex. Toward the end of our marriage, Jarret ended every argument by slamming the door behind him as he left. He made a mockery of my psychology training by goading me into childish behavior. We knew each other too well. This time, I wouldn't care if he left.

I turned toward the entrance. "It's already cool inside."

He mumbled a curse then followed me through the revolving door into the restaurant's din. Dishes clattered and conversations echoed through the early twentieth-century décor of high ceilings and low wooden booths. We stopped at the dark wood lectern near the door and waited for the hostess.

White-coated waiters bustled from the kitchen carrying large black trays of food. Diners filled tables and booths, surrounded by windows framing a view of the flats of Studio City and the mountains beyond. In the noisy bar area to our left, a strapping bartender poured drinks for patrons mingling shoulder-to-shoulder.

Jarret shuffled from foot to foot, gazing over the dining room. "Where the hell is the hostess?"

"Take off your sunglasses. She's coming down the center aisle," I said.

A pretty, salt-and-pepper-haired hostess in a black pantsuit carried an armful of menus through the restaurant toward us, smiling. "Was there a problem with your table?"

"My wi—we decided to eat inside instead," Jarret said.

She stacked the menus on the side of the stand then scanned the reservation book. "I'm sorry, Mr. Cooper. I only have patio tables available right now."

Jarret gave me a pleading look. I shook my head. "We'll wait for a booth."

"It'll be about fifteen minutes," she said. "If you want, you can wait in the bar. I'll call you as soon as your table is ready and have the waiter bring in your drinks."

"That's okay. We'll wait here." Jarret edged me to the corner between the door and the dining room. He stared out the window, jangling keys in his pocket. I glanced aimlessly through the crowd, eager to sit down and get this over with.

Someone from behind jostled me roughly aside and I tripped into Jarret, circling my hands for balance. Forrest Huber, reeking of booze, thrust his chin in Jarret's face.

"You son of a bitch." Forrest's voice carried over the clatter of plates, causing a hush at nearby tables. "What did you do to my wife, Jarret? What did you do to Laycee?"

Towering over Forrest in height and strength, Jarret put up a calming hand and said quietly, "I'm sorry, man. It wasn't what you think."

"How do you know what I think?" Forrest shoved at Jarret's shoulder. "You don't have the balls to return my messages. You used her and left her to die, you bastard."

"Forrest, please." I touched his arm, moving toward the door. "Let's talk outside."

"Get away from me." He brushed me away. "You lied to me, too. You deserve each other."

The hostess and two waiters rushed over, forming a shield around us.

"Sir," the hostess said to Forrest, "I have to ask you to leave."

He ignored her and pushed Jarret's shoulder again, raising his voice. "Were you screwing her in Atlanta, too?"

The bartender broke in and seized Forrest's arm. A waiter took his other arm and they hurried him, struggling, out the front door. Jarret and I followed them to the open walkway. Patrons dodged out of the way, stopping to watch the scuffle from a distance. A pudgy, middle-aged security guard hustled up the escalator in double steps and jogged toward us, panting.

"Let me go. That bastard is the reason my Laycee is dead." Forrest tried to pull away from the bartender. He glared at the arriving guard with contempt. "What do you want? This is none of your damn business."

"I'm calling the cops." The guard pulled out his phone while the waiter and bartender cornered Forrest against a window.

A woman bystander snapped a picture of Forrest then another of Jarret and me.

"Damn it." Jarret tugged my arm. "Come on, Liz. Security will deal with him. Let's go inside."

"Not yet." I approached the guard. "There's no reason to involve the police. No damage was done to the restaurant. We won't file a complaint. Would you be open to escorting Mr. Huber downstairs and calling him a cab? He's staying at the Sportsmen's Lodge."

"I'm not going anywhere until that bastard tells me the truth," Forrest said.

"We can get him to the elevator," the bartender said, boxing Forrest in.

Forrest pushed away, calling out to Jarret, "You're a low-life coward, Cooper."

"You and your husband better go inside so we can calm him down," the guard said to me.

As Jarret and I walked toward the revolving door, Forrest shouted from behind us, "Cooper."

Jarret looked over his shoulder. "Yeah?"

"I'll see you rot in hell."

Chapter Twenty-two

The waitstaff, diners, and two cooks behind the kitchen counter watched Jarret and me follow the hostess to a booth in the farthest corner of the Daily Grill. A lean blond waiter stopped at the table and, smiling tactfully, took our drink order—iced tea for me, a shot of scotch and a beer for Jarret.

"Great," Jarret said after the waiter left. "Did you see the people taking pictures of us outside? I'm probably all over Twitter by now. I wanted this to be a quiet dinner so I can apologize."

"Now's your chance. This better be good."

"Ira told me a scandal would trigger the morality clauses in my Dodger and endorsement contracts." He leaned forward, brow wrinkled and voice pleading. "An arrest would cost me income and jeopardize future deals. When Thad heard how much you hated Laycee—"

I put out my palm to stop him. " 'Hate' is a reckless and damaging word. You don't—"

"Okay, okay. Let me finish. Thad used your *dislike* of her to steer the police away from me. Team management is letting me suit up tomorrow, but I won't play until the police clear me. If I'm arrested, I face suspension without pay."

"In other words, you let Thad sell me out for money. You call that an apology?"

He gaped at me, incredulous. "I tried to warn you to be careful."

"Warn me?" I stared back, too angry to breathe. "How about telling the police you misled them? That you and your lawyer put me in the middle of this to take the spotlight off you?"

"I told Thad you're innocent. I didn't think a little misdirection would be a problem. After all, you did kind of put yourself in the middle, Lizzie. You knew Laycee was in town. You admit you were at the house that morning. Hell, the neighbors saw you there. Thad claimed the police would leave me alone while they check you out. I can't afford a scandal. I'm innocent."

I clenched my fists to keep from shouting. "Did you stop to think about *my* career and reputation? I had to hire a lawyer, Jarret. Pratt is questioning me again tomorrow. And by the way, you're not above suspicion. Detectives investigate multiple suspects at the same time."

The waiter appeared with our drinks and a bread basket. "Are you ready to order?"

"Not yet." Jarret downed his scotch. I fumed. Maybe dumping my iced tea in his lap would cool me off. After the waiter left, Jarret said, "Take it easy, Lizzie. I said I was sorry."

"No, actually, you didn't."

"I'm sorry. What do you want to eat?" He handed me a menu.

That was it? I got a bigger apology when my dry cleaner had trouble removing a stain from my white slacks. "Did you spot Forrest at the bar before I came in? Is that why you wanted to sit outside?"

"Yeah. The guy is crazy. Do you know he e-mailed messages to my website, threatening to go to Dodger management if I didn't call him? Thad told me to keep away from him. Forrest is a jerk and he just proved how much of a nutjob he is."

"Can you blame him? You cuckolded him."

"I told you I didn't have sex with Laycee that night."

That night. "And what about the night before?"

He glanced down at the table, red-faced.

"Don't bother answering," I said, weary and disgusted. "I know you were together. Someone saw you leave the hotel with her. You lied when I asked if you knew she was in town."

"Why would I admit I was with her?" He twirled a pack of sugar. "Laycee wasn't a great subject between us, okay? So I lied to spare your feelings. What's the big deal?"

"What if Forrest found out she went out with you that first night? He may have tracked her cell phone to your house using GPS and flown to Los Angeles to confront her."

Jarret smirked. "Good guess, but Laycee knew Forrest spied on her. She couldn't figure out how he always knew where she was. One of her friends showed her the GPS trick. Instead of changing her password, when she didn't want to be found she turned off her phone to make Forrest think she fell out of signal range."

I sat back, impressed. Laycee wasn't the brightest in the bunch but the girl had improved her cheating skills.

"So no," Jarret said, "Forrest had no way to find Laycee, and he sure didn't know she was at my house. She turned off her phone both nights." He opened his menu on the table, mindlessly twirling the sugar packet while he read.

So much for my theory. If Laycee's phone was turned off, Forrest had no fast means to find her. He assumed she was with me. I understood his fury toward Jarret after he learned the truth. Forrest was hurt, jealous, cuckolded, and heartbroken. I pitied him for the pain he suffered.

That left me with Margaret Smith and the mysterious woman who gave Schelz's pamphlet to Weisel. One and the same or two different people? I glanced across the table at Jarret—handsome, charming, with a strong instinct for self-preservation. If Jarret knew Margaret linked him to the symbol, he might lie to protect himself whether he was innocent or guilty. And worse, if I told him about her connection to Herrick Schelz, Jarret's scum of a lawyer might find a way to twist the knowledge against me.

Exhausted from making assumptions, I leaned back against the wooden bench. Panicked and paranoid—not exactly the state of mind I was shooting for.

Across the aisle, a couple whispered and glanced in our direction. I opened a menu in front of my face.

"I got the autographed baseball for your dad," Jarret said.

"It's up at the house. Do you still want to give it to him for his birthday?"

If I said yes I'd have to meet Jarret again tomorrow. Saying no meant between now and the party I'd have to shop for a replacement gift for Dad—the man impossible to shop for—and who knew if I would end up spending the day at the station with Carla, or worse. I loved Dad too much to disappoint him.

"Thank you, Jarret. Dad will love the ball."

"Good, because it was embarrassing to ask for autographs and then lose to the Cubs on the same night. The ball is on the table inside my front door. You can swing by anytime tomorrow to pick it up."

"Give me a time and I'll meet you there. I'm not going into your empty house alone again."

"The first pitch is at twelve-thirty. I should be home by six unless we go into extra innings. I'll text you after the game. We'll set a time." He glanced at the menu then closed it on the table. "I hear you've been working out at Game On."

"Only for a few days until my bathrooms are finished." I scanned the main courses. Chicken or fish? Fish or chicken?

"The gym is doing business. Kyle is turning a profit," he said.

"For your partnership or himself?"

Jarret tipped down my menu, narrowing his eyes at me. "Why would you say that? Laycee made a snide remark about Kyle's money that night at Fifth Base."

Insecure Laycee made people squirm to feel superior but she jabbed with nasty or embarrassing truths, never fiction. Did provoking Kyle get her killed?

"How did Kyle respond?"

"He ignored her. So did I. You know Laycee—she teased people for a reaction."

Our waiter appeared again. "How are you folks doing? Ready yet?"

I selected grilled salmon; Jarret ordered a New York steak, rare. Appetizers? No. Salad? No. The waiter collected our menus and left us alone.

"I assume your accountant is watching the books at Game On," I said.

"I told you, we're turning a profit. Membership is up and costs are down. Besides, Kyle wouldn't steal from me," Jarret said. "I would know."

"I noticed Kyle holds a lot of closed-door meetings with an odd cast of characters."

"That's how guys are. We like to hang out in private. You wouldn't understand." He looked down then back up at me again. "Odd in what way?"

I described Kyle's visitors and the meeting I had interrupted. "I heard Kyle was arrested for dealing drugs in Atlanta after we moved."

"Those charges were dropped." Jarret rubbed his forehead. "I'll ask Kyle about his meetings."

Hungry, and assured Jarret would be curious enough to follow through on Kyle, I buttered a slice of warm sourdough bread and popped a piece in my mouth, crunching on the savory combination. "Did the police let you go back home yet?"

"Tomorrow. I don't plan on living there much longer. That house has been bad luck for me ever since you moved out. I met with a real estate agent today. I'm going to sell it," he said. "Now I have to decide where I want to live."

"Were you with a Realtor when I called this afternoon?" I said.

"No. I spent a few hours with a friend."

"I thought you said business associate."

He took a drink of his beer. "Do we have to talk about this? You haven't been interested in my social life lately."

"Friend." No gender, just "friend." What was he holding back? "You rarely talk about your friends. Were you with one of your teammates?"

"I hung out with someone I don't see very often. No one special. There's nothing between us."

"An old friend? Like an old, old friend? From your hometown?"

He rolled his eyes. "God. You're not going to stop, are you?"

"Nope." I ripped off another piece of bread and took a bite.

"She's a girl I dated in high school, Liz. She moved out here recently and called me before I left for spring training. I took her out to dinner, curious to see how she held up. She was my first . . ." He wagged his eyebrows. "You know."

I gulped my bread. *Moved here recently?* Margaret Smith left the Bull Valley house in December. Dodger spring training began in March. His "hometown friend" fit right into the schedule. "First girl you had sex with?"

"Uh-huh." He winked. "My taste has improved since high school."

"What's her name? Janie? Mary? Margaret?" I watched his face for a flicker of recognition.

He grinned at me. "Are you jealous, Lizzie-Bear?"

"Not even close."

219

"Then what's the big deal?" he said. "Trust me, I'm not interested in her. She's not my type. Forget about her. Let's talk about something else."

Our waiter came down the aisle, balancing a loaded tray and placed it on a stand. "Hot plates," he said, handling each dish with a napkin as he set our dinners in front of us. "Can I get you anything else? Refills?"

We said no and thanked him. Jarret sliced into his steak and took a bite with relish. I picked at my fish, more interested in the woman from McHenry than in eating.

"How nice of her to contact you after all these years," I said. "It must be fun to reconnect with someone from the old hometown. Do you see her often?"

"Nope. I'm on the road half the time and at the stadium almost every night when I'm here. Hell, you probably see her more than I do. She works out at Game On in the morning. A short brunette. Plain. On the chubby side."

Jarret dated models. His idea of chubby was any woman with hips.

"What's her name?"

"Gretchen. Gretchen Kressler," he said.

I straightened back, curious. "I know Gretchen. In fact, I saw her at the game Tuesday night. Did you give her the tickets?"

"Yeah. How did you guess?"

"Gretchen told everyone at the gym that her boyfriend got her tickets."

He groaned. "Geez. Why would she say that? She knows I don't have those kinds of feelings for her. I warned her not to talk about me around there. The tabloids bug me enough the way it is. What else is she telling people about me?"

"I don't know. I've only seen her at Game On a few times and once at the ballpark. To be fair, she didn't call you by name when she talked about the tickets. And she still didn't admit to knowing you when I bumped into her at the game and introduced myself."

"She didn't recognize you? She saw your picture at the house. I told her all about you."

"Big difference between seeing me in person and seeing me in a photo. Did Gretchen know you were with Laycee Monday and Tuesday night?"

He snorted. "What I do and who I see on a daily basis is none of Gretchen's business. Kyle is the only one who knew I left with Laycee on Tuesday, and I didn't tell him I saw her Monday. Why?"

I put my fork down and covered my half-eaten fish with my napkin. "I wonder if Gretchen is the jealous type. You might not have feelings for her, but she called you her boy-friend at least once. A small-town woman reconnecting with her first love, now a Major League Baseball player, sounds like the plot of a romance novel to me. Tell me you're not having sex with her, Jarret."

He shrugged, curling his mouth into a bad-boy grin. "Maybe once. For old times' sake."

Like I had to ask. Although I detested Laycee for sleeping with him in Atlanta, she had given me a tangible excuse to escape from his street-cat morals.

"Is Kressler a married or maiden name?"

"Her maiden name. She told me she never got married," he said.

The waiter asked if we wanted coffee or dessert. I turned down both. As Jarret and I rode the escalator down to the parking lot I wondered if Gretchen had an interest in the occult. *What if she knew Margaret Smith?*

"Does Gretchen ever ask about your game-day superstitions?"

"Hell, no. My rituals are sacred ground. You're the only person who knows what I do," Jarret said. "Gretch and I talk about the old times, baseball, and my plans after I retire. She's interested in my career. She thinks I'd make a good TV sports analyst." He checked his reflection in a slim metal strip on the wall. "What do you think?"

Chapter Twenty-three

To dodge the Friday-night restaurant and nightclub traffic on the boulevard, I took back-street shortcuts through Studio City to Nick's bungalow in North Hollywood. All I wanted to do was take off my clothes and get into his bathtub, preferably surrounded by bubbles, ideally joined by Nick. My fantasy dissolved as soon as I pulled up at his house and saw Robin and Dave through the picture window, standing behind Nick at his desk.

I climbed the porch steps and opened the door to a screechy blast of haunted-house organ music. I cupped my hands to call out over the noise, "Hello? Anybody home?"

"Come here." Robin waved me over to the desk. "You have to see this."

"Hey, babe. How was dinner?" Nick said without turning around.

"Eventful. Forrest Huber attacked Jarret and nearly got

223

himself carted off to jail." The comment failed to draw attention. I edged between Robin and Dave, and rested my hands on Nick's shoulders. "What are you watching?"

"My friend at ATTAGIRL messengered me a DVD of the only TV special Billy Miles ever produced," Robin said. "He blew almost a million dollars on the production, a Halloween special on nightmares. It never aired."

"Why not?" I said.

She smiled. "Watch. You'll see."

Dave shushed us. "Here comes the good part."

Six figures with heads and bodies covered in hooded black robes, stood in a half circle in a dark, forestlike clearing lit by torches. Each character held a tall staff with a shrunken head at the top. A procession of men shuffled onscreen—feet dragging, eyes straight ahead in a daze—carrying a woman tied to a plank by chains and wearing a collar of thorns. The camera zoomed in on her eyes, fixed in a trancelike stare. Cheesy organ music swelled from the speakers.

The procession halted center screen. The black-robed half-circle parted for a bald, horned, muscular actor in a loincloth with his body painted dark red. He raised his arms and wagged his long tongue at the camera. Proceeding with dramatic, overacted strides to the side of the plank, he said to the woman, "I take you for my bride to live forever in the bowels of Hades."

She lifted her face toward him and waggled her tongue.

The four of us broke out in laughter.

"Seriously?" I said, wincing, "A million dollars? This is beyond bad."

"I am everywhere, in every shape," the onscreen devil

said to the faceless robed figures surrounding him in a circle. "I am your lover, your nightmare, your demon, your sins, and your savior."

"Why is the devil always a man?" Robin said.

"Not always," Nick said. "She-devils are scattered throughout history. The most famous is the legend of Lilith, Adam's first wife, a character from Jewish mythology. Lilith appears in several forms with different names as a seductive spirit over many cultures dating back to late Antiquity. She—"

"Fascinating," Dave said. "Save the rest for the classroom. Here comes the scene."

The hooded figures onscreen circled the devil, chanting, "Hail, Satan."

The devil figure turned, sweeping his curled tail and bare backside toward the camera. He reached for a lit torch, bent over the woman, and drew a flaming inverted pentagram on her stomach.

"The pentagram." I squeezed Nick's shoulder. "Billy used the inverted pentagram."

"He copied most of the scenes from *Häxan*, a 1922 Swedish film about medieval sorcery. The original version used an eight-pointed star instead of a pentagram," Nick said.

"Liz is right," Robin said. "This proves Billy knew the pentagram—what if he killed Laycee?"

"Why?" Dave said. "For offending him at a party?"

"After seeing this film, I doubt if Billy has the ability to be offended," Nick said.

"Maybe Laycee saw the video and gave him a review," Dave said, laughing.

"Yuk it up, kids," I said. "I'll think of you while I'm at

the police station to—" The camera panned in close on the devil's face. "Nick, pause the screen. Quick."

The face froze on the monitor. The actor's shaved head was painted red with pointed black eyebrows drawn in— but close up, the small eyes and thin mouth were unmistakable.

"That's Kyle Stanger. I'm sure of it."

Nick leaned forward and squinted. "You might be right."

"I know I'm right. Can you fast-forward to the credits?" I said.

"There are no credits," Robin said. "The project got canned before it went to post."

"You didn't recognize Stanger the first time we watched this?" Dave said to Nick.

"I only saw him once before, at the game. He had a full head of hair and wasn't in red face paint," Nick said. "And he didn't have horns."

"I'm sure it's him," I said. "Billy told me Kyle took acting classes."

"After this was shot, I assume." Robin laughed. "If I were Kyle, I wouldn't put this disaster on an audition reel."

Tidbits of information spun through my mind. Kyle's veiled resentment of Jarret. Kyle's relationship with Laycee. Kyle's absence from the gym on the morning of the murder.

"Kyle has Jarret's garage door code. He was familiar with the symbol. He left Laycee, his date, at Fifth Base with Jarret the night before the murder." I turned to Dave. "What if Kyle was angrier at Laycee and Jarret for staying together that night than he let on? Would jealousy, coupled with his knowledge of the symbol, make him a suspect?"

"Depends on the story Stanger gave Carla about that

night," Dave said. "Carla should see this clip. Stanger will be in the fingerprint database from his drug arrest. The forensics from the crime scene should be in by now. The killer could have worn gloves but, yeah, Stanger's knowledge of even part of the symbol, especially the scene of him drawing the pentagram on the body, makes *me* suspicious."

"What's on the rest of this footage?" I said.

"We watched all of it before you got here. Nightmare sequences, ghosts, and witches stirring pots." Nick ejected the DVD, gave it to me, and shut off his computer. "You saw the only scene that caught our attention—the devil drawing the pentagram on the woman's body."

I dropped the disc in my purse and then perched on a stool next to Robin and Dave at the kitchen counter. Nick pulled beers out of the refrigerator and gave us each a bottle.

"The fascination with the devil has gone on for centuries," he said, settling next to me. "Religions and belief systems on every continent conjured a dark god or spirit who caused evil and catastrophic destruction."

"Blame your troubles on the outside opposing and malevolent entity," I said. "Before contemporary psychology and the concept of the subconscious, some scientists and philosophers ascribed undisciplined emotions like anger, greed, or jealousy to possession by the devil."

"Believe me, some lawyers still do that. It's called the insanity defense," Dave said.

"Belief in the devil spread so widely that by the Middle Ages, the myth transformed into fact. He *or she*," Nick said with a nod to Robin, "became real. Hell was positioned at the earth's core, devils stuffed the damned into pots, and sinners were thrown in the fire."

"And don't forget the female healers they labeled witches," Robin said.

"Very true," Nick said. "Women were accused of signing pacts with the devil. Thousands were burned at the stake—young and pretty, old and haggard—their appearance didn't matter. Often women were accused of witchcraft as an excuse to take away their property. Diseases were labeled curses. Stories spread about witches dancing naked with the devil and preparing food made from corpses in the gallows, marinated in wine casks. Women's groups were labeled witches' councils."

I put down my beer. "What did you say?"

"Food was made from corpses in—"

"No, the women's groups and witches' councils." I covered my face, shaking my head. "I can't believe I forgot about this. Laycee and I had a hairdresser in Atlanta who called herself a witch. Laycee went to a witches' council meeting with her and came home with a book of witchcraft spells."

"And?" Dave said. "The hairdresser followed her to Jarret's house in L.A. and killed her?"

"No. I get it," Robin said. "If Laycee kept the book in their house, Forrest could have seen an inverted pentagram. When he caught her at Jarret's, he smeared the sign on her back to curse her."

"We've established that everyone on the planet except the three of you has seen a version of the inverted pentagram somewhere," Nick said. "However, only Laycee's killer understands the significance of the five. Schelz related it to vengeance."

"What's the standard interpretation?" Dave said.

"Give me a century, a religion, a sport, a science, a—"

"Are you sure you saw the number 5 and not the letter S—for Stanger?" Robin said.

Dave cocked his head, smiling. "Or Superman?"

"Five. The top edges were sharp." Nick turned to me. "Liz, earlier you said something about Forrest Huber going to jail."

"You heard me?"

"Always. Even when I'm not paying attention."

Nick and Dave both listened, wide-eyed, to recount of Forrest's outburst. When I told them about Jarret's dinner comments about Gretchen, Robin sat straight up.

"His high school girlfriend tracked him down after all those years? That's huge," Robin said.

"It got my attention," I said. "Jarret brushed her off as a casual friend with benefits, yet Gretchen referred to him as her boyfriend at the gym."

"You know, a girl never forgets her first," Robin said.

"Never?" Dave said, putting his arm around her. "Who was your first?"

Robin fluttered her lashes, poised and self-assured. "This year? You."

"Liz, what did Jarret say about Margaret Smith?" Nick said.

"I didn't ask."

"Why not?"

"The timing didn't feel right to me. I'll wait for his mother to return my call. Marion will give me details and she won't ask a lot of questions."

"This Gretchen woman's move to L.A. coincides with the Smiths losing their house in Bull Valley. Or close enough," Dave said. "Write down her last name and I'll run her through the database at work on Monday." He slid off his stool and gave Robin's blonde ponytail a gentle tug. "It's getting late."

She took Dave's hand, then gave me a knowing wink. Getting late—lover's code for let's go to your house and fool around.

"We'll see you tomorrow night at your dad's party." Robin picked up her purse from the coffee table. Nick and I followed them outside.

"Good luck at the police station," Robin said. "Don't let Carla the bulldog intimidate you."

"Oliver will be there to growl back," I said.

Dave stopped at the sidewalk and called across the lawn, "Call if you need me."

Nick and I waved from the porch as they drove off under the night sky, clear and black, punctuated by a scattering of bright stars. A forceful wind rustled through the trees, blowing dust and dried leaves across the lawn. I wrapped my arms around Nick's waist and rested my head on his shoulder, taking in the scent of summer flowers and fresh-cut grass, happy for the quiet.

He moved his hand up my back, caressing my neck with his forefinger and thumb. His slow, gentle kneading shot tingles of release across my shoulders to my fingertips and down to my knees. My body relaxed into his touch. He slipped his free hand around my waist and moved around to face me. Running his hands down my body to my hips, he began to bunch my dress up.

I stopped him, mid-thigh. "What I want to do with you tonight requires a soft bed, a dark room, and a lot of time."

Taking his hand to my lips, I slowly kissed his fingertips. "But first, I'm taking a bath."

When we went inside, Erzulie hopped on the kitchen counter, pacing between the empty beer bottles with her tail straight up, and meowing until I went to her.

"Where have you been?" I said. She arched her back, letting me scratch the top of her head. I scooped her up under the belly, hugging her close until she tired of the love and squirmed for freedom.

While Nick tossed the empty bottles and turned off the lights, I went into the bathroom and ran hot water in the tub. While the tub filled, I unpacked my weekender and put my clothes in the dresser drawer Nick left empty for me, keeping out the purple chiffon baby-doll gown I packed as a surprise. Since he was patient enough to wait for me while I dined with my ex-husband, I figured Nick deserved a little transparent eye candy as a reward. I hung the baby-doll on the back of the bathroom door, put two small drops from my vial of rose oil under the running water, and took off my clothes.

I eased into the tub, sliding down to immerse my head in the hot, scented water. *Hello bath, I missed you so.* The water dissolved days of yucky gym showers, worries, and tight muscles. I came up for air, lathered shampoo through my hair, and went under again. Came back up to lather my body and wash my face, and then I soaked in water to my chin until thoughts of Nick, waiting for me in the bedroom, became too inviting to ignore. I climbed out, toweled off my hair and body, and slipped into the cool purple chiffon.

Soft flutes hummed a slow and sexy African chant

throughout the house. In the dark bedroom, a lone pillar candle flickered beside the fertility goddess on the night-stand. Nick waited in bed, propped on an elbow against a stack of pillows with a sheet stopped at his bare waist. I walked barefoot across his Turkish rug and stood in front of him in the candlelight. His eyes drifted from my face to my chest to the edge of the baby-doll brushing the top of my thighs. He held out his hand.

I put my knee on the bed and let him pull me in. I fell into his arms and into a deep, lingering kiss. The baby-doll stayed on for a good thirty seconds, a new record for us.

Chapter Twenty-four

Erzulie nudged her nose to my cheek in the dark, waking me from a contented dream at Nick's side. I peered over her head to the clock on the nightstand. Five thirty. I scratched her behind the ears. "Go back to sleep. It's Saturday."

She jumped over my body and pawed Nick's shoulder. He stirred, draping an arm and bare leg over me.

"What time is it?" he mumbled, half asleep.

"Too early." I burrowed my head into my soft, warm pillow.

Erzulie, resolute about her wake-up-I-want-breakfast mission, climbed onto Nick's hip and meowed. He leaned into me. I heard her jump off the bed, then in an instant she hopped to my side again. She sat, staring at me. Guilt settled in. My girl was hungry.

If I got up really fast and fed her, I might be able to come back to bed and catch the end of my dream. I sat at the edge of the bed and slipped into the only clothing nearby—the purple chiffon baby-doll. Leaving Nick to sleep, I tiptoed out of the bedroom with Erzulie trotting beside me to the kitchen. The dream faded by the time I pulled a can of seafood splendor out of the cabinet and pulled off the lid.

I set her dish on the floor and freshened her water. Extending my arms above my head, I stretched a blissful ache out of my muscles. I didn't get much sleep, but we sure had a good time last night. Memorable.

An engine outside broke the silence. I heard a *plop* then another *plop*. The uncurtained living room window provided me with a full view of the pre-dawn street and the headlights of the car outside. The window also gave the driver delivering the morning paper a full view of me in sheer, thigh-skimming chiffon under the bright kitchen light. I ducked down fast, crouched next to Erzulie, and waited until the engine sounds disappeared in the distance. My impromptu neighborhood peep show jolted an adrenaline rush of embarrassment. No shot of getting another hour of sleep now. Might as well make some coffee and start the day. Better get dressed first.

Nick slept with his arms and legs sprawled across the king-sized mattress. His head rested on a scrunched-up pillow. His mouth relaxed open, inhaling soft, rumbling breaths. I watched him for a minute, battling the urge to pull off the sheet and slide between his arms. He looked too content to wake, even for a morning kiss.

Easing the dresser drawer open, I pulled out my gym shorts and a T-shirt, then tiptoed down the hall to the bathroom to brush my teeth and change. I left the baby-doll—a new candidate for the Lingerie Hall of Fame—on the bathroom door hook for an encore performance.

Back in the kitchen, I filled the well of the coffeemaker with water, scooped fresh grounds into the filter, and hit the "On" button. While I waited for the coffee to brew, I flicked on the small TV tucked in the corner next to the refrigerator.

"We're taking you on scene to John Joseph Heywood . . ."

"Do I smell coffee?" Nick wandered in, barefoot and in sweats. He came up behind me, nuzzling my neck with his scratchy chin while his soft hair tickled my cheek.

". . . two alarm townhouse fire last night at the thirtynine hundred block of Carpenter Avenue near the Carpenter School in Studio City."

I jolted to attention. The reporter onscreen stood across the street from a charred building I knew very well. "Nick—that's my old townhouse."

We stood together, watching, as the reporter continued, "Firefighters were called out to the townhouse just before one A.M. last night and found flames engulfing the south end of the building. Residents escaped safely after firemen went unit to unit, pounding on doors. Fed by high overnight winds from an approaching weather system, the fire swept through the dry trees and brush bordering the property, endangering the school and homes in the canyon. Though firefighters managed to contain the blaze, two of the townhouse units were heavily damaged."

"Thank God no one was injured." I said. "I wonder how a fire like that started in the middle of the night?"

"With this heat drying up all the vegetation, a small spark

in high winds can set off an inferno. They're lucky they caught the blaze before the fire spread into the canyon." He shut off the TV and took two mugs out of the cabinet, setting them on the counter while I brought out the milk and spoons. "Why are you up so early?" he said.

"My fault. My early trips to the gym this week reset Erzulie's feeding schedule. I tried to be quiet."

"As opposed to last night?" he said with a playful grin.

"You should take that as a compliment."

"I do. What's the plan for this morning?"

"Stan will be at my house at nine. I think I'll head over to Game On and see if Gretchen shows up. I want to ask her about Margaret Smith."

If I was going to even pretend to exercise, I needed nourishment first. I opened the cabinet and scanned the boxes on the second shelf. *What was the deal with guys and cold cereal?* Frosted Flakes, Cinnamon Toast Crunch—Froot Loops? Ah, Raisin Bran. Fiber and fruit worked for me. I reached for the purple box and filled two bowls halfway.

"I'll be back here by eight to shower and get dressed," I said, adding milk to my bowl. "What about you?"

"While you're working out, I'll go for a run and then clean up. I'll line up the Bull Valley calls. I'd like to locate Margaret today if I can."

Love him.

I cruised along Ventura Boulevard with the sunrise reflecting in my rearview mirror. The heavy winds during the night left a clear, crisp sky above and a shamble of leaves and broken branches on the ground. The only signs of life were the lights inside coffee shops prepping to open, and pigeons pecking through debris for breakfast. No delivery trucks blocking lanes, no people waiting at bus stops for rides to work. Even the early joggers and dog walkers slept in.

Turning into the Coldwater Curve lot at six-thirty, I spotted just two cars parked nose in at the Game On entrance. Lights gleamed inside and the TV in the deserted cardio room flickered news headlines through the window. I opened the door and heard a loud grunt echo from the corner of the weight room.

Earl stood beside a woman on the thigh machine. "You're up at the crack of dawn," he said to me across the empty gym.

"Nervous energy," I said, looking around. "Is anyone else here?"

"Nah. Mitzi and I open the gym every Saturday. Kyle should come rolling in pretty soon though. Need something?"

Mitzi and Earl. Two cars.

"I, uh, realized I forgot to switch my membership to my new address."

"You can do that easy. There are blank forms on the desk."

"Perfect, thanks." I went to the desk and picked up a form off the stack of blanks. As soon as Earl and his client turned their backs, I gathered up the pens scattered on the desktop and quietly dropped them into the wastebasket. "Earl? There aren't any pens up here."

"There's not?" He swung around, frowning. "Kyle has a box in his office."

"Don't leave your client," I said as he started coming toward me. "I can get them. Where's the key?"

He pointed at the desk. "In the top drawer."

I waved thanks, found the keys, and headed to the office along the wall and out of Earl's line of vision. With my pulse racing, I unlocked the door and sat behind Kyle's desk, leaving the door open to see and hear movement outside. The bottom drawer was locked. I slid open the top drawer and found the small round key I saw Kyle drop inside the day I interrupted his meeting.

Fingers trembling as I slid in the key, I opened the deep, file-sized bottom drawer. Brown grocery bags lined the bottom. I opened one and saw six brown pill bottles with a green label marked *Anadrol*. The white boxes in the second bag were labeled *Sustanon*. In the next bag, blue-and-white boxes labeled *Testostorona*.

"Anadrol" as in anabolic, and "Testostorona" as in testosterone. Steroids.

A rumbling outside drew my attention past the open door to the window facing the parking lot. The tail end of a car rolled past the gym. I returned the bags and locked the drawer in a rush, then tossed the key back where I found it.

Don't forget the pens. Where were the pens? I scanned the desktop in panic. No pens. No pens in the top drawer. Searching the floor behind me, I spotted a box of BIC pens on a stack of supplies in the corner. I grabbed two pens and dashed out.

As I secured the door behind me, Kyle pulled into the lot and parked his Jeep directly in front of the window. I raced down the aisle past the weight machines toward the desk, and dropped the office keys in the drawer.

Gretchen walked through the door and stopped, gaping at me. "What are you—?"

"I know. I woke up early and couldn't fall back asleep." I held up the Change of Address form, breathless. "Then I realized I hadn't changed my address here since I moved. No time like now."

Kyle stormed in behind her, dropped his satchel, and came at me. "What the hell were you doing in my office?" A six-foot-plus muscular mass of strength flushed with anger, he grabbed my arm with enough power to throw me across the room.

"Let me go." I pulled away, resisting him. "You're hurting me. I was in there less than a minute, looking for a pen."

He relaxed his grip but not his attitude. "Who let you in?" His demand echoed over the equipment.

"It was no big deal," I said, my heart pounding in my ears. "I needed a pen."

Earl jammed out of the free weight room, calling to Kyle as he crossed the room. "Hey man, take it easy."

"Did you let her in the office?" Kyle said, rounding on Earl.

"Yeah. So? It was Liz. I was busy."

Kyle thrust his finger at Earl's face. "What? Are you deaf?" He emphasized each phrase with a poke. "First Laycee, now Liz? Are you stupid?"

"You don't trust your partner's wife?" Earl kept his hands at his side, clenching and unclenching his fists. "I don't have to take this crap."

"This is my fault," I said, stepping between them. "My old townhouse burned last night and the news upset me. I came in here obsessed with changing the address you have on file. I wasn't thinking about anything except getting a pen to fill out the form. I'm really sorry." Kyle's hostile attitude softened to my lie. I turned to Earl. "Jarret is my ex-husband. I'm just a regular member here. Kyle has every right to question why I was in there."

"Whatever." Earl walked away, shaking his head and muttering.

Gretchen hovered in front of the cubbyholes, watching. When Kyle didn't bark back at me, she took a wide girth around us toward the cardio room.

"Members aren't allowed in the office. Understood?" Kyle said to me.

"Yes. It won't happen again." I forced a smile and picked up the pen.

He pocketed the keys from the drawer and left me at the desk, scribbling my name and address on the sheet even though I had a feeling I wouldn't be back. Once the DEA busted Kyle's side business, Game On could be history.

I finished and headed for the cardio room where Gretchen pedaled on a stationary bicycle. Taking the bike next to her, I slid my feet into the stirrups and began pedaling.

"Kyle's in a foul mood," I said. "I guess I picked the wrong day to give him my new address."

She turned. "Your old place burned last night?"

"I heard about the fire this morning on the news. Great building. I hope there's not too much damage. I moved out only a few months ago and I'm still catching up with changing my address everywhere. It's been a horrible week. First Laycee, then the townhouse . . ."

We pedaled in silence then Gretchen said, "You were friends with her, huh? The woman who died?"

"We used to be neighbors in Atlanta. We had some good times together." Flashing on Laycee and I sharing a joke in her kitchen, I swallowed back a twinge of sorrow. I said to Gretchen, "The other night at the game, you didn't mention that you and Jarret went to school together."

She jerked her head. "He told you?"

"We had dinner last night—"

"I know. I was with him when you called yesterday." Her eyes gleamed. "What did he say about me?"

"That you're from McHenry and exercised at Game On." I chuckled. "You know how bad men can be with details. So you knew Jarret when he was a kid?"

"He wasn't a kid. We met in high school. What else did he say about me?" Gretchen glowed like a smitten teenager.

"He said you had moved out here recently. L.A. is a big change from such a small town. Did you live in McHenry all your life?"

"Most of it. But Jarret made the move here easy for me. He's been showing me around a lot, hanging out. Yesterday we went out searching for a new house for him to buy." She smiled. "I wanted to help him take his mind off of his problems."

Gretchen's tone insinuated closeness. At our dinner, Jarret claimed he saw Gretchen occasionally. She rode the bike in a steady motion, arms lax at her side, eyes fixed on the TV above, only glancing at me on occasion. Her unwavering posture made it difficult to get a read on her body language for lies. Aware of Jarret's limited free time during the season, I went with his version.

"You must know Jarret's parents then," I said. "And the rest of his old friends?"

"Most of our friends from school moved away, like Jarret.

His parents and I stayed close. I used to see them around McHenry all the time."

"Marion and Bud are good people," I said. "Did any other McHenry folks move out to L.A.?"

"None that Jarret or I see."

People wandered into the gym, filling up the cardio machines. As the noise around us increased, I needed to get to the point with Gretchen before we were interrupted. I dropped the runaround and asked straight out, "Are you familiar with a woman from McHenry named Margaret Smith?"

She wrinkled her forehead. "Never heard of her. Why?"

"Jarret mentioned her name to me. Or maybe his mother did at one time or another. While we were married I didn't spend enough time in McHenry to meet his old friends, like you. Actually, I think Margaret lived in Bull Valley."

"Bull Valley is miles away. All of my and Jarret's friends lived in McHenry."

"What made you leave McHenry and your family?"

"I don't have family." She looked away, then said, "I'm an only child. My father passed away when I was ten. My mother died of a heart attack last year. The Coopers sent me flowers. Then Jarret invited me out here for a visit, and I decided to stay."

Jarret invited her? Her story and his drifted farther apart. Something about her relationship with the Coopers struck me as fraudulent. If she was so close to Jarret's family, why didn't I hear about her years ago?

"I'm sorry about your mother," I said.

"Don't be. We weren't close. I'm happier here."

"Then I'm glad you're settled in." I didn't know what else

242

to say. Gretchen was clearly smitten with Jarret and had nothing to offer about Margaret Smith. I stopped pedaling and stood up. "Have a good weekend, Gretchen."

"I will. You, too. What are your plans?" she said.

Aside from my interrogation at the police station, hunting down Margaret Smith, or turning in Kyle for dealing? "Kicking back. Going to a party tonight. What about you?"

"Jarret and I are having dinner."

Chapter Twenty-five

I circled through the weight room to the back studio. Led Zeppelin's "Kashmir" blasted over the overhead speakers. Earl slammed his gloved fists against the leather bag dangling off the ceiling in the corner.

"I hope I didn't make trouble for you with Kyle," I said over the music.

He punched at the bag. "He'll get over it. So will I."

"I didn't realize he's so touchy about his office."

A double fist to the bag. "Yeah. Tuesday afternoon he went off on Laycee, too"—lower cut to the bag—"like the jerk he is." Earl stopped and faced me. "Laycee flashed him a sweet Southern smile and more or less told him to shove it. Classic."

"She went into his office?"

"She interrupted one of Kyle's private meetings." Earl smirked. He eyed a member at the far end of the studio and leaned in close, dropping his voice. "I'm sick of the secrecy and superior attitude around here. If Jarret Cooper knew what Kyle was up to in that office, he'd fire his ass. Jarret should let me run the gym. I can bring in the clientele this place deserves. My clients are clean and they have money."

"Maybe you should talk to Jarret," I said. "Does he ever come in here?"

"Never. Jarret hasn't been around since the day Game On opened. If he wants to find out what's going on, he should spend a day here and see for himself. Some of us trainers are talking about moving our clients to the new gym down the block. Things have to change if Jarret wants us to stay. The only one making serious money here is Kyle Stanger." Earl spun around and kicked the punching bag with a wide leg swing.

I backed away and unrolled a blue mat on the floor in front of the mirror to stretch. My muscles relaxed into each long stretch as my mind exercised possibilities about Kyle, steroids, Laycee, and Jarret.

By seven-thirty, an unfamiliar weekend crowd jammed all three studios. I bought a bottle of water from the vending machine and as I gratefully downed cold water, my phone rang.

"Did I wake you?" Mom said.

"No, I'm just leaving the gym." I tossed the empty bottle into the recycle bin and walked outside.

"Then you haven't heard. Your townhouse burned last night."

"I saw the story on the news before I left this morning," I said, getting into my car. "What a nightmare. I'm glad everyone got out."

"I have a bad feeling about this, dear. I drew the Tower in my daily tarot reading—unexpected events, a life-changing jolt out of the past. When I saw the news about the fire, I knew the Tower card warning was for you."

Mom's morning tarot reads had little to do with fortune-telling and everything to do with whatever occupied her mind that day. Since I enlisted my parents' help to clear my name, I wasn't surprised she translated the card to fit me.

I drove out of the parking lot east onto Ventura Boulevard. "Please don't worry about me. I'm going to the station with Oliver today to talk to Carla Pratt. Nick and I picked up some new information yesterday about the symbol left on Laycee's body. The details may not clear me, but I'm hoping Carla will move me to the bottom of her suspect list."

"That's encouraging, dear. I worried we'd have to cancel your father's birthday party tonight."

"Better bake a file into the cake just in case, Mom. Carla is relentless."

"We already set your bail money aside," she said. We both chuckled, a welcome break from the underlying tension. "But dear, I can't shake this sense of a threat from something or someone else. I felt unsettled energy in your new house the other day. That woman was murdered in the house you lived in with Jarret, and now your old townhouse burned. I'm afraid a malevolent force is seeking you."

"Unfortunate coincidences. I wasn't in either house at the time. As soon as the plumber finishes my bathrooms, the disruption at home will settle." I eased into the left lane and turned left on Laurel Canyon Boulevard toward North Hollywood.

"Well, watch yourself, dear. And keep the doors locked. What time are you going to the police station?" Mom said.

"Eleven. I'm meeting Oliver at ten. We're going to the station together."

"Jarret left me a message yesterday. I have a mind to return his call and tell him what I think about all the trouble he's causing our family."

"Don't. Let's not give him a reason to sic his lawyer on me again. I had dinner with Jarret last night. Get this, his apology for shifting suspicion on me came with an excuse that a scandal would ruin his career."

"I suppose the team frowns on—" Mom clucked her tongue. "Never mind. The nerve. As if your career is less important than his."

"Right? You'll never guess who we ran into at the restaurant. Or literally, who ran into us." I told her about our confrontation with Forrest.

"They should have let him at Jarret," Mom said. "Just on principle."

"Believe me, Forrest tried. I'd never seen him so uncontrollable. If he suspected something went on between Laycee and Jarret, he may have been after both of them that morning and only found Laycee. The problem is—"

"Forrest didn't murder his wife," Mom said. "After we talked to you yesterday afternoon, your father and I went to the Sportsmen's Lodge and asked the bell captain and the desk clerk if Forrest left the hotel early Wednesday morning. The bellman saw him go into the Patio Café at eight."

So Forrest had a solid alibi even if he had tracked Laycee to Jarret's. I was left with drug-dealing Kyle Stanger, the untraceable Margaret Smith, a maybe jealous girlfriend in

247

Gretchen, or a random intruder as possible suspects. As Oliver would say, I was sunk.

"Is Dad home?" I said.

"He's right here." Mom muffled the phone. "Walter, your daughter wants to speak with you."

I parked at Nick's curb as Dad came on the line. "Detective Cooper reporting for duty. How's my girl?"

"I need your advice." I got out and walked toward the house, relating my office caper at the gym. Nick opened the door in a black T-shirt and jeans. When he heard me tell Dad about the drugs in Kyle's desk, Nick threw up his hands and went inside, shaking his head as I followed.

Dad exploded, blustering over the phone. "Stanger saw you?"

I perched on the sofa arm, waiting for Nick to stop pacing in front of me and for Dad to stop yelling in my ear. "What do I do now, Dad? Do I warn Jarret? Tell Carla about the drugs?"

"Screw Jarret," Nick said.

"Stanger is Jarret's partner," Dad said over the phone. "If Jarret already knows about the steroids, you'll put yourself in a very dangerous position. If he doesn't, why do you want to help the fool?"

"I don't know, Dad. That's why I'm asking you. What's the right thing to do?"

"The smart move is to take care of yourself. Jarret can solve his own problems," Dad said. "Consider how the information will affect Carla's investigation."

"If Laycee threatened to tell Jarret about the steroids, Kyle had a motive to kill her. She made a snarky comment about Kyle's income in front of Jarret the night before she died. We know Kyle had the garage door combination. Robin found proof connecting Kyle with the inverted pentagram."

"Definitely enough for Carla to interrogate Stanger again," Dad said. "What's important is how you conduct yourself with Carla today. She'll be softer on you if she views you as cooperative. Make sure Oliver has my number if he needs me."

"I will. Thanks, Dad."

Nick stood over me, arms crossed and frowning. "Stanger caught you in his office?"

"I had to find out what Kyle was up to. I found a chance to search his office and took it. Kyle didn't see how long I was in there." I started to get up. Nick stopped me.

"I don't like you taking risks. At best, Kyle will move the drugs out of the office so he won't be caught."

"And ruin his business? I doubt it." I tried to move around Nick. He wouldn't let me.

"At worst, you made a killer suspicious of you."

"Good. Let him show himself." I faced Nick nose-to-nose, which in our case meant mine tilted up under his. "I'm not going to apologize for trying to clear myself. I got the information I wanted, and more. I had an odd conversation with Gretchen, Jarret's old girlfriend from McHenry. If she stayed close to Jarret and his parents all these years as she claims, why was last night the first time I heard of it? I got the impression she's trying to revive or relive a high school fling."

Nick shrugged. "Doesn't make her a bad person. Did you ask her about Margaret Smith?"

"I did. She didn't know her. I can understand Jarret not knowing Margaret, but Gretchen lived in McHenry for years after he left. I wish Jarret's mother would call me back."

"So we're left with either Forrest or Kyle as a suspect. Or Jarret."

"Forrest is in the clear. A bellman at the hotel saw him in the Patio Café around the time of Laycee's murder. And even if I'm right about Kyle's motive, I don't understand why he killed her at the house—unless he intended to frame Jarret."

"Or Jarret committed the murder," Nick said.

"The symbol makes the least sense of all."

"I'm not giving up on the Schelz connection yet," Nick said. "There's a chance Schelz's daughter left a fake address at the prison. If we're lucky, the woman who gave Weisel the pamphlet will show up at the liquor store and we can talk to her. Until then, maybe Jarret's parents or one of the Smiths in Bull Valley or McHenry knows Margaret. We'll find her."

I read the time on the mantel clock. "We better get going. You have to meet Stan at my house in a half hour, and I should take a shower and get ready for my meeting with Carla." I froze, gut twisting with apprehension—if Carla had enough evidence to hold me, I might not be back.

Erzulie hopped on the sofa behind me and purred. I knew she would be safe with Nick. But my practice, my house, my—

"Liz?" Nick lifted my chin with his finger to face him. "You'll be fine. Meet me at your house after you're done."

"But what if—"

"'If they hang you I'll always remember you.'"

"What?"

"Joking." His eyes twinkled in affection. "It's a Bogart quote from *The Maltese Falcon*. Have confidence in the truth, Liz. And know that whatever happens, we'll get through this together." He picked up his keys and left me with a short kiss, walking out the door like he was going out for a carton of milk.

His light attitude and support calmed me. Smiling with confidence, I watched him drive away. I took a quick shower and dried my hair then put on slacks and a collarless white cotton blouse. As I added a touch of lipstick, Nick's desk phone rang.

After three rings his answering machine clicked on, echoing the message through the house. "Nicky? It's Izzy." Her voice, young with a Hispanic accent, came across as worried and questioning.

"Please, please call me back. I just left a message on your cell. We have to talk today. I haven't heard from you since Thursday and I'm going crazy. Did you have the conversation yet? You promised me you would talk to Liz before the weekend is over. I can't hide anymore. Everyone will know soon. Please call me. Love you."

Click.

Chapter Twenty-six

*L*ove *you? Be calm. Don't overreact. Maybe I misunder-stood.* I set the lipstick on Nick's bathroom sink, went into the living room, and replayed Isabella's message.

Nick promised her he would talk to me. *About what?* She's tired of hiding. *From what?* Everyone will know soon. *Know what?* "Love you" wasn't difficult to interpret. *Or was it?*

The message ended. I stood dazed, her words racing through my mind. Battling old feelings of betrayal and emotional abandonment, I tried to center myself. Stop. Be logical. Quit overreacting. How would I advise a client faced with the same situation?

Get more information. Talk to Nick. Face your fear.

Erzulie, with an uncanny knack of sensing when my body was in the room but my mind was in outer space, jumped on the desk and stared at me. I stroked her head. "You heard the message. What would you do?"

She jumped down and trotted away. Big help.

I had thirty minutes to drive to Oliver's Van Nuys office. In light Saturday morning traffic I could make it in twenty. Time to stop muttering to myself and get moving. Gathering my purse and keys, I left the house and traveled, head down, across the debris-ridden path to my car.

Buckling up, I pulled onto the street then called Nick. His cell rang once. I'd tell him about the message. Second ring. Let him explain. On the third ring his phone went to voice mail.

"Nick, it's me. Liz." *As opposed to your other girlfriend or girlfriends.* "I'm on my way to meet Oliver. Check your messages at home. Isabella called. She needs to talk to you right away." *So do I.*

I hung up without leaving my love, a substitute for you-better-explain-now. Instead of feeling better, I felt childish.

My psychology training didn't exempt me from runaway emotion. Intellectually, I understood my reaction: working myself up over Isabella's call allowed me to avoid my apprehension over meeting with Carla. I needed to talk things out with someone rational. When Robin answered her phone, I gave her the high points of Isabella's message.

"I'll kill him if he's cheating on you," she said.

"Don't do that. I'll need your support in the aftermath if it's true."

"Then I'll have Dave kill him. He'll be sad to lose his best friend but family comes first," Robin deadpanned. "But we do nothing until Nick has a chance to explain. I see the way he treats you, Liz. He adores you."

"So did Jarret."

"Do you hear yourself? Hello? Come join me here in the present. You're not the same person you were during your marriage. You're not stranded alone in a strange city, and Nick is nothing like Jarret, thank God. Where are you now? How much time do we have to talk?"

"I'm passing under the Hollywood Freeway on Victory. We have about ten minutes to locate my common sense."

"No problem. Tell me how you feel." Robin delivered my formula, solve-all psychology phrase with compassion in her voice.

"You love throwing that line at me."

"What can I say? I learned it from you. Talk."

I let go, venting my fears, suspicions, and insecurities in emotion-chocked spurts. Call-waiting beeped. I ignored it. Robin listened to me without interruption until I repeated how much I trusted Nick.

"Maybe you're afraid of how much he cares for you," she said. "You do trust him. You know he wouldn't cheat on you. You'll probably end up marrying the guy and you're terrified. Heck, you bought a house to avoid moving in with him."

"Not true. My house is an investment."

"You and Nick could have bought a house together."

"Our relationship was too new, Robin. I wasn't ready."

"Are you ready now?"

"Not if he has another woman on the side."

"And if he doesn't?" When I didn't answer, she said, "Listen, I realize you're afraid. Jarret stomped on your heart in the worst possible way. You trusted him and he cheated on you. So what? Ancient history. Forget about it and move on. Nick is amazing."

"Spoken like a woman with second chances on her mind," I said. "Anything you want to tell me about you and Dave?"

"Don't change the subject. Let's finish talking about you. It stinks that you heard Isabella's message right before your meeting with black-hearted Pratt. Are you ready for her?"

"Ready enough. Oliver will be with me," I said. "Robin, Izzy ended her call to Nick with 'Love you'."

"Big deal. I tell the barista I love him when he has my morning latte waiting for me every day at the Coffee Bean. I love Nick, too. Just not the way you do. And I will continue to love Nick until we have to off him for mistreating you—which will be never. Don't assume the worst. You forget Dave and Nick talk every day. If something iffy were up, Dave would tell me."

"He would? How did you crack through his code of silence so soon?"

"Brownies and lingerie. Not necessarily in that order. Very effective."

I stopped for the red light at Van Nuys Boulevard, smiling. I knew whatever happened, Robin would be there for me. "Okay. I'm calmer now. Breakdown is on official delay until after I talk to Nick."

"It could be worse. He could up and propose. Then what would you do?"

"Thank you. You now have managed to thoroughly distract me again. If Nick asks, you'll be the second person to hear my answer."

"I'll expect an update on the Isabella call tonight at the party. Dave and I are going gift shopping for your dad this afternoon. What did you get him?"

"A baseball autographed by the Cubs—Jarret got it for me. I don't like being indebted to him, but I know how much Dad will love the ball. Besides, I don't have time to squeeze in a shopping trip between my arrest and breakup."

"Don't even joke about that. Where is my objective friend? What did you do with her?" Robin said. "Accept the ball. Please. Jarret owes *you* after getting you involved in his mess."

The intersection light turned green. "I have to go. You're the best, Robin."

A block west of the boulevard, I turned into the driveway next to Oliver's office building and parked in the empty lot. I checked my phone. One unanswered call from Nick, no message. A small red dot on the e-mail app signaled one new message. I opened the inbox and read:

Sorry I missed your call. Got your message—we can talk later. Be strong with Carla. I love you. Nick.

I tucked the phone in my purse with a sigh. Later.

Oliver pulled into the lot in a dusty black Prius and parked in the space next to mine. He lowered his passenger window, waving a cigar at me. "Let's go."

"Let me get this straight," I said, watching him snuff the tip in the ashtray as I got in. "You drive a low-emission car but pollute the interior—the air you breathe—with cigar smoke?"

"Go figure." He brushed ashes off his legs and the coat of his tan suit, then shifted the car into gear. "Anything I should know since the last time we talked, Liz Cooper?"

"I had dinner with Jarret last night."

"What's with you? I told you not to go. Can't you stay away from the guy?"

"No—I mean, yes. I can." While we sped west on Victory Boulevard, I told him about Forrest's scene at the restaurant and my conversation with Jarret at dinner. Oliver kept his eyes fixed on the road, turning north onto Reseda Boulevard as I segued into the new info on Kyle, from the devil video to my steroid discovery.

"Geez," he said. "Are you one of those people who can't sit still? My youngest son always pokes around things, too. The kid is in constant motion. But he's nine. What do they call it? Hyper . . ."

"The common term would be childhood. And in extreme cases, a developmental disorder called ADHD. No, I'm not impulsive or hyperactive." I grimaced, irked by his lack of interest in my compelling new information. "You wanted other suspects for Carla."

"I wanted the *names* on her suspect list. Do you pay your taxes?"

"Yes."

"Then why the hell are you doing Pratt's job for her?"

I crossed my arms. "Are you serious? She'd like to arrest me."

"You done? Because now I'm going to tell you what you're NOT going to do in the interview. And this time, if you want me to remain your lawyer, you'll listen. No twitching, fidgeting, volunteering, or lying. Stifle headshakes and nods. No snide comments or any comments blaming the victim or the people you think are suspects. Don't answer any questions without looking at me for permission first. Got that?"

ROCHELLE STAAB

"Got it. Do I need your permission to cough or sneeze?"

He let my comment pass without a flicker of reaction. "Everything you say will be recorded. If she tries to provoke you, don't react, defend, or comment."

"Do you give all your murder suspects this speech?"

"Only the ones who are innocent." Oliver turned onto Vanowen, made a U-turn in the middle of the block and parked in front of the modern two-story West Valley Community Police Station. He switched off the ignition, then swung around to face me. "From now on, no more rogue investigations, Liz. I don't want you to get hurt." He opened his car door. "Come on. Let's get this over with before lunch."

The butterflies hit my stomach on the elevator ride from the spacious tiled lobby to the detective waiting room on the second floor. Oliver and I entered the empty reception area, a small lobby with six black metal chairs and a window to the street below. I took a seat facing the "WEST VALLEY DETECTIVE BUREAU" sign over the sliding glass reception window, my gaze flitting from the Wanted posters on the adjacent corkboard to the nearby exit.

While Oliver approached the officer behind the glass, I looked at my watch. We were on time. Checked it again. Same time. Oliver sat down next to me, tapping his thumbs to a silent beat. Two minutes, which felt like two hours later, a door next to the reception window opened and Carla beckoned us inside.

Oliver patted my knee encouragingly. "You're gonna do great."

We filed behind Carla past three gray cubicles down a small hall opening toward a massive room on the left with signs—"ROBBERY," "GANGS," "JUVENILE," and "HOMICIDE"—hanging above clusters of empty desks.

She opened a door into a small conference room furnished with a cherry-laminated table and eight padded chairs. Oliver rolled out a chair for me and I sat, spine straight, conscious not to swivel or fidget.

Carla took a seat across the table with what appeared to be an eight-by-ten frame enveloped in a plastic cover, facedown in front of her. "I appreciate you arranging your busy schedules to come here this morning. Would you like some coffee or water before we begin?"

"No, thanks. We're good," Oliver said.

"Then let's get started so we can enjoy the rest of the weekend. As you know, I'm investigating Mrs. Huber's homicide and I have a few unanswered questions that I hope Dr. Cooper can clear up for me. How are you today, Liz?"

"I'm—"

Oliver nudged my knee.

I smiled at her to signify my good health and carefree attitude. The picture of calm—if she didn't notice my quivering upper lip.

"Great," she said. "I don't think this will take long. I understand you weren't at your office last week. Why?"

At Oliver's nod I said, "I took the week off to finish unpacking while the plumbers were at my house."

"And to spend time with Mrs. Huber?"

"No. I had no idea she would be in town."

"Yet Mrs. Huber told several witnesses she came to visit you. Can you explain why?"

"She lied."

Carla took out a notebook and flipped through the pages.

A prop, I knew from Dad and Dave, to buy time or make me uncomfortable. She stopped on a page. "The morning of Mrs. Huber's death, her husband called you, looking for her. According to Mr. Huber, you told him you hadn't seen his wife since the prior morning. But here's where I'm confused—Kyle Stanger heard you and the victim argue the night before at the Dodger game." Carla closed her pad and stared at me. "So why did you lie to Mr. Huber?"

Chapter Twenty-seven

Air hummed through the vent in the conference room ceiling as I turned to Oliver for permission to answer Carla's question. He met my eyes with a cautious nod,

"I assumed Laycee and Kyle were on a date at Dodger Stadium," I said. "Telling Forrest I saw her at the game would invite questions I didn't want to answer. Frankly, I didn't want to put myself in the middle of the Huber's marriage problems."

Carla let out a dramatic sigh. "Smart move. Mr. Stanger, however, claims they attended an ATTAGIRL network business function together at the stadium. And then Laycee ended up spending the night with your ex-husband. Boy, she really got around, didn't she?" Carla flashed me an exaggerated, let's-get-down-and-talk-trash-about-that-floozy look.

No kidding. If Oliver hadn't warned me against attacking

Laycee's character, I might have thrown up my hands in hearty agreement. Alerted by Carla's theatrical segue from inquisitive pro to my new bestest friend, I turned to Oliver again. He stared at his hands, laced in front of him on the table. No permission. No comment.

"Are you right- or left-handed?" Carla said.

"I'm right-handed," I said. Oliver cleared his throat.

Her brow furrowed. "Let's go over your movements from the time you left the stadium Tuesday night until your conversation with Mr. Huber the following morning."

"You already took a statement from Liz. Is this necessary?" Oliver said.

"Dr. Cooper's statement only covered Wednesday morning until she met her plumber at her home. I want an extended account of her hours before and after," Carla said.

Oliver gave me a nod, holding my eyes long enough to convey *Go ahead with discretion*. I pondered a moment and then launched into details about Tuesday night, editing out the romp with Nick in my backyard, and then continuing through Wednesday morning. I ended with my breakfast at Aroma and Forrest's call.

Carla scribbled notes on her pad then turned over the plastic envelope and slid it across the table at me. "Do you recognize this?"

The clear envelope encased a framed copy of Jarret's and my wedding picture with the glass shattered into a web of cracks.

Once again, I glanced at Oliver. On his nod, I answered, "It's my wedding picture."

"And?"

Checking with Oliver was monotonous, but we got a

rhythm going. If he looked at me I would answer; if he didn't look, I didn't talk. This time he looked.

"The glass on the frame is broken. What else do you want me to say? I haven't looked at my wedding pictures for a long time. It was another life, Carla."

"Smashed. You can see the glass on the frame had been smashed." Carla frowned. "I mean, if I walked in my ex's bedroom and saw the woman who ended my marriage sprawled naked on his bed with my wedding photo there on the nightstand next to her? Who wouldn't be furious enough, in the heat of the moment, to destroy the woman and the photo?" She squinted at me. "It's almost like they had sex right in front of you—for spite. Laycee stole your husband, ruined your marriage, and then came back for more. Is that why you killed her?"

Heat flushed through my body. I inhaled, exhaled slowly, then with all the dignity I could gather said, "I didn't kill Laycee."

"Move on, Detective," Oliver said.

Carla stood the frame in the center of the table. "This was beneath the bed where the victim was found. How did it get there?"

Oliver touched my hand, stopping me from answering, then said to Carla, "You wouldn't be showing us this if her fingerprints were on the glass or the frame. How would Liz know who moved it? She already stated she didn't go into the bedroom that morning."

"I'd like Liz to answer anyway," Carla said calmly.

"She already addressed your question," Oliver said. "Move on."

The ensuing series of questions and answers bounced

like a three-way Ping-Pong game. Carla asked me, I looked at Oliver, and he either nodded permission or answered for me.

"When was the last time you were in Jarret's bedroom?" Carla said.

"I honestly don't remember," I said. "Years ago."

"Why did your marriage end?"

"Their divorce decree stated the reason," Oliver said. "Irreconcilable differences."

Bravo to Ollie for doing his homework.

"Did your differences involve your husband's infidelity?" she said.

"Don't answer, Liz." Oliver leaned across the table. "I have some questions for you, Detective. Do you have evidence that places my client in the bedroom with the victim? Fingerprints? Hair samples? No? Do you have any questions for Liz about your other suspects?"

Carla set her elbow on the table, watching him with her chin resting on her palm.

Oliver pushed his chair back. "Then I think we're done for today. I'm hungry. If I don't eat, my blood sugar will drop and I'll get cranky. We're free to leave, right?"

"Yes," Carla said in a clipped tone.

"Good." He opened the door for me and said, "Liz, I need a few minutes alone with Detective Pratt. Wait for me downstairs, will ya?"

As I exited, I tugged at his sleeve and led him into the hall with me. In a whisper, I said, "What about Kyle and the information I gave you on the symbol? Carla needs to—"

"Hear it from me. The less you say, the better," he said. "I'll meet you outside."

I handed him the DVD of Billy's movie then left without argument. Freedom was a short elevator ride away.

Instead of waiting in the lobby, I paced the small concrete plaza out front, letting fresh air soothe the remnants of my nerves. I dialed Nick, then remembered Isabella's message and my heart clunked into my stomach. I hung up before the first ring.

Oliver blew out of the station door in a whirl—loosening his tie, taking off his suit coat, and pulling out his keys. He cocked his head for me to follow, and we walked at a brisk pace to the curb.

As soon as we settled into his car I said, "What do you think? How did we do?"

"Pratt's got nothin'. I grade her a one and a half on her third-degree—hungry to make an arrest *and* she's a loose cannon." He checked over his shoulder then pulled into the heavy traffic on Vanowen. "When I brought up Schelz's daughter, she brushed me off. Then I put her on Stanger's trail with the information on the drugs and the symbol."

"You didn't tell her I—"

"Got the information? No. I let her assume McCormick did the investigation. I left you out of it." He looked over at me. "And you should stay out of it."

"What if Nick locates Margaret Smith in McHenry, or the woman who gave Schelz's pamphlet to Weisel shows up at the liquor store again?"

"You call me and I'll get McCormick to do the follow-up."

"Then what's next?" I said. "Will Carla leave me alone now? Do I get my box of books back?"

"Cool it on the books. You'll get them back at the end of

the investigation unless the killer smeared fingerprints all over the box. Now? We wait. Pratt may want to see you again. I think the pressure is off for this weekend. Go home. Have some fun. You did good. She gave up more information than she got."

"Right—the photo," I said. "When Carla showed me the frame, I didn't stop to think about why it was broken. Jealousy? Envy? Spite? Why would the killer smash my wedding picture? I don't get the connection."

"Pratt thinks she made one—Laycee broke up your marriage."

"My marriage faltered long before Laycee crawled into bed with Jarret. She was a catalyst but not the cause."

Oliver dropped me off at my car with instructions to call if I heard from Carla again, and warning me to give up playing detective for the rest of the weekend. No problem—assuming Carla backed off for the moment.

I cranked up my air conditioner and turned the local rock station on loud in an effort to block negative thoughts of a confrontation with Nick. *Nicky.* Didn't work. Despite the blaring music, I spent the drive home creating scenarios between Nick and Isabella. The ugly knot of traffic I fought through the Valley to Studio City gave me plenty of time to torture myself.

By the time I pulled up behind an old compact and Nick's SUV parked at the curb in front of my house, I had set myself up for an invitation to their wedding. At least one thing was going right—Stan's white truck sat parked in the driveway. I didn't hear the squeal of a drill blasting through the closed windows on the second floor but the plumber was somewhere inside working.

I climbed my porch steps with trepidation, opened the door, and crossed the foyer to the living room. I stopped short. A plump, pie-faced, twentyish Latina in an oversized UCLA T-shirt nestled in the corner of my couch, talking on her cell phone.

She brushed an explosion of black frizzy hair off her face and broke into an open smile. "Liz?"

"Yes. And you are?" I glanced past her into the den. Nick sat at my desk with his back to us.

"I'll call you back," the girl said into the phone. She unwrapped her tight-clad legs, rolled off the sofa, and rose to greet me. In heels, she might clear five feet in height; in her flip-flops, the top of her head barely reached my chin. She tilted her head back to look up at me, her eyes sparkling. "I'm Isabella. I'm so happy I finally got to meet you. Nicky told me many, many wonderful things about you."

Her little hand pumped mine with enthusiasm. A string of clichés rolled through my mind: "Love is blind," "Love conquers all." Maybe she was a genius. Or—

"You're free. You escaped the wrath of Pratt." Nick rushed from the den with his arms spread wide and rocked me in a warm embrace. "I thought about you all morning. Why didn't you call as soon as you left the station?"

"I couldn't wait to get home." Not a lie, just subject to interpretation. I glanced past him into the den. Seriously, where did he hide the statuesque sex-bomb I drove myself into distraction over?

"I see you met Izzy," he said.

"I did." I managed an uncertain grin. "What a . . . nice surprise."

"I recruited her help to make calls to McHenry about Margaret," he said.

"Did you find her?" I said, happy to escape utter confusion for a moment.

"No. I want to hear what Carla had to say, but first let's talk about Izzy's call this morning. Your message sounded distant. I think you may have misunderstood."

You think?

"I'm so sorry." Blushing, Izzy took my hand between hers and said, "I must have sounded crazy, pushing Nicky so hard. I consider him family and sometimes I forget he's not. I'm freaked out because my grandfather will be here on Monday for a visit. He doesn't know yet."

Neither did I. I creased my brow, still struggling to follow. The doorbell rang. Nick answered, and a slim young man in his early twenties followed him through the foyer carrying two paper bags.

Sweet-faced and well-groomed in a polo shirt and fitted jeans, the young man stopped under the living room arch and said, "Where should I put the tacos, Izzy?"

"First come and meet Liz." She bounced to his side and tugged him toward me, her face glowing with affection. "Liz, this is my fiancé, Jorge."

Fiancé. Well, I got the wedding invite right but miscast the groom. Relief flooded through me, then shame for doubting Nick.

"Very nice to meet you, ma'am," Jorge said, a shy smile

on his face. He set the bags on the coffee table, and wrapped a loving arm around Izzy.

"A complete pleasure, Jorge," I said. A *complete* pleasure. Nick grinned at the young couple like a proud uncle. I tucked my hand under Nick's elbow and said in a low voice, "You might have mentioned this to me a few days ago."

"I just found out myself. I was going to tell you, but clearing up Carla's crazy accusations toward you took priority," he said.

"Don't blame Nicky," Izzy said. "Jorge and I kept our engagement a secret from everyone." She pointed at the brown bags. "Can we tell you the whole story over lunch? Jorge brought tacos from Henry's."

"I would like that a lot," I said. "I'll get some plates. We can eat in the dining room."

"Let us set the table," Jorge said. "Izzy and I will get everything ready so you and Nick can talk." He picked up the bags and scurried Izzy to the kitchen. I'd known the kid for less than five minutes yet he was scoring points by the second.

When they were out of earshot I said to Nick, "When Izzy left you that message this morning, I thought—"

"I know," he said. "I heard it in your voice. That's why I asked her to bring Jorge here so you could meet both of them. This is my fault for not introducing you to Izzy months ago."

"No, I'm sorry for letting my old fears creep into our relationship. Next time—"

"I won't try to manage you," Nick said.

"You manage me?"

"I said *try*."

Stan appeared at the foot of the stairs. "Mr. Garfield, I'm taking a lunch break. The plaster in the second bathroom is drying. I'll be back at two."

"We'll see you then," Nick said.

After he left I said to Nick, "Stan calls you Mr. Garfield?"

"Damn right he does. We had a long talk this morning. I'm not happy with the speed of your renovations or the budget he showed me. As Melvyn Douglas said in *Mr. Blandings Builds His Dream House*, 'You've been taken to the cleaners, and you don't even know your pants are off,'" Nick said. "Pending your approval, Stan quoted a new estimate to finish the whole job, and then I reduced the number by twenty percent. He promised the shower in your spare bathroom would be usable tonight. Your master bath will be completed by Wednesday, on budget."

"And if it's not?"

"The full renovation on the second bathroom goes to another plumber."

"Did you bully him?" I pictured Stan on his way home instead of going to lunch. After he warned the plumber grapevine about Nick, I would never have a working shower in my own house again.

"Not at all. We got along famously. I earned his respect by speaking tool."

"Tool?"

"It's a derivative language spoken by artisans. Ancient. Very—"

"You can name all the thingies he carries in his toolbox."

"Correct."

Jorge and Izzy called us into the dining room. We sat around my oak table eating tacos while Izzy explained how she met Jorge in the UCLA library and they fell in love. Trapped in the lie she told her grandfather before she left Costa Rica last summer, Izzy let him assume she was still engaged to Nick. Now that her grandfather was on his way to the States for a visit, she had to reveal the truth—she and Jorge wanted to marry.

"I don't know how to tell him. Even my parents don't know about Jorge yet." She crumbled the last bite of her taco into the yellow wrapping on the plate. "After Jorge and I graduate, we want to move to Costa Rica. Nicky always talks about what a good psychologist you are. On Thursday, I asked him if maybe I could come to you for advice." She looked across the table at me, pleading. "I love my grandfather. I don't want him to be angry. What should I do?"

Jorge reached for her hand. Their eyes searched my face as if their happiness depended on my answer.

I gave them a comforting smile. "Be gentle. Sit your grandfather down in a private setting. A place you won't be interrupted. Tell him you have something you need to talk about that may be difficult to understand. Reassure him that you love him, then tell him the truth."

"That I lied?" Izzy's face creased in alarm.

"You might not want to open with a confession," I said gently. "I think it's important for your grandfather to understand where you're at right now. After you left home with Nick—a friend—you fell in love with Jorge. Focus on your feelings instead of past behavior. Avoid excuses. If he gets angry, resist the urge to fight or withdraw. The kindest thing you can do is to listen and to acknowledge how he feels about this new information. And until he arrives in town, try not to imagine a problem that doesn't exist," I said with a shamed glance at Nick. "Trust your heart, Izzy. Your whole family will be very happy for you. It's clear to me how much you and Jorge love each other. Your grandfather will see it, too."

Chapter Twenty-eight

"Your home is beautiful," Izzy said as we rinsed off the lunch dishes in the kitchen. "And I love your yard."

"Thank you." I glanced through the back window, beaming. "The lemon tree is my favorite. When I was a little girl, I felt positive I could pay my way to Disneyland with a lemonade stand if my dad would plant a tree for me. He did, and my mom and I made fresh lemonade every summer. I never quite got that stand going, though."

"I love fresh lemonade," she said, drying her hands. "Is it okay if we make some?"

"If you remember the measurements. It's been years. I can't be trusted without a cookbook."

"My mama taught me, too. If you get the sugar and a pitcher, I'll put our men to work outside." Izzy called over her shoulder into the dining room, "Jorge, Nicky—we need eight or ten of the fattest lemons from the tree."

Within minutes, we became a lemonade production line. Jorge sliced the fruit; Nick extracted the juice. Izzy made simple syrup in the pitcher with the sugar and hot water. I poured in cold water, then filled four glasses with ice.

"Izzy gets the first taste—this was her idea," I said. We watched in anticipation as she took a sip.

She puckered her lips and shuddered. *"Perfecto."*

"Killer," Jorge said after tasting. He glanced at me. "I'm sorry. I mean . . . I shouldn't have . . . Izzy and Nick told me that you . . . Oh man, did I just mess up big time?"

"Not at all," I said, grinning at his clumsy apology. "I agree with you—about the lemonade, of course."

"Tell us what happened at the station this morning, Liz," Nick said. "Are you off Pratt's suspect list?"

"For the moment." I gave them a shortened version of my morning with Carla, ending with the damaged photo she had in evidence. "Why would Laycee's killer smash an old wedding photo?"

"Laycee's husband had a reason—he hated Jarret," Nick said.

"We already ruled out Forrest," I said. "And if Kyle Stanger killed Laycee and left the symbol, why destroy the picture?"

"Again—hated Jarret?" Nick said. "The photo meant something to the killer. Nothing else in the bedroom got trashed."

"What about your ex-husband's girlfriend?" Jorge said. "Maybe she was jealous."

"I assume Detective Pratt queried Jarret about his love life. He dates around. There's one woman I know of who's infatuated with him. If a jealous lover killed Laycee and left the symbol, why smash the wedding photo, too? Our divorce happened years ago."

"But he kept the picture in his bedroom," Izzy said. "Maybe this killer thought Laycee was you."

"Me?"

"The photo of Laycee in the news looks just like you," Izzy said. "I noticed the resemblance as soon as I met you."

"I can see it, too," Jorge said. "You're both pretty, same dark hair, same size."

"They have a point, Liz," Nick said. "Remember, the moment I saw Laycee lying facedown in Jarret's bed, I confused her for you. The curtains were drawn."

I downed my lemonade and set the glass down slowly, mulling their idea. Jarret joked about using me as a buffer when women got too close to him. Did one of them mistake Laycee for me? I wasted my morning visualizing Nick in an affair with Izzy though I knew nothing about her and little about their friendship. It wasn't far-fetched to think one of Jarret's women viewed me as competition. Wrong, but not far-fetched.

"I'll accept the jealousy angle," I said, turning to Nick. "Carla accused me of killing Laycee out of jealousy. I practically accused Forrest of the same. Nick, you said Laycee was found lying facedown. It's crazy to imagine a killer deciding it was me in the bed without seeing a face. Besides, *any* woman in Jarret's bed might trigger a seriously unstable lover to commit a crime of passion."

"Schelz's version of the symbol introduced the section on vengeance," Nick said.

"It fits the theory—retaliation for stealing Jarret." I leaned on the counter. "Anger acted out with violence often connects to low self-esteem or a history of childhood abandonment."

"Leading us back to Margaret Smith again." Nick put his glass down. "In essence, Schelz abandoned his children when he got sent to prison."

"Valid point. But even Gretchen didn't know the mysterious Margaret."

"Yes, what about Gretchen?" Nick said.

"She's certainly infatuated with Jarret, but Gretchen would be able to tell Laycee and me apart—she saw us together at the gym Tuesday morning. What would Gretchen be doing at Jarret's house that early? And how would she get in? From what Jarret told me, he doesn't see her that often."

"Maybe he had a fan stalking him," Jorge said.

"The killer needed access to the house," I said. "Kyle Stanger had a possible motive, opportunity, knowledge of the symbol, and Jarret's security code. He could have bumped the photo off the nightstand by accident then stepped on it. Nick, do you remember anything else about the room?"

He tapped his fingers to his mouth. "I saw Laycee face-down on the left side of the bed with her hand draped over the side, a sheet half covering her legs. A pink shirt, white pants, and purse were on a chair next to the nightstand."

An icy shiver ran through me. Laycee wore the pink Dodger T-shirt to the game. Gretchen saw me in an identical pink shirt that night.

"What is it, Liz? You're pale."

"I have to find Jarret's parents," I said. "Will you excuse me?"

Izzy tugged at Jorge's sleeve. "We have errands to do this afternoon. Let's leave so Liz and Nick can be alone."

"Promise me you'll call me right after you talk with your family," I said to Izzy as we escorted them out to their cars.

"I promise." Izzy wrapped her arms around me. "Thank you, Liz. You're a goddess."

I turned and pecked Jorge on the cheek. "Be patient with her family. You're wonderful. They'll love you."

"I hope so," he said.

"Cute couple," I said to Nick as they drove away. "Izzy's great. Now I understand why you helped her."

Stan returned from his lunch break. After I approved the updated renovation estimate, Nick followed the plumber upstairs. I headed to the den and dialed Marion Cooper, the only person other than Jarret who might have additional insight on Gretchen. No answer. I flipped on the TV to the Dodger game. The visiting team was at bat with two outs in the top of the ninth inning and no one on base. The Dodgers led ten to nothing. I watched the last batter strike out, giving the Dodgers the win.

I puttered around, cleaning up the dirty glasses in the kitchen and taking out the garbage. I missed little Erzulie following me around. Being there without her made me realize how much she made our house a home. My phone signaled Jarret's incoming text—he'd be home in forty minutes.

Raucous laughter came from the top of the stairs then Nick's voice. "Let's hope anything that can go wrong, won't."

"Not this time, Mr. G.," Stan said. "I gave you my word."

"Assure Liz, not me."

Nick walked into the kitchen alone and smiling. "Looking good upstairs. The plaster in the spare bath is drying now. You can shower here tomorrow if you want to. On Monday, Stan's putting in your new tub. After the tiles seal and dry, your master bathroom will be ready Wednesday."

"Thank you. That makes me very, very happy. I won't be showering at the gym after Kyle gets busted for drugs or arrested for murder."

"You don't accept the theory the killer mistook Laycee for you?"

"Would you, if you were in my position? It would mean someone out there hates me, and right now only one guess comes to mind." I told Nick about the matching T-shirts and Gretchen's infatuation with Jarret.

"Maybe it's time to tell Carla your suspicions," Nick said.

"Not yet. If I accuse Gretchen on a hunch, I'd be doing to her what Jarret's lawyer did to me. She saw me in the T-shirt, but so did thousands of other people at Dodger Stadium. I'm going to run up to Jarret's to pick up Dad's birthday gift. I'll ask him about Gretchen again and give him the dirt I learned about Kyle. I'll meet you at your house later."

Traffic moved quickly along Ventura Boulevard from my house through Sherman Oaks. My phone rang at the light at Beverly Glen Boulevard and I fumbled through my pocketbook, catching the call just before it went to voice mail.

"Liz? It's Marion Cooper. Yah, I hope it's not too late to call you. I got your message last night. Bud and I spent all day at the county fair. We ate chicken-fried bacon and fried Twinkies. Can you imagine?" Her hearty chuckle trailed into a smoker's cough.

I imagined a heart attack and lung disease, but laughed with her nonetheless. "It sounds like you had a good time. Thanks for calling me back."

"Bud wanted to see the tractor pull and visit the animal barns. I held my nose all afternoon hiking past animal poop. He wanted to stay for the pageant but my feet were killing me."

Fascinating. "I won't keep you for too long. Do you remember Jarret's high school friend Gretchen Kressler?"

"Gretchen? Yah. Sure. Jarret dated her the year before he left for college. We haven't talked to her since you and Jarret became engaged," she said. "Why?"

Check off Gretchen's claim of continuing friendship with Marion and Bud as a lie. "Before I answer, is or was there a family in the area named Schelz? Three children, one of them around Jarret's age?"

She paused. "Not that I can think of. When did they live here? Did you ask Jarret?"

"They would have come sometime in the late eighties or early nineties. Jarret didn't recognize the name. What about Margaret Smith from Bull Valley?"

"Smith is Gretchen's married name. Gretchen is a nickname for Margaret. She began calling herself Margaret after she married Randy Smith from Bull Valley." Her voice slowed with suspicion. "Why?"

I tightened my hold on the steering wheel. The left turn lane at Sepulveda backed up a half block, giving me time to grasp at my fast-draining composure. "Jarret mentioned Gretchen to me last night. Will you tell me more about her? I'm surprised I didn't hear about or meet her over the years."

"You can thank me for protecting both of you. Gretchen was a troubled, moody girl. I honestly don't understand what my son saw in her. I warned her to stay away from Jarret after your engagement."

I dismissed moody—what teenage girl *isn't* moody, and said, "Troubled how?"

"Clingy and possessive," Marion said. "Bud and I thought Gretchen was far too serious about Jarret. We tried our best to keep him busy, but she was always around. If she wasn't with him, she called the house every hour looking for him."

"How did they get together? I thought Jarret lived and breathed baseball in high school."

"He did. But she was on the pep squad and, to be honest, I think she joined to be near him. Their teams practiced on the school field at the same times and, of course, the pep squad went to every game. We hoped for a breakup when he left for college and she stayed in town, but when he came home to visit us, she wouldn't leave him alone. Once I woke up and found her in my kitchen, cooking Jarret breakfast. You don't know how happy we were when he met you."

Or how devastated Gretchen must have been. Possessiveness led to jealousy, and jealousy could prompt irrational action. Carry a torch for twenty years? Absolutely. If she confused sex for love—as a teenaged girl might—her unresolved feelings could carry into adulthood. In fact, time and distance added to over-romanticizing an old relationship, especially if her marriage soured.

"I never heard you talk about her," I said.

"You and Jarret were so happy together. I thought it best to put Gretchen in the past."

"Gretchen goes by her maiden name now. What happened to her marriage?" I said.

"Randy left her for another woman last November," Marion said. "We never tell Jarret anything about her. That first weekend he brought you home from college to meet us, Gretchen sat in her car in front of our house. Bud finally went out and told her to leave. After she married Randy, we thought her obsession with Jarret would be over, but she sent Jarret letters and birthday cards at our address for years. I threw everything away, unopened. It wasn't easy to avoid her—Bull Valley is only a few miles away."

"What about her family?" I said.

"The father died before they moved here," Marion said. *Schelz is in prison for life. Close enough.* "She had an older sister and a much younger brother." *Three children—same as the Schelz family.*

"Had?" I said.

"About a year after Gretchen married Randy, her mother, sister, and little brother died in a horrible house fire," she said. "There were rumors about arson but no arrests."

I had heard three stories about fires within twenty-four hours: The address Margaret Smith gave the prison burned last December, a month after Gretchen's husband left her; Gretchen's family died in a fire; and someone torched my former townhouse last night. Coincidence or connected? As I edged closer to Jarret's neighborhood, I ticked off a list of Gretchen's lies—her name, her marriage, her lack of siblings, her relationship with Jarret's parents, and the timing of her mother's death.

"Did Gretchen know your garage door code?"

"All of Jarret's friends did," she said.

"One last question. Did you ever hear Gretchen talk about devil worship?"

"I would have barred her from my house if she did. Liz, you're worrying me. Was Gretchen the woman who died at Jarret's house?"

"No, Marion. The victim was Laycee Huber, a woman Jarret and I knew in Atlanta. Jarret told me a little about Gretchen last night. Margaret Smith's name came up during the investigation. I didn't know Gretchen and Margaret were the same person until you told me. She moved to Los Angeles a few months ago using her maiden name."

Her voice sank. "Jarret didn't tell us. I pray he's not involved with her again. That woman is disturbed."

Chapter Twenty-nine

I passed the entrance to the 405 on Sepulveda and as I drove under the freeway bridge marking the end of the business district and the beginning of the upscale residential section, the driver behind me tooted his horn. I glanced in my rearview mirror and saw a familiar red sports car with the convertible top down. Jarret tipped his Ray-Ban Aviators and, oozing charm, flashed his celebrity smile.—the wide, cocky grin he broke out in public. A heart-melting, bad-boy expression a girl could and would fall for. I did, a long time ago. So had Gretchen.

He maintained a car length's distance behind me until the turn on Royal Oak Road, then he playfully tailgated me on the slow wind through the sunlit arc of lush green trees leading up the hill. Two blocks from his street, he eased back. In the rearview mirror I saw him talking on his headset. Definitely not smiling. I swung my car up his asphalt driveway and stopped at the apron of pavement in front of his garage. Jarret parked next to me, still deep in conversation. I heard him before I got out of my car, his voice resonating loud through the quiet of the sheltered neighborhood.

"For God's sake, Ma, I saw Gretchen once and only because she begged me. I wouldn't be seen in public with her, much less date her. There's nothing going on between us. There never will be. I dumped her years ago—why would I care about her now?" From the agitated twist on his face, I assumed Marion Cooper had hung up from me, made a pot of coffee, lit a cigarette, and called her son to offer an opinion on his renewed contact with Gretchen.

I stood away from his car to give him privacy although he spoke loud enough for anyone within driving distance to hear the contemptuous description of what he called a one-time pity dinner with Gretchen. While I waited for him to finish, I gazed at the house with a tinge of melancholy. The front door stood centered between bushes lining the windows to a gourmet kitchen suitable for a master chef, and the sliding glass doors to the bedrooms we had planned as guest rooms or offices. The living room, great room, and master suite created an *L* across the back of the house, facing the pool, custom brick outdoor kitchen, and the landscaped yard.

After Jarret bid his mother good-bye, I turned, bracing for the backlash.

He got out of his car, his tan barely masking his red-faced anger. "You riled my mother over a pathetic case like Gretchen? Are you *serious*?"

"Very serious, and stop shouting." I walked ahead of him to the front door stoop then turned. "You must realize

Gretchen is infatuated with you again. There are a few things we have to talk about before you see her tonight."

"See Gretchen? What makes you think I'm seeing her tonight?"

"This morning at the gym she told me the two of you are having dinner together," I said.

"That's crazy. I'm staying home, alone. Why are you talking to Gretchen and why the hell did you call my mother about her?"

"Please listen to me, Jarret. Gretchen's been lying to you."

He folded his arms. "About what?"

"Do you know who Margaret Smith is?"

"No. And why should I give a damn?"

"She's the daughter of Herrick Schelz, a devil worshiper serving life for murder in the Indiana State Penitentiary. I saw the symbol the killer left on Laycee in a pamphlet Schelz wrote, and a copy of that pamphlet surfaced recently at a liquor store in Sherman Oaks. Dave traced Margaret Smith to an address in Bull Valley. I called your mother to ask if she knew her."

"What the hell does all of this have to do with Gretchen?"

"Gretchen *is* Margaret Smith, Jarret. She's known the symbol since childhood. Your mother confirmed Gretchen knows your garage code. I think Gretchen came here that morning to surprise you, saw Laycee in your bed, and killed her out of jealousy."

He staggered back a step, wide-eyed. "Pratt asked me about women I'm dating. I didn't even think to mention Gretchen. What a freak. Are you sure?"

"Sure enough to take this information to the police. I'm worried Gretch—" The front door flew open behind me.

"Liz!" Jarret lurched forward, sweeping me to the side with his hand. I stumbled off the stoop into the bushes, stunned, as Gretchen plunged a knife into Jarret's left shoulder, ripping through his flesh. I scrambled to the pavement on my knees, grabbed at her legs, and jerked her off him. Jarret staggered back. The knife clanged to the pavement.

"Why won't you die?" Gretchen yanked a fistful of my hair. "I stabbed you in his *bed*. I burned your house. What are you? Why won't you die?"

I shoved at her chest. She lunged for my throat. Jarret wrapped his right arm around her waist, yanking her off me.

He held her mid-air, blood pouring from the slash on his shoulder. She thrashed, wild-eyed and kicking. His face blanched from pain—I knew he wouldn't be able to hold her mid-air for long. I bent my knees, loaded my strength, and drove my fist into her stomach. The impact knocked the wind out of her. Jarret let go. Gretchen fell to the pavement, facedown and gasping.

Jarret pinned her down with his knees, blood seeping from the gaping wound on his shoulder. I ran to my car, pulled out my phone, and called 911.

"Let me go, Jarret," Gretchen pleaded. "You love *me*. You've always loved me. I'm not going to let her have you again."

The operator confirmed an ambulance and squad car on the way as I dashed into the house, phone to my ear. I turned on the kitchen faucet and dampened two hand towels. An unopened bottle of Jarret's favorite scotch and two raw steaks on a broiler pan sat on the counter next to the sink. A salad bowl filled with lettuce stood beside a sliced tomato on a chopping block. Gretchen must have let herself in, and was preparing dinner for Jarret when we arrived.

Outside on the driveway, she begged Jarret to let her go, her voice so clear I realized she had heard all of Jarret's insults and my accusations. I wrung out the towels and rushed back to Jarret.

"Don't let her touch you. She's not human," Gretchen said, struggling to turn beneath the pin of Jarret's knees as I ripped his shirt away from his wound. "Let me go. We can be together."

"Shut up, Gretchen," I said.

"I'll never shut up. I'll never stop hating you. I'll find a way to kill you somehow. You stole my life. I'll get vengeance. You'll see."

Jarret winced in pain as I gently wiped blood off the slash in the muscle curving around the top of his shoulder and arm—his pitching arm. Gretchen spewed a continuous stream of obscenities. But neither Jarret nor I spoke.

Both of us knew the damage to his shoulder would end his season, perhaps his career. I pressed the towel on the open wound to control the bleeding and used the other to wipe the sweat off his forehead. Worried he would pass out or go into shock from the loss of blood, I draped the towel around his neck to keep him cool as sirens blared from down the street.

EMTs lifted Jarret to a stretcher and took him by ambulance to Encino Medical Center. Gretchen, arrested on the scene for attempted murder, was handcuffed and put in the back of a squad car for a ride to the Van Nuys jail. I gave the remaining officers a statement and asked them to contact Carla Pratt, and then got in my car to meet Jarret at the hospital.

On my way down the hill I phoned Nick.

"Where are you?" he said. "Did you get my messages? Weisel called from the liquor store. He snapped a cell phone picture of the pamphlet woman. I e-mailed you her photo."

"Let me guess. Short-haired brunette around my age in a green dress? Bought a bottle of scotch?"

Two hours later I waited in the Encino Medical Center Visitor's Lounge for news on Jarret's condition with Nick, Dave, Robin, and my parents seated in club chairs around me. Mom, still in the calypso-themed canary yellow pedal pushers and ruffled blouse she wore for Dad's hastily canceled party, rose every five minutes to inquire at the desk about Jarret. As soon as she heard he saved my life, her attitude toward him shifted from furious back to fond, bordering on doting. His agent, Ira, paced in front of us, fielding calls from the press on his headset.

Robin sat at my side staring at Nick's phone with Weisel's photo of Gretchen in the liquor store on the screen. "I can't believe Gretchen thought it was you when she killed Laycee."

"After my conversation with Marion, I realized Gretchen resented me all these years for marrying Jarret. Meeting me at the game personified her hatred, and then, when she stole into Jarret's house the next morning, recognized the shirt I was wearing on his bedroom chair, and saw a naked woman with my shape and coloring in the bed—she went berserk. Her sheer hatred for me blinded her from seeing Laycee."

"It takes a cold heart to stop and mark a victim like she did," Dad said.

"Sealed the vengeance. A message to Liz." Nick's words made me shudder. "And Weisel can confirm Gretchen's connection to the symbol."

"If the case gets to trial," Dad said. "She might plead out. Or she could try pleading insanity."

Dave shook his head. "I doubt if she walked into the bedroom knife in hand. Going back for the knife signals intent."

"Her indifference to her mistake is stunning. Amoral. She showed no signs of empathy or remorse at the gym on Thursday. Gretchen barely flinched when Tess and I talked about Laycee." I stiffened. "Oh my God—Tess's dream."

Nick looked at me with puzzlement. "What are you talking about?"

"The night after the murder, a woman at the gym had a dream about me, Laycee, and a cheerleader fighting over Charlie Sheen on a lifeboat. I thought Tess was out of her mind, yet Marion Cooper told me Gretchen was on the pep squad in high school. How strange is that?"

"Not strange at all," Mom said. "Dreams are important. The lifeboat represents uncontrollable emotions."

"And the Charlie Sheen appearance in the dream is obvious," Nick said.

"To you, maybe," I said. "What did I miss?"

"I seriously have to catch you up on movies," Nick said. He looked at Dave and together they said, *"Major League."*

"Charlie Sheen played the role of a baseball pitcher," Nick said. "Jarret?"

I shook my head. "I don't know whether Tess's dream impresses or frightens me."

"I'd say Gretchen is more frightening than your friend's dream," Dave said. "Criminals are either ignorant or arrogant. But failing two—make that three, including today—attempted murders in the same week classifies Gretchen as one of the dumbest or craziest killers on record."

"Her father preached vengeance as a right," Nick said. "Once she had Liz in her sights, Gretchen felt entitled to take her due."

"The smashed photo didn't fit until Jarret's mother described Gretchen's obsession," I said. "Carla pinned the motive—jealousy and revenge."

"She just didn't dig back far enough in Jarret's history to find the real killer," Robin said.

"Pratt would have gotten there," Dave said. "And now that Gretchen confessed to starting the townhouse fire—"

"After she hacked into the gym's computer for my address then rummaged through my backpack to confirm I hadn't moved just so she could torch me *and* my home," I added.

"I'm sure the Illinois authorities will reinvestigate the fire at the Bull Valley house last December and the blaze that killed her mother and siblings," Dave said.

"What happens with Kyle and the steroids now?" I said.

"He won't be in business for long," Dad said. "This morning after we spoke, I tipped a contact at the DEA about Stanger's sideline. He'll be busted as soon as his next customer leaves Game On with drugs. I wouldn't go back to that gym, Lizzie."

"Don't worry. I won't." I tucked my arm under Nick's, whispering, "I'm going to fly to Atlanta for Laycee's funeral. I need to forgive her and wish her peace. Will you come?"

He squeezed my hand. "Of course."

In the midst of the excitement, I realized I hadn't notified Oliver. I took out my phone and dialed his private number.

Oliver answered with, "If Pratt's with you, try for God's sake to keep your mouth shut. Do you need a bail bondsman or the national guard?"

"Neither. You can call off your private eye and relax for the rest of the weekend. Laycee's killer is in custody."

"Jarvis confessed?"

I laughed, and then gave him the details on Gretchen's attack and subsequent confession.

"No fooling?" he said. "I'm happy it worked out but I'll miss working with you."

"Me, too, Oliver."

"Stay out of trouble, kid. But if you can't, you know how to find me."

A young doctor in green scrubs and straight blonde hair tied at the nape of her neck, entered the waiting room and said, "Is Liz Cooper here?"

Mom and Robin rose with me to face her. Ira swerved around, pocketed his phone, and joined us.

"I'm Dr. Adler, Jarret Cooper's emergency room physician. Which one of you is Liz?"

"I am. How's Jarret?" I searched her face, hoping for good news.

"He lost a lot of blood. We have him stabilized. I'm keeping him here overnight to monitor his blood pressure."

"What about his shoulder?" Ira said.

"Fortunately, the knife didn't cut the radial nerve, but he will need surgery to determine the extent of muscle damage." Dr. Adler smiled at me. "Jarret asked if you were here, Ms. Cooper. You can go up and see him if you like."

Of course Mom followed me up to Jarret's room. She had the decency to wait in the hall to give me a moment alone with him.

Jarret reclined in the hospital bed with his left arm and shoulder bandaged. He looked up, his lips curled in a loopy smile. "Hi Lizzy-Bear."

"How are you?"

"Almost in one piece."

I leaned over the bed to kiss his forehead. "Thank you for pushing me out of the way. I owe you one."

"You sure do." He reached at me with his free hand. "Come closer. Let me cop a feel."

"I'm almost grateful enough to let you, but my mother is right outside your door, ready to burst in. Plus I'm thinking you should keep your hands to yourself for a while."

"Hell, no. Did you meet Dr. Adler? Did you *see* what she looks like? And she's single. Find out if she makes house calls."

"Yoo-hoo." Mom peeked in, taking Jarret's weak wave as permission to enter.

"Hey, Viv." Jarret sunk into the pillow, his eyes struggling to remain open.

She went to the bedside and straightened his sheet. "Don't you worry—we'll make sure you get the best doctors. I'll bring you breakfast in the morning so you don't have to starve to death in here."

"No food. Going home tomorrow."

"Not to that house, you're not," Mom said. "You're coming home to stay with Walter and me for a while so I can help you recuperate."

I shook my head, smiling. Jarret living with Mom? There was a bizarre sense of justice in there somewhere.

Ex–cemetery tour guide and reluctant medium Pepper Martin is dying for a break from communicating with the no-longer-living. But returning a legendary Wild West star's ghost to his hometown is proving one killer of a road trip . . .

FROM
CASEY DANIELS

WILD WILD DEATH

A Pepper Martin Mystery

Her job has been cut, she's low on cash, and her detective sometime-boyfriend refuses to even *talk* about her ability to see the dead and solve their murders. So Pepper is most certainly down for a vacation to get her spirits up. But when her cute scientist friend Dan is kidnapped, Pepper soon stumbles upon another deadly mystery that brings her to New Mexico. And she's after a clever murderer . . .

PRAISE FOR
THE PEPPER MARTIN MYSTERIES

"There's no savoring the Pepper Martin series—
you'll devour each book and still be hungry for more!"
—Kathryn Smith, *USA Today* bestselling author

"Entertaining . . .
Sass and the supernatural cross paths."
—*Publishers Weekly*

penguin.com
facebook.com/TheCrimeSceneBooks
caseydaniels.com

Cozy up with Berkley Prime Crime

SUSAN WITTIG ALBERT
Don't miss the national bestselling series featuring herbalist China Bayles.

LAURA CHILDS
The Tea Shop Mysteries are the toast of Charleston, South Carolina.

KATE KINGSBURY
The Pennyfoot Hotel Mystery series is a teatime delight.

For the
detectiv